I0604509

The Book Keeper

Also by Amelia Grace/Julieann Wallace

Amelia Grace (print and eBook)
Adult fiction
The Girl with the Flaxen Hair
The Colour of Broken - long-listed to be made into a movie.
All the Colours Above
A Dream of Light

Julieann Wallace (print and eBook)

Young Adult
You Before Me

Middle Grade Chapter Book (print and eBook)

Captain Vertigo, and unfortunately... Fart Man
(a superhero with a cochlear implant)

For Children
Picture Books (print books)

Forever and a Day, Love Mama
Henry Bear
Darth
Who Said?
Lily's Lollies
THING
THINGY

Ménière's disease (print and eBook)
(donating profits to medical research)

Vanilla Swirl (children's print book)
Blueberry Swirl (children's print book)
Dear Ménière's - letters & art (#1 on Amazon)
Ménière's Woman
Daily Ménière's Journal
It Will Change Your Life - a cochlear implant journey

Amelia Grace is the pen name of Australian author, Julieann Wallace. Her best-selling adult novel, The Colour of Broken, was longlisted to be made into a movie, twice and was #1 on Amazon in its category.

Julieann is also an artist and secondary arts teacher, empowering students to be change-makers to create a better world for themselves and for future generations.

When she's not writing, teaching or creating art, Julieann tries not to scare her cat, Claude Monet, or her mini sausage dog, Pablo Picasso, with her terrible cello playing. Her deaf cat, Jameela, is her #1 cello music fan.

Julieann lives in Brisbane with her husband. She is the mother of three amazing grown-up children and has a gorgeous grandson. She has a cochlear implant and is an Ambassador for Ménière's Australia.

www.julieannwallaceauthor.com

The Book Keeper
Lilly Pilly Publishing, 2024
lillypillypublishing@outlook.com
www.lillypillypublishing.com

Text Copyright ©2024 Julieann Wallace, writing as Amelia Grace

The moral right of the author to be identified as the author of this work has been asserted.

This is a work of fiction. Names, characters, places and incidents are products of the author's imagination or are used fictionally. Any resemblance to actual events, locales or persons, living or dead, is entirely coincidental.

All rights reserved. No part of this book may be reproduced or transmitted by any person or entity (including Google, Amazon or similar organisation), in any form or by any means, electronic or mechanical, including photocopying, recording, scanning or by any format, storage and retrieval system, without prior permission in writing from the publisher.

Bible verses from The Holy Bible, New International Version* NIV* Copyright ©1973,1978,1984, 2011 by Biblica Inc.* Used by permission.
All rights reserved worldwide.

All errors belong to the author.

ISBN: 978-0-9942044-6-2 (print book)
ISBN: 978-0-9942044-7-9 (eBook)
Cover design by Lilly Pilly Publishing
Cover image: 123rf image ID: 208075536 teacup: beehouse studio
Interior art: beehouse studio

PROUDLY

The Book Keeper

Amelia Grace

Life is about choices.
Some we regret, some we're proud of.
Some will haunt us forever.
The message: we are what we chose to be.

Graham Brown

Chapter 1

The long, bony index finger slid down the page of names, searching for the *terrena nomen dedit* of the man standing before him. It stopped at the empty space between other names, alphabetically.

His name was not there. It had vanished.

'Sir, your Earthly Given Name does not appear to be in The Book. You must return, Earthbound—perhaps it is not your time, or—' His voice was deep and grave, his eyes soulful.

The solitary man looked into the eyes of the unknown figure, searching for answers to questions not yet asked. And then he looked to the ridiculously large book that rested upon the golden lectern, each page edged in fine gold.

Tears pooled in his weary eyes as he shook his head in disbelief.

My name is not in the book?

My. Name. Is. Not. In. The. Book...

He clutched his chest and then blackness fell upon him like a plague, surrounding him as the silence moved in to torture him.

Chapter 2

A rough tongue traced the underside of my foot as it hung over the edge of the bed, waking me. Mr. Meowgi. The unwelcome neighbour's mangy cat that seemed to take a liking to me. It sat, glaring at me.

I shook my head to free myself from the grogginess. It abated, but lurking in my mind was an awkward memory that left an uneasy feeling in the pit of my stomach. I shuddered.

I moved in an unbalanced sort of fashion to the window of my bedroom, disturbing the chaotic, colliding dust motes in the filtered beams of morning sunlight that had crept in.

The street below was busy with cars travelling at a hasty pace. A dog was at the fence barking at some children running past on their way to school. It all looked very familiar.

I pushed my hand through my hair and shook my head.

Something was different. If only I could pinpoint that particular element that had caused the change...

I turned from the window but stilled, as my reflection caught my eye. Memories from the cognizance came flooding back to me.

The Book.

I plastered my hands over my face as flashes of memory returned to my conscious mind.

The dream—it was wrong, so, so wrong.

I sat on the floor and put my head to my knees. The cognizance seemed so real and yet, surreal. I closed my eyes; *the dream was not fact—my name is in the Book of Life!*

I looked up at the sound of loud splots of rain hitting the windows. It was the summer rain that I so loved; the sound, the smell, the expectation, the muted light... my room had darkened.

I stood to turn on the lamp, and there sat a book on the top of my bedside table.

Covered in dust...

It wasn't mine! I'm not a book nerd. I don't read books. I don't buy books.

I looked away from the book and to the soft light of the lamp before I ran my hand over my face, trying to figure out the mysterious appearance of a book by my bed.

Odd things have happened—weird things.

With my curiosity piqued, I leaned over and blew the dust off the top of the book. It flowed into the air like a wave turning over on itself, leaving the worn brown leather cover naked to the eye.

I ran my fingertips lightly over the cover. It was smooth and soft like the skin of a newborn baby. But then I felt some bumps at the top right-hand corner.

It was blemished, damaged.

I lifted the leather-bound book in my hands, raised it level with my eyes and looked closely at the area of damage. It wasn't damage on the leather at all, but an embossing. The words were unknown to me—*Mutato Nomine De Te Fabula Narratur*—Latin, I think.

I raised my eyebrows, confused by the appearance of the book. I just... don't read books.

I placed it back onto the bedside table while I figured out what to do with it.

I. Don't. Read. Books. Simple as that.

I rubbed my forehead then left the bedroom, only to return to fetch the book.

The aggravating, stupid book!

I wanted it to repel me like all frigging books did. But it didn't—I was drawn to it.

I. Don't. Read. Books!

I swung my hand over the leather cover and let my fingers fall heavily onto it, then begrudgingly picked it up. I wanted to slam it down onto the wooden floor.

Why did it incite anger in me? It was just a book!

Repulsion began to pulse throughout me, but also an obsession at the same time. I ran my hand through my hair again (yes, again) in exasperation and took a deep breath, turned and walked into the kitchen with it. I placed it on the kitchen table to deal with later.

My mood had now been set for the rest of the day. I swung my work satchel over my shoulder and left the apartment in haste, hoofed it down the three flights of stairs onto the street and ran to catch the bus, but missed it. And with it, I missed the connecting train as well.

Now I would be an hour and a half late for work. The boss would not be happy—join the club!

'Cohen, nice of you to make an appearance at work today!' Sarcasm spewed from the mouth of my ever-pleasant boss as I arrived at work, late. Perhaps I should have delivered a vanilla latte to her as I walked in the door—a peace offering. Sometimes it worked.

'Aye. Couldn't get my designs wet in the rain—played it safe,' I offered as an excuse to soften the blow.

She lowered her head and raised her right eyebrow. No smile in sight. 'Bring them to my office immediately, Mr. Darcy,' she ordered before she turned abruptly, her skirt swishing around and then settling as she walked off with intent.

I took a deep breath, closed my eyes and followed her to her glass-walled office. She closed the blinds—our conversation would not be seen or heard.

She stood behind her walnut-coloured desk that was her battle station. Her arms were folded. Her non-receptive stance. She held a scowl on her face. 'Shut the door, Mr. Darcy.' Her words froze the air.

I looked into her green eyes momentarily before I smoothly turned and closed the door with the faintest click.

'Don't bother to sit. You won't be here long.' Her words were curt.

I took a deep breath before I turned and looked at her. I took a step closer to her and stopped as my stomach tightened.

I am about to be fired.

I tensed my body and waited for the words of unemployment to come from her mouth—the mouth that was framed by perfectly formed lips. How could such piercing words of poison leave such a place of beauty?

She walked around her desk and stood directly in front of me. I could smell her citrus perfume and feel her breath on me, sweet and minty. She looked directly into my eyes with the face of need and of innocence. 'Cohen, I received a directive this morning. You will no longer be here with us. You need to report in at CAI by three o'clock this afternoon. They have... needs... only you can fulfil.' Her voice was soft and full of regret. It was like she was two different people.

She moved her hand to the back of my neck and lightly ran

her fingers in my hair. She was sending such confusing mixed messages. One minute she was closed and icy; the next, warm and seductive.

She looked deeply into my eyes before she moved her lips gently onto mine, kissing me lightly at first, and then with intent.

I put my hand to the side of her face and ended the kiss. 'Catherine ... no.' I shook my head. 'You are my boss...' my voice trailed off.

She looked into my eyes once more, then ran her warm, soft hand over the side of my neck and along my jaw line before brushing a finger over my bottom lip. I wanted her to stop. I had no romantic feelings toward her.

'Not anymore,' she whispered suggestively.

I brought my eyebrows together. 'I... don't do... sex is for marriage,' I said with a gentle tone.

She took a small step back from me and raised an eyebrow at me, then removed my work bag from over my shoulder. She placed it onto the chair behind her without taking her eyes off me.

I pushed my fringe to the side and suppressed my desire to flee.

Catherine placed both hands onto my chest and slid them up over my shoulders, around my neck and hugged me, tightly, pressing her body into mine. I kept my arms by my side.

She placed a light kiss below my right ear. I reached up to her arms and peeled them off from me. 'Catherine... I am not interested in you in that way... and... I want to keep myself for my wife of the future.' I rotated the ring on my fourth finger on my right hand. My pledge.

'One day you will regret that you had refused me, Cohen— remember that!' she whispered into my ear, before biting my ear lobe lightly. Then she stepped away. In an instant she became cold and business like—detached. 'Collect your belongings, Mr.

Darcy. Talk to no-one, and leave by 12 o'clock, or you shall be escorted out by security—understood?'

'Clearly,' I replied, raising my eyebrows questioning her reaction. I grabbed my leather- work bag of designs and promptly left the office. I bee-lined for my desk, ignoring the eyes that burned into me as I walked past colleagues and friends.

I placed my satchel onto my worn chair and closed my eyes in frustration.

First an uncomfortable dream. Then that book. And now, I am to work at the offices of the CAI. I shook my head as my stomach churned. What was the CAI after? This was neither a promotion, or a reward.

I busied myself, packing my belongings into a small brown cardboard box that had been placed onto my desk. I didn't have much, mostly my drawing and designing implements. No photos, no decorations, no personal oddities, like co-workers around me. I must admit, their "stuff" made the office less hostile, and the bobbing head on the Albert Einstein figure was a good distraction when I needed to zone out a bit. I'm going to miss the good people here. My friends.

I grabbed my satchel, my cardboard box and turned around to silent stares and saddened faces. I nodded to them, saying goodbye in my silent way, the only way I could after being told not to talk to anyone. And then left. Exiting the office area along the long walkway.

Catherine stood outside her office, her face serious, sour. 'Good day, Mr. Darcy,' she spat in an acidic tone.

I looked at her and half smiled. 'I assure you ... I will never regret it, Miss Williams.' My voice was even and controlled. I gave her a salute and walked out the door, down the internal stairway, through the foyer and to a waiting taxi.

Chapter 3

The rain obliterated the skyline for the entire hour-long journey to the new office space. I sprinted from the taxi to the revolving door, where I was then escorted up to the twenty-seventh floor of the communications giant.

Everything was white. Sterile. The information desk was occupied by a woman dressed in a white business suit with white bleached hair, her teeth scarily too white.

I felt like I had been sanitized.

'Mr. Darcy, welcome to Communication Alliances Incorporated,' her voice squeaked, 'Mr. Rubin is waiting for you. You may enter now.'

I smiled at her, wondering about how her psychological health was affected from working in this area of sensory depravity. Poor woman. She seemed to have been stripped of any personality. So cruel.

Mr. Rubin sat in his high back, red leather chair when I entered his office, facing away from me.

'Mr. Darcy, good to see that you can follow orders. Now sit... please.' His voice was deep and spellbinding. He turned in his chair to face me.

My eyes widened in shock at his unexpected appearance. I always imagined managerial staff to have a certain type—tall, healthy, well-fitting suit. I hoped he did not notice my negative reaction to him. His voice did not match his physical attributes. He appeared to be a small-framed man as he sat slumped in his oversized leather chair. But perhaps it appeared that way because of the disproportional height of the seat. His face was white and rounded, puffy even, topped off with a bald shiny scalp. He looked up at me with small, beady, dark eyes.

'It seems you have something we need. The drawing... hand it over.'

Fire skirted over my skin as my body responded to flight or fight. 'I don't understand, sir. I have no knowledge of what you are talking about,' I replied, trying to keep my voice steady. *What did I have that was so important to the company?*

'Mr. Darcy, our security data has shown that you have drawn a design that is of great significance to us. It has the potential to revolutionize communications. It is the eye piece that is implantable we seek.'

My mind went into an electrostatic buzz—*not the drawing of the eye implant that allows internal brain visualization and was a thought scanner mind-reading device. It was imperfect. It was also science fiction, meant for imaginative purposes only.*

'Sir, the implant is not real. I was fooling around with my imaginative juices to create a state of subliminal awareness to locate the missing piece of the seventh key to the seventh communication sense,' I explained with a composed voice while my mind was in a panic.

'That would be the one that we seek, Mr. Darcy.' He raised his left eyebrow, his face deadpan. 'Hand it over. It is now the intellectual property of Communication Alliances Incorporated.' His dark eyes pieced mine with threatening domination.

I wanted to stand tall and deflect his aggression but thought the better of it. It would be smarter to play along at this stage, learn the rules of the game, and play it better.

I opened my satchel, flicked through the drawings and designs and handed Mr. Rubin the piece of work he was asking for. Little did he know that the original was stored in a fireproof safe at my residence.

Play the game, play it better.

'You will continue to work on it here until the technology is perfected, Mr. Darcy. That way we can be assured of maximum security. You have no idea how your work will change the world. You have become our most valuable employee. And we look after what we value. Tomorrow, you start work at 9am, twenty-eighth floor. Do not be late. Your work records show your tardiness. Good day, Mr. Darcy.'

He picked up the design and turned his chair away from me—the epitome of rudeness. I burned my eyes into the rear of his aggressive red leather chair.

The light touch of a hand on my arm alerted me to the pitiful White Girl's presence. 'This way, sir,' she squeaked. She indicated to the doorway of Mr. Rubin's office, then led me to the third elevator, which was waiting for me.

I stepped inside.

'Which floor, sir?'

I looked at the Elevator Operator's name badge. Alex. 'Ground floor, please.'

'Indeed, sir.'

I smiled at White Girl as the doors closed. She didn't bat an eyelid.

Challenge on.

The elevator doors pinged on arrival at the ground floor. 'Have a good day, sir,' Alex said with a polite nod.

I tilted my head with a smile and stepped outside the elevator.

The uninvited book entered my mind as I exited through the ridiculous revolving doors. Who has revolving doors these days anyway? And how is that maximum security?

Outside the opulent building, a taxi waited in the pouring rain. At first, I thought it was good timing. But then the taxi driver welcomed me by name—this was no co-incidence. I took a deep breath as my skin prickled, and kept my mind alert, noting details about the taxi and the driver.

By the time I had arrived at my apartment, the storm had moved in. Green skies threatened to release a violence of hail while powerful lightning left its evidence as a thunderous crack sounded throughout the atmosphere.

I fumbled with my drenched hand as I inserted the key into the door lock of my apartment. It opened with ease. In a blur, the old mangy cat flew out of my apartment and back next door to where it belonged.

Good.

I ventured into the kitchen and poured a whiskey, hoping it would subdue my unnerving, erratic emotions.

What a day! The cognizance, the book, the seduction, the unlawful act of stealing my work. The promise that my life would never be the same.

Maybe I could do a system restore of my life to an earlier time and bypass the events of today.

I dragged my feet as I walked over and sat on the sofa, put my head back, closed my eyes and let out a deep breath.

Could the day get any worse?

Chapter 4

A blast of icy cold wind stung my face, startling me from a sleep that had crept over me. At the same time, the sound of rattling papers taking flight around the room caught my attention.

To my right, the organza curtains billowed in the gusty wind. Rain thumped against the closed windows, but one window was open, and the rain entered, unwelcome. I moved at speed to close the window, but my legs gave way on the slippery wet floor and I came crashing down with a thud. I crawled to the window instead, stood and slammed it shut. I turned to discover the room was now a complete mess; papers strewn everywhere. I ran a hand over my face and closed my eyes, hoping that when I opened them, the room would be tidy. But of course it wasn't.

With resignation, I lowered myself onto my knees and collected the papers, haphazardly piling them untidily on the floor, slamming the very last piece down on the top in exasperation, only to find a smaller white piece of paper shoot out before my eyes.

I watched it as it gently glided down onto the floor like a

feather falling from the sky.

The paper was white and unmarked. Not new though; a little aged in appearance. It looked smooth, but on closer inspection with my hands, it was slightly bumpy.

Confused, I ran my finger over the paper again, trying to place where the paper belonged.

The book! The piece of paper belonged to that book!

I went to the table where the book sat. Its leather cover was open like it was exposing the internal intelligences of the written word.

But there were no words. The pages were unblemished by ink, by words, letters or illustrations. Yet the book looked used and worn. I slid the escapee page of the book back inside with the other pages and slammed the cover closed. It would make great fuel for the fireplace.

I walked away from it, only to return to it like I was a piece of steel attracted to its powerful magnet. It had sunk its nasty little hooks into me. I removed the extrovert page, now named the escapee. My curiosity needed quenching so I could rid my life of the power of this book. At once I made my way to the study room and turned on the desk lamp. I placed the paper onto the glossy glass top. Without looking up, I reached for a soft sketching pencil and another piece of paper, then proceeded to do a texture rubbing over the blank page.

Initially, flowers appeared on the rubbing with vines with leaves. Quite childish really. But then some lettering appeared.

A name. It was female.

I smirked. Well, the female name didn't surprise me really. Boys didn't tend to go about drawing pretty daisy flowers and scrolly vines on paper.

My smile faded when, to my surprise, an address appeared, complete with an email and phone number. So, the book was not as old as I had assumed it was. I raised my eyebrows, then frowned, perplexed by the details I had extracted.

I sighed. This book belongs to someone. Did she break into my apartment and leave it here? I didn't see any signs of break and enter. Besides, I was asleep. I would have woken if someone was in my room.

I thought back to the night. Nothing. I recalled nothing of that night except for the dream.

I returned to the table and placed the page back into the book and closed the worn leather cover.

I covered my face with my hands and growled in frustration. I could not simply burn this book as I was thinking of! It had a person's name and address in it. It had an owner.

I released a loud, exasperated breath.

Bloody book!

I grabbed my laptop. The computer purred as I engaged it and keyed in my security code. I went immediately to emails— new message.

FROM: Cohen Darcy
SUBJECT: Your Book!
DATE: May 08 16:37
TO: Georgia Harrison

Hello,
I have found your book. How can I return it to you?

Cohen Darcy

Send...

I watched the computer screen for a few minutes, cupping my hands in each other and twiddling my thumbs while I waited for a reply. Twenty-five minutes later, the ping of a new message alerted me.

FROM: Georgia Harrison
SUBJECT: Your Book!
DATE: May 08 17:02
TO: Cohen Darcy

Hello Cohen,

It is not my book. Is this a pick-up line?

Georgia Harrison

Great—girls! Always assuming a guy is trying to romantically connect with them. My fingers twitched with agitation as I replied.

FROM: Cohen Darcy
SUBJECT: Your Book!
DATE: May 08 17:05
TO: Georgia Harrison

Georgia,

The book has your name, address, email
and phone number contacts in it.

IT IS YOUR BOOK!

You need to claim it before I use
it as fuel for the fire.
Books are not my thing!

Cohen
#thefireisburningbarely

Send…

FROM: Georgia Harrison
SUBJECT: Your Book!
DATE: May 08 17:13
TO: Cohen

Dear, Dear Cohen,

I have not lost, misplaced, deserted,
thrown out or ditched a book.
Feel free to use it as fuel for the fire.

Georgia

FROM: Cohen Darcy
SUBJECT: Your Book!
DATE: May 08 17:17
TO: Georgia

Dear, Dear Georgia,

Your wish is my command.
I will begin destruction of YOUR BOOK
in exactly 60 minutes and counting.
The fire is hungry!

Cohen
#temporarykeeperofYOURBOOK!

Send...

End of communication.

Good. I had permission to cast the intrusive book into the violent bowels of the raging fire, to be eradicated, all evidence of its existence obliterated. I smiled lopsidedly. The book problem was about to be solved.

As I bided my time, I absent-mindedly flicked through the pages of Georgia's book. The one she claimed wasn't hers.

Nothing but empty pages. Some sort of journal I assumed.

One she hadn't used.

I angled the book towards the flickering flames of the fire in the hope of being able to read the inkless book in case it was written in a secret ink, or whatever it was that girls sometimes did with their friends. I leaned forward to concentrate a little more on the inkless text, but then snapped it shut.

It was personal.

I had no business reading the personal diary of Georgia Harrison. And besides, I couldn't see anything on the pages.

For a moment I pondered on what secrets it held. Obviously, none too important if she was happy for me to dispose of it in the fire.

My shoulders rose as I inhaled deeply.

I don't do books—Fiction. Comics. Fantasy. Dystopian. Action & Adventure. Mystery. Horror. Thriller. Historical Fiction. Romance. Contemporary. Magic Realism. Graphic Novel. Short Story... perhaps... Non-fiction—only for work purposes, Memoir, Biography, Recipe—*well... yes*, for obvious reasons, Art... yes, History, True Crime, Science & Technology... depends on my research.

Simple. I don't do books. Unless it's necessary for work.

I looked up at the wall clock. It was well past the allotted sixty minutes I had given Georgia to claim her book. Clearly, she didn't want it. I flicked through the pages again, aerating the pages so they would catch alight quickly, and then tossed it into the not so raging fire.

The book started to crackle and spit embers as the ping of the laptop caught my attention.

I opened emails.

FROM: Georgia Harrison
SUBJECT: Your Book!
DATE: May 08 18:30
TO: Cohen Darcy

Hello Cohen,

Please don't burn the book. YES, IT IS MINE!

Georgia.

My eyes widened in panic as I watched the book being consumed by the fire. I raced over to the hearth and fished the book out with the fire tongs.

The book was blackened, damaged and still ablaze on the edges. I dropped it onto the slate and stamped on it with my shoe. Smoke rose to the ceiling and the book looked like it had been exposed to the violent flames of a fire wielding dragon. At least it wasn't burnt to cinders!

I returned to the laptop.

FROM: Cohen Darcy
SUBJECT: Your Book!
DATE: May 08 18:40
TO: Georgia Harrison

Hi George,

I still have it. Where can I send it to?

Cohen
#thekeeperofYOURBOOK!

Send...

FROM: Georgia Harrison
SUBJECT: Your Book!
DATE: May 08 18:43
To: Cohen Darcy

Hello Cohen,

Meet me at Flowers for Fleur – the café section, at 3pm.
And don't call me George!

Georgia
#I'mgladthatyoudidn'tfeedmybooktothefireofdoom

FROM: Cohen Darcy
SUBJECT: Your Book!
DATE: May 08 18:47
To: Georgia Harrison

Apologies George.

What do you look like? How will I know that it is you?

From Cohen
#iamstillthekeeperofyourbook!

Send…

There was no reply.
And now there was another complication with the peculiar
book—I had to meet a girl to get rid of it.

Chapter 5

My *personal* taxi was waiting for me when I exited my apartment in the morning, compliments of CAI. I climbed in to hear a *personal* welcome. Personally, I didn't care for any of these pre-meditated, controlled frivolities. I preferred to have control of my own destiny, and not have another person choose my pathway in life, including taxi conversations.

Play the game. Play it better.

I was *personally* escorted up to the twenty-eighth floor of CAI, hand-scanned for entry and *personally* escorted to my new office. I shared it with no-one, personally. Thank goodness it was not sterile white. Instead, it had three different ghastly wall colours; blue, green and purple, plus an entire wall of floor-to-ceiling windows overlooking the city. Perhaps white walls would have been better?

My drawing desk was white however, the work desk white, and my high-backed leather chair, white. I had only settled into my new flashy office for ten minutes when Mr. Rubin walked in, unannounced.

'Mr. Darcy, I trust you are happy with your office and

location.' His voice was serious with no frills.

Play the game. Play it better.

'Yes, thank you, sir.' Politeness was not warranted, but it was part of the game.

'Your designs, Mr. Darcy. Update me at 2pm daily, without fail, without tardiness.'

He drummed his knuckles on top of my desk and pierced my blue eyes with the icy coldness of his beady dark eyes. Then he turned on his heel and left the room.

Rudeness exemplified.

I looked around my little abode to find the security cameras. Maximum security meant that I was being watched. I located the cameras: all five of them. According to my calculations, there was a blind spot with their overlap. I could have perfect invisibility if I played my cards right. The plan formed in my head and the prototype was designed in my mind. I moved my desk and chair. I felt happier about my circumstances then, if that was even doable. I think it was the thought that I could possibly beat the firm at their game.

At 2pm I descended a level to Mr. Rubin's office. White Girl was there.

I bowed my head and smiled at her as I walked past.

'Mr. Darcy, Mr. Rubin is waiting for you,' she squeaked, exposing me to her blinding white teeth.

I squinted and walked past her. I entered the open door to Mr. Rubin's office. The rear of his red high-backed chair was facing me again.

'Mr. Darcy, you are two minutes late. I despise tardiness. You and I will get on better if you lose the trait of bad time management. Project details?'

And I despise bad manners, Mr. Rubin. I doubt that we will ever get along.

Play the game. Play it better.

'I have spent a large portion of my time today revisiting my design and making notes. As you are aware, the mind-reading communication device was only a creative outlet for my mind, a purely science fiction piece of work. I will need to get details on the anatomy of the brain and eye, medical procedures, and a timeline, to see if I can produce what you are wanting in this field of communication. I... cannot guarantee that this idea of an eye implant for mind-reading will work. Furthermore, I request a flexible time schedule, to allow me to come and go as I see fit. For instance, to visit medical universities for research, to watch eye or brain surgeries, and to visit places of creative inspiration. And... I do not need a personal taxi or escorting on or off the premises,' I asserted in a polite manner.

Mr. Rubin stared at me, his left hand supporting the weight of his bald shiny head in a handgun formation under his chin, as if in deep contemplation of my debriefing and request while giving a subtle subconscious gesture of power play.

I maintained eye contact with him as he considered my request.

'I shall permit all your requests, except the personal taxi service and escorting on and off the premises. I repeat to you again, Mr. Darcy, you are currently our most valuable employee, and we look after who and what we value. Vacate my office. 2pm again tomorrow, and daily unless I choose to change the time to suit my needs.' His voice was devoid of emotion, very business-like. He turned his sterile red high-backed leather chair away from me and I shook my head in disapproval of his contempt of me. I turned and exited his office, fully aware of the security cameras watching my every move.

As I passed White Girl, I gave her a coy smile and a nod, acknowledging her presence.

'Mr. Darcy.' Her large brown eyes followed me, but her face remained expressionless. I liked a good challenge. She will smile at me soon!

At precisely 2.45pm I left my office, scanned my handprint and briskly headed to the Café at Flowers for Fleur, by foot.

I stopped before the entrance to the flower store and took a deep breath before I pushed the door open. When I stepped through onto the wooden floor a metal bell dingled, announcing my arrival.

I scanned the faces of the patrons. What on earth did she look like? E-mails didn't give a clue about appearance. At least over the phone you could form a possible image of someone by the sound of their voice. Was she young or old? I had absolutely no idea! No-one even looked up at me as I entered the café.

Maybe she wasn't here yet?

Maybe she was running behind schedule?

Or maybe she was leading me astray because she thought I was trying to pick her up?

I sat down at a vacant square wooden table and tucked my bag under the chair. Before I even had the chance to look up, I heard a soft worded 'hi' and saw her delicate hand resting on the table.

'Hi!' I replied and lifted my face to hers.

Her cornflower blue eyes sank into mine as she smiled at me. Her wavy mid-length brown hair framed her heart-shaped faced perfectly and my heart accelerated.

'Georgia?' I asked, raising my eyebrows.

She nodded once.

'Please, sit. Would you like to join me for a tea or coffee?' I asked, suddenly unsure of myself—way out of character for me. I don't do books, and I don't ask unknown women to join me for tea or coffee.

'Yes please, tea,' she replied and sat down.

Her voice weaved a thread to my soul and took my breath away. I had not expected such a reaction to her. The only reason she was here was so I could offload her book. I tipped my head down with a small smile and nodded my head like my ex-co-worker's ridiculous Albert Einstein Bobble Head figurine, before I rose from the table to place our order.

I returned to our seating the long way through the café. I needed to observe her, to assess her character. She didn't give much away. She sat with her back straight and her hands clasped on the table in front of her as if she was in deep thought. She emitted an intelligent gentleness, her face peaceful. Approachable.

But what was she thinking right now? I needed to know...

I sat opposite her and connected my eyes to hers, then looked away quickly to the table. She made me feel unbelievably self-conscious.

'Thanks for meeting me to change hands with the book, Cohen,' she said, her voice soft.

I looked at her and raised an eyebrow. 'Glad to get it off my hands. I still don't understand how it came to me. And... I don't do books. I'm not a book type of guy.' I tilted my head and winced with half my face.

She smiled then looked at the table, stealing her beautiful blue eyes away from me. Had I said something wrong? What was she thinking? I wish I knew. Girls are so hard to read—a closed book sometimes, so to speak.

Our cups of tea arrived then, with a teapot. Georgia took the liberty of pouring the tea into our fancy white teacups. 'What is it that you do, Cohen?' she asked, not looking at me until she finished pouring the tea.

I took a deep breath. 'Oh, you know—research, design, create, design, research. Nothing too exciting really.'

'Really? Your eyes tell me a different story,' she stated in a curious voice.

I blinked at her, looked down and sipped my tea.

I watched as she lifted her teacup to her lips. 'And what is it that you do, Georgia?' *Tell me exactly what you do.*

'Research, design, create, design, research. Nothing too exciting really,' she replied, her cheeks dimpled.

She was playing games. Maybe she knew my motto.

'What field are you in for your research?' I asked. I was intrigued.

She shook her head. 'I can't say… and you?'

'Same,' I replied, connecting my eyes to hers, wishing at that moment that I could read her mind.

'Did you know, Cohen… that… digitally, you don't exist?' she said matter-of-factly.

My eyes widened and I placed my teacup down before I spilt it. I stared at her, shocked.

'I googled your name, searched data banks and profiles, and you don't exist.'

I narrowed my eyes at her then. Why on earth would she be collecting data on me? Is there something wrong with her?

I cleared my throat. 'I like to keep a low profile,' I replied, keeping a cool and calm exterior, while inside I was starting to panic. Had the CAI deleted my life details on digital data banks. What is their plan for me?

I looked away from Georgia to my left and caught sight of a man staring at her. He had short, dark hair with neatly trimmed sideburns, blue eyes and a day-old growth of facial hair. His chiselled face sat perfectly with his perfect nose. Uncannily, he looked similar to me.

'Is that your boyfriend over to your right, dark hair, staring at you?' I asked, watching as Georgia followed my directions. Her eyes stopped searching when she had found the guy I was talking about. Her face lit up with her smile then, sending warmth through my body. I inhaled sharply and shook my head. Like books, I don't do girls. They are way too complicated. Unpredictable.

Her big blue eyes found mine. She was still grinning as I sipped my tea. She leaned toward me, close enough that I could smell her flowery perfume. 'No. He's not my type,' she whispered.

My heart sank. If he's not her type, then I'm not her type. End of story. Why was I hoping anyway? I don't have time for a girlfriend.

I reached down and grabbed the book from my leather bag and placed it carefully onto the wooden table and winced. I left my hand partly over the cover and watched Georgia's expression. I wanted to see her immediate reaction to the condition of her book, after I had tossed it into the fire to burn.

Her eyes widened and her mouth opened as she let out a small sigh. I rubbed the back of my neck. To be fair, she didn't get back to me in the allotted amount of time. I wanted to sing my apologies to her for damaging her book.

When she reached for it, her hand lightly brushed against mine, leaving a tingling path in its wake. She looked up at me as she dragged the book towards herself. A small tear fell from her eye, and she brushed it away quickly with the back of her hand. I wanted to do that for her. I wanted to touch her.

And I wanted to apologise to her a thousand times over.

'Cohen…' She choked back emotion.

My heart was heavy. 'I… I'm sorry, Georgia. I did tell you I was going to feed it to the fire, and I did give you a time limit, that you never adhered to…' my voice trailed off in apology.

'No, Cohen. It is in a far better condition than when I lost it. Did you clean it up, reattach pages, polish the leather cover?' she asked, full of wonder.

My mind was in a whirl as my heart thumped against my chest. Better condition than when she lost it? It was in perfect condition when I set my eyes upon it beside my bed that morning.

'You think?' I questioned her, trying to hide the confusion on my face.

She pulled out a pair of glasses from her bag and put them on. 'Yes, oh yes!' she said as she riffled through the pages. 'And the writing is so clear now. I hope you didn't read it!' She looked up at me and blushed.

I stared at her like I was frozen in time, and then I looked at the book as she flicked through the pages again. There was no writing! Not a mark visible to the naked eye!

I was at a loss for words. Either Georgia was deluded, or I had something terribly wrong with my vision.

I wished I could read her mind right then and there. What was going on?

I clasped my hands in front of my mouth and ran my finger over my bottom lip as I watched her while she went back and forth through the pages of the book, like a small child opening a long-awaited birthday gift.

Finally, she closed the cover and looked up at me. Her lips lifted at the corners of her mouth, and her blue eyes sparkled with happiness. I was glad I had my hands in front of my mouth. I didn't want her to see the deep, sharp intake of air I took.

'Thank you, Cohen. You don't know what this book means to me,' she whispered as she removed her glasses and a tear rolled down her cheek.

I reached over and wiped it away with my thumb, gazing into her beautiful eyes. Her skin was warm and soft, and I wanted to place my lips onto hers, and kiss her tenderly.

I looked down and blinked, confused by my reaction to her. A girlfriend was not on my agenda, I reminded myself as I took in a deep slow breath to gather my senses.

I lifted my head. 'I'm glad you wanted it back, Georgia. And I'm glad it's found its rightful owner. I feel a ton of weight lifted off my shoulders now that it's in your hands.' I looked down at her hand on the book, and then to the table and closed my eyes briefly, before I looked up into her eyes again. 'I must go now.

Things to do. Places to go. I wish you happy reading and happy memories with your book.'

I bent down to grab my leather bag.

'But… but—' Georgia frowned. 'Don't you want to know what's in this book?' Georgia said, placing her hand over mine on the table.

I looked at her perfectly shaped hand and fingers draped over mine. They were warm and her magnetism reaching into my being. I looked up at her. She was waiting in anticipation of my answer.

Hope, that's what it was. She was hoping I would stay a little longer to hear about her book.

I raised my eyebrows, trying to find the right words before I spoke. 'Thank you, but no. I have no right to any of the information you have in your book. I don't know you; you don't know me—heck—you couldn't even locate any information about me over the Internet. Remember… I don't exist,' I said, trying to fob her off.

I wanted to stay for an eternity and look at her beautiful face and listen to her soul connecting voice. I wanted to take her in my arms and make her mine forever, mentally, emotionally, physically.

She stared into my eyes for a moment before she looked down at the book in her hands. She lowered her head and pressed her lips together, and my heart pained for her.

'Oh,' she said softly and slouched in her seat.

I wanted to say tell me all about it. We have a lifetime together because you are mine. But that was not the truth, and it never would be.

'I'm sorry…' I muttered, grabbed my bag and stood, looking down at her saddened face.

She looked up at me and stood. 'The least I can do is give you a thank you hug, Cohen.' She stepped towards me and wrapped her arms around my shoulders. In politeness I wrapped my arms around her back and held her gently. She felt so right in my arms. I closed my eyes and lowered my head closer to her neck and inhaled her apple-scented hair, feeling my quickening heartbeat.

'Thank you, again,' she whispered into my ear. She released me from her embrace and stepped back from me.

I looked into her eyes with a crooked smile. 'You're welcome,' I said gently before I turned to leave the café, the doorbell announcing my departure.

Chapter 6

A blast of cool air slammed into my face like a bucket of icy water, stopping me in my tracks outside the café door. My mind and heart were telling me to retreat, to return to her, to swoop her into my arms to live happily ever after.

But I didn't.

Women can be confusing and complicated; trouble in my experience—no matter how appealing she was to me. Instead, I turned to my right to head home, only to be approached by the taxi driver.

'Good afternoon, Mr. Darcy, at your service. Where would you like to go?' he asked. The personal taxi driver's voice was impersonal—business like.

I let out a silent scream. I was being followed by CAI and I was not impressed.

'Home, thank you, sir,' I answered abruptly, annoyed that my civil liberties had been removed from me. And if I am truthful with myself, I was annoyed that I walked away from Georgia, the only positive emotional reaction I had sincerely had to a woman.

But I didn't believe in love at first sight, did I?

Was it possible?

Was love a measurable emotion?

Was it real?

What was I feeling, and what had caused it?

She was a human being just like me… or was she? She could see words on the pages of that book—I couldn't. Did she have a gift I had never heard of?

I looked out the window of the taxi as we journeyed to my residence. I had many more questions about the book now: Where did it come from? How could it be in perfect condition when I had found it, to being thrown into the fire and damaged, blackened, to Georgia thinking that it was in better condition now than when she had lost it? Why did she affect me that way? What is the plan for me at CAI?

I had no answers. I closed my eyes in frustration.

Play the game. Play it better.

I climbed the three flights of stairs to my apartment, two at a time. I had never felt so alive. Was it the act of releasing the stupid book from my life, or the physical and emotional connection with Georgia?

My mind was in a distant place when I opened the door to my apartment and walked to the kitchen. I stopped. I froze at the smell of a homemade dinner, and then by the appearance of a note on the kitchen bench top.

Cautiously, I placed my bag onto the dining chair and picked up the note. It was typed.

Mr. Darcy,

Domestic and cleaning services at your disposal.
R.

I slammed the note down onto the table. They had been in

my apartment.

I looked around. My own personal space had been cleaned—sterilized even, by a tidiness that took away my personality and my own presence in my home.

I hightailed it to my study at the realization they weren't here to clean—it was a decoy—a lie to cover the fact they had searched my apartment. I rummaged through my working drawings on my desk—all tidied painfully, and excruciatingly, and obsessive-compulsively ordered, alphabetically.

I was about to search my secret hiding place of documents, but then stopped. I could hear the eyes of security filming my every move. That infinitesimal buzz of the electrical energy driving the mechanisms of digital recording. My apartment had been wired for surveillance.

Play the game. Play it better.

I turned as if I was checking other paraphernalia in my study—*my decoy*. I was absolutely aware I was now owned by CAI. My life was being watched, scrutinized, counted, tracked and recorded. And my digital identity, erased.

I exited the study and headed back into the kitchen, finding the peace offering of a home cooked meal they had left me. I found a container and pushed the meal into it and placed it into the freezer for analysing later. That way, on their surveillance film it would appear that I was saving it for another day. I didn't want to arouse their suspicions that I didn't trust them.

I walked over to the television and turned it on, then sat on the sofa and watched the football. This decoy was to conceal my body language from the fact I was problem solving and concocting plans to deceive them at their own game.

My first plan of attack was to deactivate certain visual fields of their surveillance, effectively creating black spots, one by one, fooling them into believing that nothing was happening with their surveillance. And then I would install my own surveillance, alerting me to their unlawful break and entry of my apartment, tracking their movements inside my own personal space.

I feigned the start of a horrendous headache and went to the kitchen for some paracetamol tablets, taking two. Then I found my dark sunglasses and put them on, as if stopping the bright light from entering my vision and making the headache worse. I sat back down on the sofa for some time, acting out the perfect scene of a genuine bad headache—migraine even, pretending to run to the bathroom to vomit.

I rested again on the sofa with my head tilted back and started scanning the room for the hidden surveillance cameras. The dark sunglasses were a perfect barrier to conceal the movement of my eyes as I searched intricately for my targets. I found two lenses. One here in the right corner of the room, and the other located in the kitchen, covering the entry from the front door, the kitchen and a partial view of the study room.

I rubbed my forehead, faking the recurring pain of the bad headache, and then retreated to the study. I positioned myself flat on my back on the floor in the centre of the room. I had a perfect view of every facet of the study. Again, I gently massaged my head, as though my headache was excruciating, all the while searching the room for the surveillance cameras. I found three lenses; one directly next to the light in the middle of the room, another implanted near my computer so that the keyboard and screen were seen, and the other just above the skirting board, obviously for a view under surfaces in the room.

I proceeded with the rest of the apartment in the same manner. My acting was superb, Oscar worthy even. In my mind, I had formulated the plan for revenge. Their sight would be taken before their very eyes, without their knowledge or recognition of loss of vision. There were two cameras in every room, except the study where there were three. Even the bathroom was no longer private.

I needed to use my laptop. In fact, it was imperative. I was desperate to Google Georgia Harrison. But I dared not. If my apartment had been searched, sterilized and had surveillance installed, my laptop would also have been tapped, recording every word that I typed and every website I visited.

I figured using any technology in this apartment would be fatal to the game—for me. I could not even trust my cell phone now. My calls were probably being tracked and monitored as well, GPS of my whereabouts was certain to be installed from the CAI intelligence office.

I decided to ditch the phone. I would leave it at the University library tomorrow, or accidentally on purpose drop it into the dark and deep fishpond, for personal use by the overfed goldfish.

No, that would certainly arouse suspicion and make them watch me more closely. Instead, I would keep it for normal conversations with my work colleagues, friends and family, and so Mr. Rubin could contact me. I would leave it in the apartment when I did not want to be tracked.

Play the game. Play it better.

I went to bed but did not sleep. My mind was overloaded and way too alert to enter the REM zone.

Chapter 7

As dust motes floated about in the filtered beams of the morning sunlight that crept into my bedroom, I rose from my pretend slumber, dressed and headed to the gym for a workout—no cell phone.

The workout I imposed on myself was intense. I pushed myself to my absolute limit, propelling my mind from the knowledge of lack of control of my life, forced upon me in such a short, unwelcomed time.

I jogged home, showered, and dressed in my faded jeans and long-sleeved white cotton shirt, grabbed my phone and leather work satchel, then headed out the door to go to breakfast before the University library for research.

My personal taxi driver was waiting outside the apartment building: a most objectionable sight. I tensed in revulsion at my lack of freedom.

Play the game. Play it better.

I opened the taxi door.

'Mr. Darcy, good morning. Where are we headed on this beautiful day, may I ask?' the driver inquired, his manner polite.

'To Flowers for Fleur Café for breakfast, please. And may I ask, what shall I call you, since you have been given the privilege of chauffeuring me around?' I was smart to make connections to those involved with me, building alliances so to speak.

He looked at me through his rear vision mirror and studied my face. He hesitated before he answered. 'You may call me Max, Mr. Darcy. We will arrive at the café of your choice in approximately twenty minutes, sir.'

I looked at his eyes through his rear vision mirror and nodded, once, acknowledging his reply. 'Well... if we're going to be spending all this time together, let's have some music, Max. Your choice today,' I instructed him. I was testing him, to see if he was to follow my orders, or Mr. Rubin's.

He looked at me through his rear vision mirror again, studying my face, and then gave me a thumbs up. He switched on some music; classical, surprising me. It would have been my choice as well.

'Thank you for the lift, Max. How shall I contact you when I finish breakfast. I need to go to the University library for research next,' I said as I exited the taxi.

'Use this number on my card. You are my number one priority, Mr. Darcy.'

I took the card from him, then closed the door of the taxi noting the number plate as he departed.

I entered the Café, the dingle of the doorbell welcoming me. I sat at the same table I sat at yesterday with Georgia, and looked over the breakfast menu: eggs, bacon, toast, coffee. Excellent. It wasn't my normal practice to eat out for breakfast, lunch or dinner. But I had decided I would do it more regularly. That way, I wasn't being watched as I would be if I was still in my apartment.

At the clang of the doorbell heralding my exit, I loped off down the busy street towards the University, choosing not to be driven there by Max. The walk was a good thirty minutes, refreshing me and giving me time to clear my head. I needed to focus on the research I was planning to do.

I walked through the enormous glass expanse of the entry doors to the library and headed up to the fourth floor via the stairs, landing me in the home of medical information.

I found a table with a comfortable cushioned seat and organised my gear. I was going to be here for a while. I gathered my thoughts and wrote down the necessities of my research before I left the table to hit the nerd shelves.

Yes, I was officially, now a nerd! Except, I didn't have the glasses or the over controlled hairdo going on. Cliché I know. My eyes were still perfect, and my hair dark, in a business cut, short sides and back, manicured sideburns, and longish fringe—that had a mind of its own.

I scoured the shelves containing the anatomy of eyes and carried a few books back to the table to study in detail. I needed to plan where the mind-reading implant would be fitted into the eye structure, and the sizing of the components for maximum effect.

Hours passed as I thoroughly researched the subject, making copious notes and drawing extremely detailed diagrams. When I sat back, satisfied with my research gathering, my stomach grumbled, so I headed down to the cafeteria.

I sat among a thriving metropolis of nerds and geeks. It was my happy place. I just didn't want to admit it. I played a game of people watching, labelling them as popular or unpopular, psychopath or not, doctor or engineer or teacher.

Then I spotted a guy trying to pick up a girl. I decided this would be entertaining to watch as I ate. I observed their body language, their facial expressions, the games the girl would play, word wise, body wise. The games the boy would play, word wise, body wise.

It was like a dance of sorts. I watched how he would react to her, mimic her, and how he manoeuvred around her body language and other messages she inadvertently sent, consciously or not.

I had a girlfriend once. Twice. Four times. With each of them, that indefinable something was missing. And... I had been burned at the stake far too many times during my quest to find a suitable partner.

This guy, though, he had an interesting tactic. He maintained total eye contact the entire time and mirrored her body language. If she stepped away, he would step towards her. He smiled at her a lot and made her laugh, he touched her shoulder, arm, hands, a lot. He seemed to compliment her much, because of the way she would look down and blush, or throw back her head and laugh. And then he carried her food tray to her table for her and sat down beside her. This guy was good at the game. I bet that he has done this a million times before. I was watching a master at work.

I sighed as I continued to watch them interact. Wouldn't he love to know what she was really thinking? Wouldn't she love to know what he was really thinking?

I laughed to myself. How ironic—a mind-reading device—my specialty, apparently.

I returned to the fourth floor of the University library for phase two of my research—the brain. This was going to be far more problematic than research into the eye. Grey matter, and the mapping of areas involved in the mind-reading implantation from the eyes was extremely complex. I wasn't sure if I could conquer this part of the research. I really needed to talk to a medical professor with intimate knowledge of the workings of the brain, I think. But today, I would give it a go at least, and then I would request a medico from Mr. Rubin.

I walked to the medical book section and ran my finger

along the spine of the books, looking at the titles. My cell phone vibrated in my pocket, and I looked at my watch. Split! It was 2.05pm. It was Mr. Rubin.

I closed my eyes and answered. 'Hello, Mr. Rubin. I'm at the University library conducting research on various facets of my design, sir… time simply got away from me. I did not realise how late it was, sir… I cannot tell you over the phone, sir—it would not be wise… yes, I will report at 9am precisely tomorrow, sir… and I apologize that I did not make it to report to you at 2pm today … no, it will not happen again… sir—'

He hung up on me. Absolute impoliteness! He needs to take crash course Manners 101.

I sighed and opened my eyes then shoved the phone back into my pocket and clenched my teeth in frustration. I looked above the shelf I had been searching, to no avail. But then, there was the book I wanted. It had been placed entirely in the wrong area.

I reached up to grab it and was hit by the scent of her sweet perfume: Georgia's. My heart accelerated. I removed the book from the shelf and turned. I wandered up and down the library isles looking for her. She wasn't anywhere I could see. My heartbeat slowed as I became disappointed. How can the memory of a smell do that to someone? And besides, perhaps it was a popular perfume choice by many women. Georgia couldn't be the only one who wore it.

I moved along the isle to locate another book I for my research. I found it easily and removed the large book from the shelf, effectively creating a gap between the books so that one could see into the next isle.

I could only see half of her face framed by her wavy brown hair. But it was definitely her. Butterflies fluttered in my stomach as I realized that Georgia was close.

I opened the book and spoke, not making any eye contact.

'Miss Harrison, we meet again.' From my peripheral vision, I saw her move to the open space to look at me.

'Mr. Darcy,' she said, her voice full of surprise. 'Our paths cross again. What brings you here today?'

I smiled to myself. That's Georgia, straight to the point.

'You know… design, research, create … I'm in the research phase, and you? What brings you to the heart and brain of the medical floor?'

'Psychology research,' she said matter of factly.

I looked down at my book and grinned. How apt, psychology, reading people. That was something I needed to do with her. She was unreadable, unpredictable.

'Are you smirking at me, Mr. Darcy?' she asked, her eyes serious. Then she appeared before me in the same isle.

'No, not at all, Miss Harrison,' I replied, keeping my voice even, refusing to make eye contact with her.

'Liar, liar pants on fire, Mr. Darcy,' she said without an ounce of humour in her voice.

Then she snapped her book closed and bumped into me as she moved away. She turned to face me, walking backwards. 'There is a whole chapter devoted to people who exhibit your character traits, Mr. Darcy,' she called after me, this time with a hint of humour in her voice.

I stopped reading the brain book and stared straight ahead of me.

What character traits is she talking about?

Her voice then came from the book space on the other side of the shelf again. 'The chapter is titled "Stalkers",' she added assertively.

I turned my face towards hers.

'What? You think that I am stalking you, Georgia? How sad and boring your life must be if you believe that!' I spat the words at her fuelled with bitterness. I snapped my book shut, grabbed the other two brain books and stormed off back to my workspace, dropping the books down and creating a loud ear-splitting crack, disturbing everyone working on the fourth floor. I looked around at the eyes that pierced me like daggers.

I breathed slowly to release the tension from my muscles from our altercation. I rested my forehead against my left hand and returned to working on in solitude, blocking out all reality in the library.

Study of the brain made for fascinating reading, but it left me with more questions than when I started out.

What is it that generates thoughts and where do they come from?

What is conscience, and how is it formed?

Why do some seem to be void of conscience, knowing right from wrong?

What about creativity—how can one think up something from nothing?

Why are some people gifted without even having had to learn what they are gifted in?

What about belief in God and faith? Where does that come from?

Why do some believe and others not?

What about conscious thought compared to unconscious thought? And dreams—Why? How?

I sat back in the chair and sighed in deep contemplation. There seemed to be an area of brain function that cannot be explained or measured. Frustrated was a word used lightly to as how I was feeling right now. Was it the brain research or Georgia's derogatory comment that pierced my heart and made me feel aggravated?

Whatever it was, she was just like the rest of them. How could I have fallen for a little bit of hope that she was different to other women? Stupid, stupid idiot!

I ran my hand through my hair and looked at my watch. 7pm. Time to head home. I called Max, gathered my stuff and headed out of the library doors. Max was there waiting me. For once I was glad to see him.

'Straight home please, Max.'

'Yes, sir,' he replied, looking at me in his rear vision mirror.

The rain pelted onto the car and the sound of the squeak of the windscreen wipers began hypnotising me. It was Max's voice informing me of our arrival that pulled me out of my distant place.

'8am tomorrow, please Max,' I said as I left the taxi. I sprinted to the apartment building entrance through the pouring rain, then slowed my pace considerably, walking slowly up the stairs to the apartment.

I inhaled deeply as a sadness settled over me. It used to my apartment. My bachelor pad. But not anymore. I now shared it with the prying eyes of security at the CAI, and goodness knows who else.

I unlocked the door and entered my dwelling, gently closing the door behind me. The aroma of another home cooked meal assaulted my nostrils. Beef Stroganoff, I think. I placed my bag into the study and wandered into the kitchen and stirred the pot of food. My stomach growled.

They won't kill me yet, I thought. *I haven't finished their most valuable project. When I do, I am pretty sure that they will dispose of me. I will be a high security risk to them otherwise. I know too much. I was officially living on borrowed time.*

I jumped at the knocking on the front door. I waited and hoped whoever it was would go away. But it continued, becoming more aggressive each time until it became an urgent thumping on the door.

I made my way to the door and stopped and listened again. I heard one more thump, and then a faint, 'Please open the door.'

I smelled her sweet perfume before I saw her when I opened the door a fraction, thinking twice about talking to her. She was the last person I wanted to see after she accused me of being a stalker.

How did she get my address if I "don't exist"?

'Cohen, I know it is you. I followed you here from the library,' she said, her voice assertive, answering my unspoken question.

She pushed on the door forcing it open, taking me by surprise. I stopped her from opening the door fully, keeping the door more closed than open. It was for her safety.

'Cohen, let me in. I want to apologise to you.' Her voice was sincere and full of regret. Then she barged in, taking advantage of my moment of weakness.

Bossy.

I blocked her way into my apartment. I couldn't let her venture further in because of the heavy surveillance. I didn't want her involved in any way. I had to protect her.

I wrapped my arms around her and pulled her against me. It was the only thing I could do under the circumstances.

'Cohen?' her voice was full of shock.

I moved my lips close to her ear and spoke in a hushed tone. 'Listen to me. You need to leave. My apartment is under surveillance. Every move I make is being watched, recorded and analysed. If you are smart—you will leave.'

She placed her hand around the back of my head sending a tingling sensation down my spine. She kissed the side of my neck and then put her lips close to my ear and spoke so quietly that her voice was barely audible. 'Then let's make it dramatic for them, whoever they are. Kiss me, Cohen, and then I will slap you across the face and storm out of your apartment. That will give them something interesting to watch and analyse.'

I couldn't believe what she was suggesting. It was way out of left field.

'Georgia… I… I… can't. I don't know you. I won't feel comfortable kis—' My words were taken away from me as her lips were on mine. Her warm, soft lips, weakening my knees and taking my strength. I wanted to melt into her. I could very easily lock lips with her forever.

Then she pulled away, looked angrily at me and slapped me across the face. Her slap bit into my cheek and the sting echoed about through the layers of my skin. My immediate reaction was to put my hand over my smarting cheek, and then I watched her storm off, slamming the front door behind her.

She was good. Very good. Even I believed her. I stared at the front door for some time and relived our kiss. And then I ran my hand through my hair, about turned and walked through to a large sash window overlooking the road. I watched as she stepped into a cab and disappeared into the distance.

Why had my life suddenly become so complicated, dangerous even?

Why couldn't I have met Georgia under pleasant circumstances?

I breathed out in disappointment and touched my burning cheek again.

I turned on the sports channel, grabbed my Beef Stroganoff and settled down in front of the television, wishing that my worries could be taken away, even for just a short while.

There was so much to plan to stay ahead of the game; so much to do.

Was I running out of time?

Chapter 8

'**M**r. Darcy,' White Girl's voice squeaked, as bubbly as ever.

'Good morning… aaahhh…' I was waiting for her to fill in her name, but she didn't. Must I prompt her like a child? 'How shall I address you?' I asked. Still no reply. 'What is your name?' I asked again—for heaven's sake!

'Me?' she asked, her voice impossibly higher. I pinched my lips together in frustration and looked to the floor to control the laughter that was about to erupt from me. I looked at her and nodded, raising my eyebrows.

'Oh… Mia, sir. Go right through. Mr. Rubin is ready for you.'

'Thank you… Mia.' I smiled slightly at her before I walked through the door of Mr. Rubin's office.

His red high-backed leather chair was turned away from me, as usual.

'9am as requested, Mr. Rubin,' I said, speaking to the chair.

His chair turned slowly, and he gave me three slow claps. My blood began to boil. I looked at his face and narrowed my eyes at him. At this point in time, there was nothing to like about this pitiful excuse for a man. What is his job description in this corporation anyway? I would love to know what is in the mind of this man.

'Progress update, Mr. Darcy!' He spat saliva as the words left his small repulsive mouth.

'I am in the important research phase of the design, sir. I cannot make further progress on the implant until I have intricate details on eye and brain structure. Once these details are sorted, then I can move forward with the drawings of the mind-reading implant... and then build a prototype. Do you have a subject chosen for the testing of the device, Mr. Rubin?'

He stared at me before answering my question. I could see his dark mind turning over as he considered my question. He twiddled his thumbs around and around one another as he continued to look at me. 'Mr. Darcy, I have two possible worthy candidates under consideration for trialling the device. How much more research time do you need?'

'Time wise... it's hard to pinpoint at this stage. Thoroughness is vitally important, including discussions with medical professors—ophthalmology and neurology. If any mistake is made, it could result in blindness, or irreparable brain damage, or both. Mr. Rubin, I need you to allow me to conduct my research as I see fit, in the hours that I need to work, without having to return to the office to report to you. It is most frustrating when I am in the middle of deep thought and problem solving, and then it's interrupted. I can't get back to that particular, essentially important moment... that particular genius creative moment. It would considerably speed up the process of development of the implant if I could report to you once I have made significant progress.'

He stared at me in his accusational, derogatory Mr. Rubin way, and then sat back in his red leather chair. 'Mr. Darcy, if that is the way you are going to make the quickest progress on the development of the new technology, I give you permission to work your own way. I must remind you though, that the implant is of the highest priority, and it has been deemed top secret by the company. You are not to speak to anyone about your work. A contract is being drafted as we speak. We will have a lawyer to thoroughly navigate the contract for you to sign.' He cleared his throat. 'You are now wasting valuable time standing in my office. The meeting is closed. Good day, Mr. Darcy!' He turned his chair away from me.

His blatant disrespect of me made me see red. I was infuriated. What was it that he did in his sterile office daily, anyway? I turned on my heel and escaped the suffocating, arrogant, hostile Mr. Rubin. The less contact I had with him the better.

I stopped at White Girl's desk, but she did not look at me. She didn't even bat an eyelid.

Challenge on.

'Can I get you a tea or coffee, Mia?' I asked in a warm, smooth voice.

She looked up at me expressionless. 'Oh… Mr. Darcy. No, thank you. It is not my break time yet,' she bubbled with her squeaky voice.

'Ah, but you would not have to move. I would be getting you the beverage. How about white milk to blend in with the whiteness around here, or some snow perhaps?' I asked, adding humour to see if she had any.

She put her hand over her mouth and let out a quiet giggle. 'Oh… Mr. Darcy. No, thank you. It is not my break time yet,' she responded in the exact same words and tone of squeakiness.

I stared at her briefly and noticed that she was writing excessively small words on a small piece of white paper. She slid it over to me in the smoothest of movements; precise and hardly noticeable at all. I took her hint and moved my hand over the barely visible piece of paper and hid it in the palm of my hand. 'Good day then, Mia,' I said formally, and left for the elevator, ascending one floor to my own office.

I sat at my desk to read the note but thought the better of it—surveillance. I walked over to the massive windows, stood closely to the glass, and inconspicuously read the note.

We are being watched. Mx

Point taken. So, I'm guessing Mia is not who she seems. Is Mia her real name?

I went back to my desk and my designs. I also retrieved the research from the nerdy floor of the University library yesterday. It was time to start melding the technology to the human eye and brain. It was still purely science fiction. Didn't Mr. Rubin see that?

I could not see how it would work. And to be truthful, I didn't want the mind-reading implant to work. There could never be any good come out of it. It would get into the hands of the wrong people who would use it to the detriment of humankind, for the power and money hungry whom have no compassion for others, only their own self-indulgences, gratifications and wealth in mind.

Play the game. Play it better.

I returned to the copy of the original drawings I had given Mr. Rubin and studied them closely, checking and cross checking. I poured hours upon hours into going over the design until I was certain I could not make any improvements on the technology. Then I stepped away from it and let it settle in my mind. My brain would continue working on it without any conscious thought about the implant, and then bring to my consciousness, any problems or improvements. The brain was absolutely and totally fascinating in that way.

I left the office and walked three blocks to the park. I craved to connect to nature, and to the laughter and peacefulness of normal humans, and to soak up the warmth and brightness of the sun. It was essential for my health. My nature supercharger.

I grabbed a hot dog on the way and perched myself against the trunk of an ancient oak tree. At first, the sounds of nature spoke to me: the gentle breeze zigzagging its way around and through the leaves and branches, the chirping of the birds, the barking of playful dogs, and the laughter of children as they played.

And then my eyes settled upon a couple—a man and a woman—relaxing on a blanket lost in each other. He was talking to her, his eyes connected to hers the entire time of the conversation. He kissed her. He pressed his body against hers and ran his hands over her back and along the side of her face, only to receive a shove from her. I bet he would love to be able to read her mind.

And what about her? Would she like to be able to read his mind and then know what he had planned to do to her?

Would a mind-reading device be a good thing for people?

Would it take away from relationships, or would it give to relationships?

And do you really want people in your head with your private thoughts and ideas?

There had to be a shut off point for mind-reading technology. Surely it will not be offered to the general population.

What would be the point of it? The only way that the technology could be used is for intelligences, spying, espionage, criminology. Such a device like this would have to be top secret, never to be revealed to living souls. Perhaps I should also invent a memory extracting device to erase any memory or information of the existence of mind-reading technology to spare the lives of those accidentally caught up in its use.

Is this even possible?

When the trees cast long shadows on the lush, green grass,

I returned to work and gathered my leather work satchel and walked home at a leisurely pace. The world as I knew it was going to change, and dramatically for some. For others, life would remain the same, and they would remain utterly clueless as to what was going on in the technology and communications field.

Blessed are the pure in heart.

I continued to walk to my apartment with the feeling that I was being followed. My life was not my own now, and never would be. I opened my apartment door to the smell of roast chicken and vegetables.

'Thank you to whoever is making me the delicious dinners. You are spoiling me,' I said out loud, knowing the message would be passed on to the chef—woman or man—I did not know. The more allies I had the better.

Play the game. Play it better.

I ate my meal at the dining table, cleaned up and then headed to the lounge room and turned on the sport—football.

Establish a routine.

Stick to it.

Arouse no suspicion.

Now, it looked as though I was watching the football. And I wanted it to look as though I was watching the football, but in reality, I was not. I was planning the slow and unnoticed blackness of their vision into my apartment—the security cameras.

At the end of the football game I headed to the shower, using ample hot water to fog up the bathroom, and hence their security cameras. Under the limited vision of the steamy bathroom, I prepared for attack on security, drawing a detailed map and listing the steps to freedom in blind spots around my apartment. The cover of darkness was critical in the accomplishment of this mission. They will have no idea that they are about to be beaten at their own spy game.

I climbed into bed and drew nonsensical illustrations on a

piece of paper, then folded it into a paper plane and threw it for their amusement, before I turned off the lights—but not to sleep—to await the appointed time to attack, little by little.

At exactly 2.27am, I dressed in black clothes under the covers of the bed—long sleeved shirt, long pants, gloves, balaclava, socks and sunglasses. I pulled my black permanent marker from my pocket and made my way to the very first surveillance camera and carefully added one black dot to the edge of the rim of glass, three quarters around the edge of the circular camera. I then proceeded to do this to each camera according to my calculations on the plan to create a blind spot in their vision, where I could have invisibility in my own apartment, without their awareness. Thank goodness I had double doors at the entrance; one side would be visible, the other not.

Within thirty minutes I was back in bed, and this time I went to sleep. I was pleased with my progress, and thus my defiance of CAI surveillance.

I hit the gym before work as was my routine schedule, showered at gym, headed to the Flowers for Fleur Café for breakfast without surveillance, and then called Max for my transport to CAI Headquarters. I efficiently hand scanned into the security system and entered my office.

It had been tidied!

I was seething.

Now I would have to waste time tracking where my information was and then get my head into the mind-reading eye-implant zone again before I could make any forward progress.

I would have a word to Mr. Rubin. This was absolutely not acceptable!

I stormed out of my office and rode the elevator to the floor below.

'Mia,' I said curtly, not looking at her as I walked past by and assertively headed towards the doorway of Mr. Rubin's office.

'Mr. Darcy!' Mia squeaked after me.

I ignored her. I had a bone to pick with the obnoxious man.

'Cohen!' Mia called louder; all signs of her squeakiness gone. Her voice was a much lower pitch. Normal even.

I turned at once. I took her more seriously with her "new" voice.

She lowered her face, frowned and shook her head quickly, warning me not to go into the office. I walked over to her and stopped closely in front of her. I tilted my chin down and looked deeply into her eyes. The glare in her eyes told me to step back. She was trying to tell me something, desperately trying to tell me something, but couldn't. She was gagged for some reason.

Did she fear for her job, her safety, or her life? I wish I knew. The mind-reading device would be quite advantageous right now.

I stared into her eyes for a moment longer and then stepped back from her and made my way back to the elevator. I must try to talk to her at some other time, away from the eyes of the security cameras. Maybe in a park, or perhaps in a loud music environment, where our conversation could not be overheard. I would slip her a note as she did to me yesterday.

I re-entered my office and went about rearranging it my way, the way my brain and personality liked to work. Agitated, I sat down and tried to penetrate the design zone in my mind. It was not so easy once my feathers had been ruffled.

I pulled out my cell phone and loaded my ears with earphones. I found a very sombre piece of cello music: *Deathzone* by Apocalyptica, closed my eyes and put my head back to dissolve into the melody to carry me to my creative place, my place of dark rainforest trees with swirling mist, a quietness akin to the premonition of danger lurking, upping the adrenaline surging through my body alerting every sense, making my brain neurons fire with ferocity.

Within a short amount of time, the creative Cohen was

present.

I removed my music and headed to the tidied working drawings to find my detailed sketches of the working eye, and my drawn prototype of the eye to brain implant—some details missing at this point in time. I wanted to start to marry the two together.

I needed to draw what I saw in my head. The A0 paper size was not large enough. In my anger, I screwed the paper into a ball and threw it at the wall, watching as it bounced off and fell to the floor. I repeated the act again and again and again and became amused by the landing space of the paper balls.

In my insane moment of amusement, I saw the wall space as my new working drawing: my canvas. I attacked it with passion, ensuring that exact details were meticulously drawn. I knew it would be deadly to miss any detail, no matter how insignificant it seemed. Every structure of the eye was vitally important.

I worked like a madman, seized by an all-encompassing passion and insanity.

At 8.30pm I left the office, exhausted.

Max was waiting for me outside the CAI headquarters and greeted me politely before driving me home. I entered the apartment to the delicious smell of lasagne.

'Thank you!' I called before I tucked into the food. The home cooked meal filled my ravenous stomach. One human need was satisfied.

I made myself a strong coffee to keep me awake. I had a routine of sport to watch on television, followed by my hot steamy shower to add progress information to my plan of altering their security vision, and then to wait for 2.27am to add more "graffiti" to their surveillance cameras.

The next morning, I headed to gym as per my routine, stopping at the Flowers for Fleur Café for breakfast.

I took the table by the window as it was the only one left and buried my head in the daily paper.

I smelled her sweet perfume before I felt her presence.

She placed her warm hand onto my arm and my skin tingled under her touch. I took a deep breath before I looked up at her with a half-smile.

She sat opposite me. 'You know you are being followed, Cohen,' Georgia said in hushed tones.

I smiled to myself. 'Yeah—by you. Who is stalking who now?' I jeered.

I heard a quiet giggle. It was nice to hear.

'Seriously, Cohen, see the man in the dark corner with dark glasses and his ear turned in our direction as if he has bionic hearing? He followed you out of the gym, keeping his distance. He stopped walking when you stopped. I followed him, stopping when he stopped. It was quite a fun game really,' Georgia said in whisper with excitement plastered all over her face.

I peered over the top of the newspaper at my tracker and committed his face to memory. Then I locked eyes with Georgia. 'You need to stay away from me,' I said, my tone low and serious, warning her off.

She stared back at me with a challenging, defiant look in her eye.

'Please leave... Georgia. It would be safer for you. I don't want you to get involved,' I said in a quiet stern voice. I looked away from her and shook my head. 'Please… go!' I implored. I looked back into her eyes, warning her with mine, unsure of what she would do. She was so unpredictable. That mind-reading implant would come in handy.

She tilted her head to one side and her eyes saddened. She looked down before she stood and looked at me despondently before walking off. My heart hurt as I watched her leave the café. But it was for the best. I ran my hand through my hair and looked over at my tracker, then decided to leave as well.

Max was waiting for me outside the café. It was such a welcome sight.

Chapter 9

Oddness greeted me in the reception area outside my office. Once upon a time, the reception area was bare, with white marble floors, white walls, a white ceiling, no furniture and no personality. Sterile, just like the floor below where Mr. Rubin resided.

But today, there were two white chairs: one occupied by a man reading a newspaper. He was dressed in a black business suit, black shirt but no tie. His hair was dark, and he sported a manicured short growth of facial hair.

As I walked past him, he glanced up at me, then cast his eyes back to his newspaper. I scanned my hand and entered my office then bee-lined to the enormous glass window. I placed my hands on top of my head as I looked out over the city. More people seemed to be appearing in my daily walk of life. I wasn't imagining it. It was real and it worried me.

I went to my desk and found a small spiral bound notebook and started a diary of peculiarities that were popping up here and there. I detailed them in the notebook to look for a pattern, if there was any. I also wrote a detailed description of trackers and other peoples who seemed suspicious, just like Black Suit Guy outside my office.

Next, I cut out a particularly small piece of white paper and wrote a meeting time and place on it to give to Mia. I did not write her name on it, nor mine.

I exited my office and stood before the elevators. Black-Suit-Man was still sitting there reading the newspaper.

'Mr. Darcy, good morning,' Mia squeaked as I entered the twenty-seventh floor.

I stopped in front of her. 'Is Mr. Rubin in? May I see him briefly?' I asked, sliding my hand over to hers to pass her the small square of white paper. I tapped my middle finger twice when she didn't follow my lead with the message passing.

She looked at the computer screen, picked up a file and placed it where my hand was, covering the little note I was trying to give her. She picked up the phone and spoke in a bubbly voice to Mr. Rubin, informing him that I was here to see him.

The office door clicked, and Mia indicated for me to enter the office.

I nodded to her, and she tapped her middle finger twice as I did. I understood it as she had the piece of paper. She was smarter than she looked.

Mr. Rubin sat in his disproportionate red chair with the high back facing me as usual. He turned slowly with his elbows resting on the arms of the chair. His hands were together, but only his fingertips touching.

'Mr. Darcy. I have been expecting you. What seems to be the problem?'

'Mr. Rubin, my progress was considerably slowed yesterday because my office had been tidied. I request that tidying does not occur again as I have a specific working arrangement of my designs, research and notes. When you interfere with my office, you interfere with the flow of work and the amount of output. It is not to your advantage to intrude on my intellectual mapping in this manner,' I said. My voice was assertive, but not aggressive. I also wanted to ask him if he had people tracking me, but I needed to make more observations of placement of people around me first. Perhaps it would be better to play ignorant in this area. The less he knew what I observed going on, the better.

'Mr. Darcy, tidiness of your office space is easier for security purposes. I am also offended by your use of the wall as a drawing area. It is akin to graffiti. I abhor graffiti. It will be cleaned off at 4pm today.'

I shifted my body weight onto my other foot. He was getting under my skin and rubbing me the wrong way. 'Mr. Rubin, if you erase my working drawings of the MR Implant, I will cease to work. Do you understand how much thought, energy, precise transfer of the anatomy of the eye went into that "graffiti" as you call it? Did you even consider asking me as to why I chose to work on the wall?' I challenged him, using my hands for added effect and persuasion as I spoke.

'Humour me, Mr. Darcy! Why did you draw on the wall like a two-year-old with crayons?' he retorted, belittling my work idiosyncrasy.

'For security purposes, Mr. Rubin! If I had drawn the images onto the computer and saved the data on the hard drive, the system could have been hacked, and the work stolen. My next wall graffiti will consist of an enlarged drawing of the brain. When that is complete, I will need to consult medical professionals, of your choice, to discuss positioning of the mind-reading implant.'

Mr. Rubin cleared his throat and sighed, like I was boring him.

'I hope I have humoured you to your liking, Mr. Rubin,' I lied, but it sounded feasible. I tried to keep all sarcasm out of my voice. It was hard to do as his arrogance irritated me. It was like rubbing salt into a wound.

'Conceded, Mr. Darcy, the graffiti will remain.'

I relaxed my stance. Victory. I had won. 'The next time I will see you, will be when I need to consult medical personnel and a biomedicalmechanic department. Thank you for your time, Mr. Rubin.'

I nodded my head at him slightly before I turned on my heel and left his office. The door locked behind me. I glanced over at Mia as I headed for the elevator.

'Mr. Darcy, enjoy your day,' she squeaked in her bubbly voice.

Black-Suit-Man sat in the chair of my office floor. This time with a briefcase by his side. His elbows rested on the arms of the chair, his fingers entwined in front of him, and his head was tilted back against the wall. He stared at the numbers above the elevator door without blinking.

I scanned my hand and entered my office. I stood back and looked at my eye "graffiti" and smiled to myself. Perhaps I should develop my own "tag" to sign next to my design drawings when I finish, then Mr. Rubin could call it "graffiti"!

Taking my detailed eye diagram over to the wall, I continued with the intricate details, double checking and cross checking when I thought I had finished. The proportions were perfect. Maybe I should have been an artist instead of a technology engineer. If I was, I certainly wouldn't have landed myself in this situation. But then again... Leonardo da Vinci...

The beeping of the alarm on my cell phone alerted me to the possible meeting with Mia. If I left now, I would be there before her. I would prefer it that way. Then I could judge her body language and demeanour, guiding me in how to conduct the secret meeting.

I looked over my eye graffiti once more and then left the office, opening my door to an empty lobby. No Man-in-a-Black-Suit. Was I reading into the situation too much? I mean... my office wasn't the only one on that floor.

I waited less than twenty seconds for the elevator to arrive. The doors opened, and there standing before me was Black-Suit-Man, staring at the numbers above the elevator doors. He reeked of suspicion!

'Ground floor, please Alex,' I said to the elevator operator.

Black-Suit-Man followed me out of the elevator and through the stupid revolving doors. I hightailed it three blocks to the bar where I was meeting Mia. I ordered a drink, sat and waited.

At fifteen minutes past the arranged meeting time, Mia had not turned up. Either she did not get the note, or she would not, or could not, meet me. I downed my beer and was about to get up when Black-Suit-Man sat beside me. He slipped a note to me under the table. He raised his glass to me. 'Cheers,' he said, then stood and offered me his hand to shake before nodding his head and leaving the bar.

I looked around me, feeling paranoid. Nobody moved or even glanced my way. Nobody seemed to be acting out of sorts. I opened the note under the table and placed it into the palm of my hand to read.

It was the exact piece of paper I had given Mia this morning—for credibility, I guess. There were no names, as I had done with her.

Change of plan. Same place, 8.30pm tonight.

I flipped the paper over to the other side. It was definitely authentic—my original note from this morning. Did Mia and Black-Suit-Man know each other? Great couple they would make—White Girl and Black-Suit-Man—opposites, they attract apparently.

I returned to the office. This time Black-Suit-Man was sitting in one of the chairs with his phone, his gaze securely glued to the screen. I scuffled past him. Still no eye contact, no form of acknowledgement whatsoever.

I entered the great graffiti room again and sat at my desk. I needed to start on the working drawing of the brain. It had to be drawn to scale with the eye. Maybe I could be an anatomical artist. I could even publish my own book, "The Human Body— Beauty in the Eye of the Beholder" by Cohen Darcy. I snickered to myself before I studied the brain diagrams I had drawn at the university library recently.

On closer inspection of the drawings, I discovered I had missed some details. I would have to return to the geeky nerd floor of the university library. Oh joy of joys! I rubbed the back of my neck before I stood, gathered my gear, and headed out the door again.

Black-Suit-Man appeared to be sleeping with his head tilted back against the wall. I had the urge to go and feel for his pulse in his neck to see if he was dead. But I didn't.

Instead, I pushed the button for the elevator and then banged on the metal double doors of the elevator shaft to see if that would wake him from his beauty sleep. It didn't. Maybe he was dead after all?

I turned and walked over to him.

'Sir, could you please tell me the time on your watch. Mine seems to have stopped,' I said, forcing him to interact with me.

He lifted his head from the wall, looked at his watch, and then spoke with a deep alto voice, '4.52pm.'

And that was that. Would it kill him to use some social interactivisms. He was so stoic. He still did not make eye contact with me.

'Thank you kindly, sir,' I added to his response, smiling at him. By the end of our in-depth conversation the elevator had arrived, and I entered it to descend to the ground floor to the mysterious revolving door.

Max was waiting for me in the taxi. At least he gave me a few more words to chomp on than Black-Suit-Man.

'Hi, Max. Would you be able to take me to the university library again? I have to hit the nerd bookshelves. I won't need you after that. I'm heading to a bar to meet a friend for a drink.'

Max looked at me in his rear vision mirror and waited before he spoke to me. He always seemed to do that. Odd.

'Certainly, Mr. Darcy. But I see you as more of a geek that a nerd!' he responded.

So... he does have a sense of humour! I chuckled to myself.

'Have a good night, Max! I'll catch you later,' I said as I left the taxi, meaning every word. He seemed like a nice bloke.

The nerdy fourth floor of the university library was crowded with super geeks. It was difficult to find a study table. But eventually I did, between someone who looked like Clark Kent and another guy who reminded me of Peter Parker. I was in the Metropolis of Nerdville. And, I felt very comfortable.

I headed to the brain shelves and spent a considerable amount of time studying the details of brain diagrams, finding the book that gave me the intricate details I needed for the mind-reading implant.

Feeling incredibly pleased with my geekiness, I headed back to the Metropolis of Nerdville with Superman and Spiderman.

When I sat at the long timber table, I glimpsed her wavy brown hair from the corner of my eye. My heart leapt before it sank, remembering our last encounter at the Flowers for Fleur Café, and the look she gave me before she left.

I wished it had not ended that way. But I had to protect her.

I looked over at her. She rested her forehead in her hand as she concentrated on her study. I pushed a breath out of my pursed lips. *I'm sorry I hurt you Georgia...*

Back to my brain book.

I had a huge task ahead of me, drawing the brain in detail accurately. I decided to grab a coffee to increase my alertness.

I returned from the cafeteria with two cups. A coffee for me, and tea for Georgia.

Approaching her silently from the side, I placed her cup of tea on her desk.

'Peace offering. Tea, white, with one sugar,' I said in quiet voice.

She looked at the cup before she looked at me, her blue eyes connecting with mine. I soaked them in, filling every cell of my being.

'Very observative, Cohen,' she replied quietly, smiling gently at me. 'Thank you.'

I smiled shyly to myself and looked away from her, unable to slow my rapid heartbeat and settle the butterflies trying to escape from my stomach. I became lost for words, tongue-tied. Why did she do this to me?

'I should get back to my study. Enjoy your tea,' I said gently, not wanting to move away from her. I needed to protect her. As I turned to walk away from her, my heart wanted her to tell me to stay, but she didn't.

To Nerdville it was then. At least I would get my work done.

Thankfully, Georgia was out of my line of view as I drew. And as I became lost in the intricacies of drawing a detailed diagram of the brain, I soon forgot all about her, and finished what I had come to the library to do.

I gathered my work together, closed the large brainiac book, and stilled. I smelled her sweet perfume and felt the light touch of her hand on my shoulder. My skin tingled were her hand rested. What sort of spell was she castling on me? And what was the antidote, should I desperately need it?

'There is a book jammed on the shelf that I need, Cohen. I can't free it. Would you have a go at it, please?' she asked in a clear voice, unknowingly singing to my soul.

How could I not fulfil her request? I looked up at her and nodded.

She smiled at me and mouthed, 'Thank you.'

'Lead the way,' I said, bowing at her with a serious face. She giggled quietly and turned. I followed her to the shelves of books in question. If you asked my heart, it would follow her anywhere, but my mind would hesitate. To protect my heart.

She stopped and pointed to the jammed book titled "Higher Intelligences". As she moved her hand away, I reached up to pull it out. It was indeed jammed. I moved my eyes along the shelf further and found a smaller book that would be easier to remove. I wriggled it out of the shelf. Then I returned to "Higher Intelligences" and removed it with ease and handed to her.

'Thank you,' she replied with a grin. Her hand brushed mine lightly as she took the book from me. I inhaled a sharp breath of air in response to the warm tingling feeling her touch gave me. Our eyes locked for what seemed for like an eternity, but I knew that it wasn't. I dragged my eyes from hers with reluctance.

I don't have time for a relationship.

'So, is your tracker here with you tonight?' Georgia asked out of the blue.

I smiled coyly at her. 'No,' I answered, relieved she had spoken to break my emotional soul connection with her.

'Good. I need to talk to you about the book. Is here a good place?' she asked, raising her eyebrows at me.

I looked at my watch. It was 7.30pm. I drew in a deep breath and shook my head. 'No. I need to meet someone at 8.30. So… I have to go… about now,' I said, disappointed that I would have to leave her.

'A girl?' she asked, looking into my eyes and melting me into hers.

'Yes,' I answered quietly.

She looked away from me then, before she looked to the book in her hand. Her face was unreadable. She looked back up at me and with a crooked smile. 'Well, enjoy. Hopefully I can catch up with you later about the book. Can I email you to arrange a time?' she asked as her voice cracked a little.

'No!' I answered sharply. 'Give me your phone details and I will contact you. My name will be different, but you will know that it is me by the content of the email.'

'Hmmm. Mr. Mysterious. You need to explain this peculiarity to me sometime. Follow me and I will write down what you need,' she said, eyeing me with suspicion.

I'm sorry, Georgia. My life is becoming so complicated...

As she handed me the little piece of yellow paper with her phone number on it, I looked deeply into her eyes. If she knew what I was working on she would stay well clear of me. I was about to become humanity's most liked and most hated human being. She would despise me if she knew about the mind-reading device. I had to cut ties with her as soon as I could. I would talk to her about the book and then end communications with her pronto—in the nicest possible way of course.

I pocketed the yellow piece of paper and leaned in close to her ear. 'Soon,' I whispered to her, then collected my gear and left the university library to head to the bar to meet Mia.

This should be interesting to say the very least.

'Mr. Darcy, very punctual,' she squeaked from behind me.

I turned around but could not see White Girl. Instead, an attractive red-headed woman stood behind me, smiling with sparkling green eyes. I frowned at her and then looked to my left and right, for Mia.

'Tardiness is not accepted,' she squeaked again. I turned back to her and impolitely stared at her, and narrowed my eyes. She did not look like Mia, but her voice was so convincing as Mia.

'Cohen, relax. It's me... Mia,' she said in a lower tone of voice. 'Minus the white hair wig, minus the brown eye contact lenses, and thankfully, minus the irritating squeaky voice!'

I shook my head at her in disbelief. 'Spill the beans, White

Girl,' I said with caution.

'I have come here to warn you. Mr. Rubin is a very dangerous man. We have been monitoring him for quite a while, gathering evidence, using higher intelligence to nail him. He is planning to use you as the guinea pig of the mind-reading implant, and then deal with you, if you know what I mean. You have been very clever in your ability to outwit him so far. He doesn't like you having the upper hand over him. He is tracking you. We are tracking you. And we are tracking his trackers. The game is on. Act naturally, at all times… and you need an SOS word so that we can step in to save you. What will the word be, Cohen?' Mia was straight to the point, no frills attached.

I frowned and looked at her for a moment longer, half-shocked, half-surprised, wholly filled with fear.

'RED!' I responded, no frills. "Red is my SOS word to save me from whatever occurrence that you think is going to happen to me.'

'Red it is, Mr. Darcy. And now for a code to use to see who's hands you are in. Remember this, Mr. Darcy—your line is—you wish—and our trackers will answer with—*jellyfish*.'

I looked down and laughed. How absurd. How ridiculous; "you wish jellyfish!" I could hear the sarcasm in my own mind voice.

'You find the situation amusing, Mr. Darcy? Believe me, when you look death in the eye, you will not find it amusing.' Her face was void of emotion.

I raised my eyebrows at her and lifted my glass of scotch. 'Cheers!'

She nodded back at me.

'Does he know, Mia? That you lead a double life?' I asked.

'If he did, he would have my head as an ornament. I have protectors all around me. They are even here in the pub, as are your trackers and their trackers. It is like a game, though deadly.

And we must use our higher intelligences—outwit, outlast. Our mission is as peacekeepers on the earth. There are technologies that must not be shared with some. Do you understand what I am saying, Mr. Darcy?' Mia said, her green eyes piercing the depths of mine, searching for my conscience.

'Yes,' I answered, maintaining her piercing eye contact.

She left me then and headed to a corner booth. She sat with a strikingly handsome man. Was he her protector, a tracker, or a boyfriend? Only observation of their connections would establish the answer to that, and I did not have the time to sit here to be a spectator of life. I had a lot to think about.

I headed out of the bar and Max was there waiting for me.

Who paid his wage, I wondered.

Do I trust him, or not?

Chapter 10

I entered my apartment via the right double door to be visible on their surveillance. The aroma of chicken cacciatore awakened my dormant stomach. In silence I served it on a dinner plate and sat at the dining table to eat it.

Will my life be forever like this? Monitored, analysed and interfered with?

Is it possible to press the eject button and disappear off the radar?

Tempting… if it was at all possible.

I did not watch the sport on television tonight as I had done routinely since my awareness of the surveillance cameras. Instead, I headed in to the shower, turned it on to fog up the bathroom to add to my plans of interference with their surveillance vision—I had nearly finished.

I reclined in bed in the darkness of my room after my shower, wide awake, trying to make sense of the new information I had been given.

According to Mia, the White Girl, who is not really the White Girl, Mr. Rubin has bad intentions with the mind-reading implant. He has me under surveillance. He has me tracked and will use me as the guinea pig for my invention, after which he will then kill me.

But, Mia who claims to be like a secret agent, has trackers following my trackers, who will step in to save me if I use the SOS word RED.

She called it a game. Outwit, outlast were her words.

Play the game. Play it better—those were my words.

I must be astute, alert at all times and one step ahead while looking behind me.

I also had to deal with Georgia as soon as possible and end our contact. It was for her safety.

Under the darkness and protection of the thick blankets, I turned on my Blackberry.

FROM: Tim Jennings
SUBJECT: Book Questions
DATE: May 13 23:23
TO: Georgia Harrison

Dear Georgia,

I was rather pleased to read your book.
You obviously used higher intelligences to write it.
I would like to meet you at Flowers for Fleur Café tomorrow at 3pm to discuss possible publication of your piece of fascinating, intriguing writing.
Please reply if you are unable to make this appointment.

Tim
#booksmakeforverygoodfirefuel

Send...

Within three minutes I received a message from her.

FROM: Georgia Harrison
SUBJECT: Book Questions from me.
DATE: May 13 23:26
TO: Tim Jennings

Dear Tim,

3.07pm would be preferable.
I am sure with your higher intelligence after your
brain studies you should be able to organise your time
schedule to meet at that exact moment in time.
How was your date?

Georgia
#theownerofthebookthatyoulovesomuch

FROM: Tim Jennings
SUBJECT: 3.07PM
DATE: May 13 23:35
TO: George Harrison

Dear George,

My schedules can only be arranged hourly.
3.07pm does not exist in the higher intelligence
scheme of things. Meet me at 3pm.
Shall I order tea for you?

Tim
#the3pmtimeisnotnegotiable
P.S. It was not a date.

Send...

FROM: GEORGIA Harrison
SUBJECT: 3.07pm
DATE: May 13 23:40
TO: Tim Jennings

Dear Timothy,

George is a boy. I am not. Perhaps you should date some girls to understand us better. What if I don't feel like tea tomorrow?

Georgia
#teafortwosoundsnicebutitdependsonthecompany!

FROM: Tim Jennings
SUBJECT: The Tea Company?
DATE: May 13 23:45
TO: Miss Georgia Harrison

Dear Georgia,

I do not know the name of the company that makes the tea, but I shall order tea for you anyway.
See you tomorrow at 3pm.

Tim
#SuperGeek@MetropolisofNerdvilleUniversityLibrary.

Send…

There was no reply. I concealed the Tim Jennings Blackberry in an inside pocket of my black clothes and awaited 2.27am; the final instalment of Operation Black Dot on CAI surveillance cameras.
Play the game. Play it better.

I was up at 6am, went to the gym and showered before I grabbed breakfast along the way. Then it was work as per my usual routine. Nothing out of the ordinary.

The graffiti wall of eye and brain art was coming along slowly. As my hands worked on the transferral of the detailed brain diagram onto the wall—in the correct position and scale to the eye—I visualised the workings of the mind-reading implant over and over in every single detail to the nth degree.

When finally, I had finished drawing the brain, I stepped back to consider the reality of the device that would be implanted. It was good, but I had to admit I was out of my depth. I now required the professional medical knowledge of specialist doctors to continue this quest. But who would choose the doctors—Mr. Rubin, or me? Perhaps I should talk to Mia about it. She would advise me on what to do in this instance for sure.

The Tim Jennings Blackberry vibrated in my pocket. It was time to meet with Georgia at the café.

I hightailed it out of my office, past Black-Suit-Man, down to the ground floor and out the irritating revolving doors. I arrived at the café at 2.55pm, ordered tea for two, and sat and waited.

The door jingled at exactly 3pm. I looked over and saw Georgia entering the café. She looked amazing in her light summery dress. I stood and smiled at her, then sat down at the table after she did. It was good manners—gentlemanly.

'All before 3.07pm, Georgia. Very impressive,' I commented with a smirk.

She smirked back at me, her beautiful blue eyes sparkling, and then placed the book down on the table in front of me.

'Ah… fuel for the fire, I assume?' I teased.

She frowned at me, annoyed by my comment. 'No, Cohen. Some pages are missing. You must have them,' she accused.

I shook my head at her. 'Only one page came out, but I put it back into the book,' I explained.

Our tea for two arrived and Georgia proceeded to pour the tea into our cups. 'Look inside the book, Cohen. Look at the page numbers. Some are missing,' she insisted.

I opened the book and flicked through the pages looking for numbers. But I saw nothing but white paper—it was an inkless book to me. I shook my head.

Georgia grabbed the book off me, put on her glasses and flicked through to a certain page and gave it back to me.

'Read it out loud to me, followed by the very next page,' she whispered aggressively.

I hesitated and sipped my tea, wondering how to respond to her request. 'Georgia... this book has intrigued me since it turned up at my apartment. When I look at the pages, I don't see anything. It's completely… blank.' I decided to be honest. There was no other way around the fact that I could not see words on the pages of the book.

Her jaw dropped open, and she snatched the book from me. She flicked through the entire book rapidly, as if in a panic.

'That is impossible! Clearly there are blue handwritten words in this book—look again.' Georgia thrust the book back into my hands.

I hesitated before fingering through each of the pages, and saw nothing. I looked up at her and shook my head. 'Read to me, Georgia. I want to hear what I cannot see,' I insisted, keeping my voice calm.

'Not here, Cohen. We will have to meet again at a different place. A place where your trackers will not be. How did you know I owned the book if you cannot see any words in the book?' she asked in a whisper.

I leaned in closer to her, her floral perfume making me less focussed for a moment. 'I discovered some indentations of words in the front and did a soft pencil rubbing. That's when your name, address, email and phone number appeared, and I contacted you.'

Georgia blinked at me, closed the book and wiped a tear away. 'We really must talk Cohen, but not here.' Georgia sipped her tea and looked into my eyes. 'I will organise a time and place to meet, Tim. And, you should really get your eyes tested, Cohen. You obviously can't see properly.'

I smiled at her audacity. I had only known her for a split second and she was telling me what to do.

I sipped my tea and held her eyes in mine for longer than necessary. She returned my gaze, then closed her eyes and bit her bottom lip before opening her eyes again.

Maybe I could have a girlfriend again?

'Well, if we are done here, I will go,' she said as if detached from the situation, puzzling me.

I chuckled. 'You are the one who wanted to meet, Georgia. If you say we are done, then we are done,' I said, and stood when she did.

'Good then. I am sure that if we had met at 3.07pm, the outcome of this meeting would have been different,' she remarked.

'Time is relative, Miss Georgia. I enjoyed tea for two with you. The company was interesting, and pleasant.' I looked down with a small smile, then looked back at her.

Her cheeks flushed. 'Cohen,' she breathed as she rolled her eyes at me, before she turned and left the café.

I watched heads turn to admire her as she walked confidently out of the café. I must agree with them—yes, she is beautiful.

I left almost immediately after she did. I decided it was my turn to be a tracker.

I followed her from a safe distance along the street. I didn't know what she did for a living. She had said that she designed, researched, created. She also said that she could not tell me what she was working on, or where she worked.

After some time, she turned into the entrance of a Medical Research Centre before she was lost to my view. At least I knew where she worked now.

It was mid afternoon. I didn't want to return to CAI or my apartment, so I headed to the park to clear my head. I sat under the shade of a beautiful old oak tree overlooking the lake. My tracker and his tracker were within my proximity. They did their best to look "normal", but their odd little behaviours told me they were working, watching me closely, reporting my behaviour and location.

I smiled. What an odd occupation. It was like playing spies at school at lunch time; hiding behind trees, watching others, pretending you're invisible. I wondered whether the tracker knew he was being tracked. Surely, he would. If you were a tracker, wouldn't your acute observation of surroundings and people be astute? Surely, he would know if he was being tracked.

I relaxed and emptied my mind. I was good at that. I had discovered the ability to disconnect to my surroundings when I was young. I stumbled across my own visualisation technique to take me away from the severe growing pains I experienced in my legs at night. Even though visually in my mind I was somewhere else, my consciousness was alert enough to my real time presence to quickly bring me back to the now.

The rhythmic, pulsating vibration of my Tim Jennings Blackberry against my leg brought me back to the present. It was Georgia. She was the only one with this email address. But she would have to wait for my reply tonight under the cover of darkness and under the security of my thick blanket.

It was time to head home. I felt like giving the trackers a

"come on let's go" whistle in my sarcastic mood. I wanted to skip over to them and give them a high five. But I had to control my impulses and act naturally, like I wasn't aware they were there.

I wondered if I had a red hunting target painted on my back? I would have to check it out in the shower tonight.

I varied my speed as I walked home. I thought I would keep them on their toes and make their late afternoon more interesting, and perhaps a little more challenging. At one stage, I about turned and walked towards them. It was entertaining watching them pretend not to see me and to avert their eyes away from me when I looked at them.

The trackers disappeared once I reached my apartment. But in reality, they probably had their surveillance operating, compliments of their cameras in my apartment.

I entered my living quarters and was harassed by the aromatic smells coming from the kitchen to romance my stomach. Tonight, it was a beef stir fry that seduced my digestive juices. I savoured my dinner, cleaned up, watched sport on television before I packed it in for the night and showered in a very fogged up bathroom before I went to bed.

After a while, I pulled out Tim Jennings Blackberry, and opened up the message from Georgia.

FROM: Georgia Harrison
SUBJECT: Optometrist
DATE: May 14 17:35
TO: Tim Jennings

Dear Tim,

Did you book an appointment with the optometrist yet?
I am worried about your eyesight.
I would like to meet you in the park tomorrow at 3.07pm.
Have a look for four errant pages from my book please.

Georgia
#youneedtoeatmorecarrots

Yep. Bossy as. She was on my back about an optometrist. And there was that seven minutes past grievance she wouldn't let go of.

Geez! Errant pages? What? Did she think they removed themselves from the book and ran away like the gingerbread man?

AND CARROTS—good for eye health—but they don't improve your vision!

FROM: Tim Jennings
SUBJECT: Carrots
DATE: May 14 23:35
TO: Georgia Harrison

Dear Georgia,

Orange is an interesting colour. Especially in food! I
will meet you at 3.07pm in the park tomorrow, only
so that you get past that ridiculous time thing!
Where exactly would you like to meet?

Tim
#pumpkinandorangesareorangeandmustbegoodforeyestoo!

Send…

FROM: Georgia Harrison
SUBJECT: Reading Books for Higher Intelligence
DATE: May 14 23:40
TO: Tim Jennings

Dear Tim,

Orange smorange! Apparently, no word rhymes
with orange! How odd!
There is a large and very old oak tree by the lake. I will
wait for you there.
I look forward to seeing you there at 3.07pm, with the
errant book pages—four of them in all.

Georgia
#ihopethatyoulikemereadingtoyou

FROM: Tim Jennings
SUBJECT: Do you think that I am illiterate?
DATE: May 14 23:45
TO: Georgia Harrison

Dear Georgia,

The old oak tree is stunning. I will bring the gingerbread
men (errant pages) if I find them.
I will try to time my arrival for 3.07pm.
I look forward to knowing the contents of the book
you so vehemently denied was yours.

Tim
#iwillbringmyhearingaidsandglasses.

Send…

Then darkness overcame me, and my conscious brain
entered the dream realm, of which secrets and life's ponderings
are explored, and the fears of consciousness are confronted and
challenged, only rarely to be remembered…

An assault on my ears by the blaring alarm clock shocked me into action as the new day arrived.

Oh… the ridiculous book and its errant pages and 3.07pm.

I grabbed a broom and pretended to sweep the floor, while in fact looking for Georgia's four elusive, errant pages. I shook my head. I would have come across them by now if they were here somewhere. Or, my obsessive cleaner would have bought my attention to them.

The path of the broom led me to the study room. I drove the broom head directly to the floor beneath the window and opened the shutters so I could see better, then about turned, sweeping the wooden floor looking all about the study.

My desk revealed a pile of tidied papers, compliments of CAI, or Mr. Rubin at least, in his interfering, intrusive way.

One third of the way down the pile of neatly constructed, obsessive-compulsive, tidied, loose papers, I spied the four smaller errant pages from Georgia's book.

I slid my fingers into the pile and smoothly extracted them, trying to hide them as I pushed them into my pocket. Then I continued with my super sweeping spree, ridding the floor of dust until the floor was spotless.

Perfecto! Mission accomplished! I had found the errant gingerbread men!

Chapter 11

Gym was busy at 6am and there was standing room only at the café for breakfast. So entering my secure, self-absorbed office suite was heavenly, until the meeting request from Mr. Rubin.

9am. Great! I'm not in the mood for His Royal Rudeness.

I stood back from the wall of "graffiti" and studied my work. The eye was spectacular in its detail. My "graffiti" of the brain a little less so, due to lack of definite visible structures—it truly was a miraculous organ. With all the advances in science and medicine, there was still no explanation about how the brain worked.

And the workings of the mind? How? And the fact that some people can hear our own voice whilst talking to ourselves or reading in our head? Even more intriguing!

Backing away from the wall of "graffiti" further, I stood at the drafting table. The design drawings of the mind-reading implant lay across it. I studied it in detail once again, going over the device thoroughly step by step until, a sudden pang of fear hit my stomach.

The mind-reading implant was ready for the next step in its development—the discussions and conferencing with medical professors.

It was time for it to become a reality!

My stomach quivered. I felt terribly insecure and became unsure of what I was doing. Was it because the technology was about to cross the realm of science fiction to reality, or was it because of the possible hideous ramifications of its use.

I closed my eyes and inhaled deeply.

Is this right or wrong?

Do I continue to assign myself to it, or totally distance myself from the creation and run for cover?

If I run for cover, I will have no control over its destiny whatsoever. It will definitely find its way into the hands of unscrupulous men. At least if I stay with it, I will have control and input into the device.

Now I had a moral obligation. What monster had I created? *What have I done?*

I exited my office and descended one floor to the reception occupied by White Girl the secretary. Instantly my eyes found Mia's and I nodded.

'Mr. Darcy, good morning,' she squeaked unnaturally. A friendly smile widened over her face as usual, and her big brown eyes looked up at me. A perfect cover for her naturally red hair and green eyes. 'Mr. Rubin will be available in one minute.'

'Can I get you a tea or coffee while I wait, Mia?' I asked, knowing the exact line the she would respond with.

'Oh, no thank you, Mr. Darcy, it is not my break time yet,' she squeaked.

I smiled crookedly at her and nodded. Then the door to Mr. Rubin's office clicked. It was my cue to enter.

The high back of his red leather chair faced me, as expected. Then he turned slowly to address me. 'Mr. Darcy, update me,' he said. His voice was low and threatening. He did not bother with greetings, just straight to the point.

'Mr. Rubin, all systems are go, for intervention and input from medical professionals. I will need to speak to them myself so I can make adjustments to the implant design if needed.' I spoke confidently, clearly and assertively, my eye contact unwavering. This man did not intimidate me.

He continued to look me in the eye. He was trying to dominate me, but I would not let him have power over me. He could not make me feel inferior—my abhorrence of the man saw to that.

He broke eye contact first.

Good… Play the game. Play it better.

'Miss Rubin will make the appropriate arrangements. Let her know who you need. Good day, Mr. Darcy.'

I tried very hard to stifle my sound of shock, obviously successfully, because Mr. Rubin did not bat an eyelid.

Miss Rubin? Is Mia his daughter?

He turned in his chair so it was facing away from me again. I exhaled my sudden astonishment, and slowly turned and exited the office. I felt giddy and grabbed on to the receptionist desk as I tried to catch my breath.

Mia was his daughter?

'Mia,' I said in a low voice as I slowly walked past her desk. I did not make eye contact with her. I couldn't. She had double crossed me.

'Mr. Darcy,' she called after me in her fake squeaky bubbly voice. 'I believe you need to make an appointment with Miss Rubin. Her office is to the right.'

I turned to her and frowned.

'She is available today at 11am. I will email you a list of medical professors suitable to work on the project with you. Shall I book an appointment with her?' Mia White Girl asked, her brown eyes staring back at me with her right eyebrow raised and her head nodding ever so slightly as if she were telling me something.

I turned to her confused and pierced her with my eyes. 'Tell me your last name…'

'Rueben.' She held up her identification badge. Mia Rueben; it was spelt differently. I narrowed my eyes and looked back to her face, and nodded.

'I will return at 11am. Email the medical professors to me immediately. I will need to study their qualifications, specialties, experience and achievements of excellence.' My racing heartbeat and stressed voice were calmer now that I realised the orthographic difference in their names. Mia was not related to the man behind the door. But what would his daughter be like, and did she share his genetics of arrogance and rudeness?

I returned to my office and opened my emails on the CAI server. Mia was as good as her word and had sent the list of medical professors. Efficient. But how do I read into the slight nod of her head? Had she chosen these people herself, and were they working on her side.

Was this a conspiracy?

She had supplied me with a list of two ophthalmologist professors, and two neurology professors. One ophthalmologist and neurologist was in green, and the others in red. Was this a code … like choose green, and stay away from red?

Her next email was all about traffic lights. It had attachments of you tube footage of cars running red lights and then crashing—spectacularly.

I chose to go with the green ophthalmologist and neurologist. But should I trust Mia? I really did not know her.

I decided I had to take the leap of faith. If she is not technically working for Mr. Rubin, then she must be against him. If he is bad, then she is good.

Logical? Wasn't it?

For the next hour I researched the medical specialists. It was best to be armed with knowledge.

At two minutes to 11am I returned to the twenty-seventh floor of CAI. At once Mia directed me to Miss Rubin's Office.

The high back of her hot pink leather chair faced me, a chip off the old block. I stood and waited for her to face me.

'Ah... Mr. Darcy,' her voice smoothly addressed me, but still she did not face me.

I shook my head. I could not believe she would be arrogant.

And then, she turned her chair towards me and stood to shake my hand.

She was tall, slim, with her make-up applied like a professional. Her black, short skirt suit hugged her beautiful figure, showing her long flawless legs. Her blonde hair was braided to the side so that it fell over her left shoulder.

I took her hand in mine as we greeted each other, her light brown eyes to my blue. She smiled gently at me, and I returned the smile, but it did not touch my eyes.

We were in a game of chess. She had made her move and I had mirrored hers. What chess piece would she move next? She was a Rubin, and I was very wary of her.

'Miss Rubin,' I said, nodding my head at her, raising my eyebrows.

'Please sit,' she said, indicating for me to sit on a hot pink leather chair opposite hers at her white desk. She sat in her own head poncho chair with an amused look on her face. I narrowed my eyes at her. Trust was not in my vocabulary with her.

'So, according to Miss Reuben, you have chosen your preferred ophthalmologist and neurologist. My father has expressed his wish, no, ordered me to be present at each of your meetings with the medical professionals, Mr. Darcy. See it as a type of insurance policy. You have the power to talk to the medical staff about the implant, but do not have final authority to proceed with the mind-reading implant. Do you understand, Mr. Darcy?' Her voice was assertive, no… it was aggressive.

How does she know the two medical professors I had chosen? I did not email my preferences to Mia.

'Do you understand, Mr. Darcy?' her loud repetition of the question broke into my thoughts.

'Just a little clarity first... Miss Rubin. Name the two medical professors I chose, and secondly, I would like to know your qualifications and how they will benefit the device that CAI is about to patent and trial,' I said in a non-threatening manner, trying to pull the power back to myself.

She looked down. Yes, I had cut her confidence. She turned her computer screen towards me and pulled up her emails and showed me the names of the medical professors Mia had guided me to choose.

'And my qualifications... Mr. Darcy... I direct you to visit my employee profile for a detailed CV on my credentials and career. You will not be disappointed; I can assure you. Now, I will arrange for the good doctors to come for briefing tomorrow. I will email you the time and place. Good day, Mr. Darcy,' she said. Her voice was cool, perhaps indicating she felt threatened.

'Miss Rubin, the meeting place must be in my office. It cannot take place anywhere else. I will be ready for the briefing tomorrow,' I said.

She looked at me and smirked, annoying me. 'Yes, Mr. Darcy, of course. Your, hmmm, graffiti wall will be the centre of the discussion, I am sure. My father spoke of your ah—style,' she said and smirked at me.

I narrowed my eyes at her. The words rude, arrogant, and self-righteous came to mind immediately.

Play the game. Play it better.

'Thank you, Miss Rubin. I will look forward to seeing you

tomorrow. Do be on time,' I added and stood.

'I will, will you?' she questioned me, raising her right eyebrow, mocking me.

'Well, I don't want to ruin my reputation, do I?' I shot back at her, smiling and bowing to her before I turned and left her office.

I glared at Mia as I headed to the elevator.

'Wishing you a good day, Mr. Darcy,' she squeaked as I walked past her. She was as white and as pleasant and as detached as ever.

Instead of returning to my office I decided to get out of the CAI building before it suffocated me. I bolted through the revolving doors and out onto the pavement. The cool air blasted onto my skin, having the same effect as a slap on the face. I really needed it. It was like a wake-up call. I couldn't let the Rubins get to me.

Play the game. Play it better!

I sucked in a deep breath, ran my hand through my wayward hair, about turned and entered the CAI building once more.

My handprint was scanned and unlocked my high security office as usual. I sat in my inexpensive low backed chair and put my feet up on the desk in rebellion of the Rubins. They certainly would not approve of my feet resting on the desk. In fact, they could probably see me right now in their camera surveillance. Shall I give them a finger salute as well?

I put the earbuds of my phone into my ears and listened to Apocalyptica. I closed my eyes and let the music weave its way throughout my body, relaxing and calming, helping me to see the situation very clearly.

Almost instantly, my mind was totally left field in its creation.

I opened my eyes at the revelation.

It wasn't a mind-reading implant invasively inserted into the eyeball and the brain that I saw, but a mind-reading contact lens that used organic matter to infuse with, and grow into the flesh of the eye, becoming one with the person.

My heartbeat accelerated significantly. This was serious intellectual upload. I ripped the earbuds out of my ear canals and sat bolt upright at my desk, panicked. I couldn't contain the adrenaline surging through my body. I rose from my desk and paced the room. My mind was lit with the fire for the new device.

I couldn't draw it. And I couldn't write it down anywhere because that would be my undoing. I didn't want to be railroaded into developing another device that would hurt humanity.

I stilled. I could never let the original mind-reading implant work, ever. I had to make certain that it would never work. I did tell Mr. Rubin the whole concept was science fiction. I did warn him, didn't I?

I returned to my desk and wrote specific details and questions for the doctors who I would meet tomorrow. Then I returned to my detailed drawings of the implant that would go into the fovea of the eye, where the greatest acuity of vision occurs.

I deleted one seemingly inconspicuous connection—rendering the implant useless. Only the ophthalmologist may pick it up, if he knew about my engineering side of the implant. But my guess was that he will be looking at where and how to implant it into the eye and miss the micro technology all together.

I sat back in my chair and closed my eyes. My thumping heartbeat gave away the fact that I was misleading Mr. Rubin by lying to him. But I had to do it for the sake of humanity.

The ramifications of a mind-reading implant would be catastrophic. If one was going to be built, it was not going to be built by the CAI Organisation. Was the CEO and the Board even aware that Mr. Rubin had employed me to produce this implant?

I raised my eyebrows.

I looked at the monitor of the computer. I could easily check to see if he was sending copies of our emails to others at CAI. But now was not the time to start being a detective. I would add it to my list of things to do.

Play the game. Play it better.

The beeping of my watch alarm alerted me to the time to leave to meet Georgia at the park for a personal reading of the book. 3.07pm she specifically requested.

3.07pm!

Weird!

Odd!

Strange!

Compulsive?

Obsessive?

Crap. I haven't had my eyes checked. She will give me the third degree and a scolding at my lack of concern for my eyesight. Bossy.

I left my office and hightailed it to the park.

Thirty meters from the old oak tree I saw her. She was sitting under the ancient tree, dressed in a pretty pale-blue sleeveless dress. Her feet were crossed at the ankles, and she looked relaxed. I slowed down and caught my breath after running to get here in time. My watch time was 3.05pm. I had two minutes to reach her and present myself exactly at 3.07pm.

Within the minute, I stood, hidden behind the tree. Her perfume filled the air, sweet, like pink roses. I closed my eyes and enjoyed the assault on my sense of smell, then opened them and watched the digital time on my watch.

At exactly 3.07pm I stood before her, lowered my head and bowed to her rolling my hand in front of me towards her as perhaps a servant would do.

Georgia burst out laughing and threw an acorn at me. I looked into her eyes and smiled shyly, then sat beside her, leaning against the trunk of the ancient tree as she was.

'3.07pm exactly, Miss Georgia!' I exclaimed with pride, smirking at her.

'Exceptionally well-timed, Mr. Cohen!' she replied. 'Do you have my errant pages?'

'No, but I found the gingerbread men... and they are naked!' I laughed quietly to myself at the attempted joke of the four inkless pages, and then looked up into her eyes as I handed her the pages to the book, our fingers lightly touching.

She scowled at me. 'You didn't get your eyes checked, did you?'

Here we go...

'Actually, I am meeting with an ophthalmologist tomorrow,' I replied, tilting my head on the side and raising my eyebrows at her. She didn't need to know it was about the mind-reading implant. But it would get her off my back at least.

She considered me for a moment, then looked down demurely. 'Good,' she said in a quiet voice, and then proceeded to place the loose pages back into the book.

Once she was done, she rested her head back on the trunk of the oak tree and closed her eyes. Was she regretting something?

'Are you wishing for me to leave, now that you have the missing pages?' I asked, confused by her aloofness. She didn't answer me, and nervous butterflies of rejection started to flutter in my stomach. My heart of hearts was telling me it was time for me to leave before she delivered her stab of disappointment.

I looked down at the grass and ran my hand lightly over the top of it. I was in a quandary—what should I do? She wanted me to meet her here, and yet, I am receiving the signal that she doesn't want me here.

Damn. I wish I could read her mind! I smiled to myself. How ironic! The mind-reading implant would do wonders for me and my relationships.

'Cohen,' Georgia said quietly, interrupting my thoughts. 'If

I start reading this book to you, I need you to tough it out to the end. You can't ditch half-way through. I have never read or shared it with anyone, ever. This is your get-out-clause before I start.' Her face was gentle, serene even as she spoke to me. Her eyes searched the depths of mine as I felt her trying to make a connection deep within me. I felt like I had melted into her. She was so peaceful. I wanted to stay in that place, but I pulled my eyes away from hers.

'Why choose me, Georgia? Why not a close friend who knows and understands you? I could be a very bad person, for all you know,' I said to her in a hushed tone, confused by her need to lock me into the book once she started reading it to me.

'That is exactly why I chose you. You don't know me. You will listen and see the events of the story without prior knowledge of my life imposing on it. You will see it with new vision and a different perspective. And, I intuitively know you are not a bad person. I can see through to your pure heart,' she added. Her eyes pleaded with me to stay and listen to the contents of the book.

I looked away from her into the cloudless blue sky and took a deep breath, considering my position. Every bone in my body was telling me to stay. I was undeniably attracted to this woman in the pale blue dress. I wanted to wrap my arms around her to protect her for some reason.

'And, if I have no opinion or advice to give you once I hear the contents of the book?' I asked, looking back into her eyes.

She looked down at her hands. 'I have faith in you,' she said as she looked back up into my eyes. 'The fact is… I need you more than you need me. I am even willing to put up with all of the trackers around us. In fact, I like the challenge they bring to us. When I have finished reading the book to you, I will release you from it. In fact, I can—' She stopped talking suddenly and looked away, as if considering what to say next.

I need that mind-reading device.

'—I can pull the memories from your mind if you request it,' she finished, looking into my eyes with a probing gaze.

I narrowed my eyes at her. *How can she pull memories from my mind?*

'Very intriguing, Miss Georgia. Your last statement has me extremely curious, and equally cautious. You will have to explain how you would do that at some point.' My voice was low and quiet. We held our eye connection for what seemed like an eternity. She held her composure and remained calm and... trusting.

What are you thinking, Georgia?

'We will need to meet at different places over the course of the book, you understand. And there will be times when I cannot meet you because of my job,' she added. She stopped talking and frowned.

'Yes, I can see your need is greater than mine. I take on your challenge of listening to the story contained in your book from beginning to end, but make no promises for beyond,' I said and tilted my head to the side, watching for her reaction.

'Thank-you,' she said, choking on her words from emotion. A tear rolled down her cheek.

I nodded. I wanted to wrap my arms around her and hold her to console her for whatever reason she was crying. But I didn't.

She ran her hand lightly over the leather cover of the book and fingered the symbol and words embedded into it. I wanted to ask what it meant. But I didn't. It wasn't the time for that yet.

Her eyes found mine, as if asking if I was ready to listen to the contents of the bizarre book—except she would not have used the word bizarre. That was my term.

I nodded.

Why did this feel like such a big deal?

It was only a book.

Chapter 12

Another tear rolled off her pale cheek and dropped onto the leather cover of the book. With a quick hand she wiped it off and then dried the wet trail from her tear off her face.

Why was she so emotional about this seemingly plain book? If only I could get inside her head to understand her reaction to it all.

Her long slender fingers caressed the leather cover before she opened to the second inkless page. She put on her glasses. My eyes wavered between her eyes and the page to see what she could see. I saw nothing on the page, yet she saw blue handwritten words, apparently.

Perhaps there was something wrong with her eyes, not mine. My thoughts were interrupted by her voice as she started to read from the book.

" 'He barrelled through the automatic glass doors like a bull at a gate. His brown hair was knotted and dishevelled. He was breathing heavily like he was out of breath from running a marathon. I froze on the spot as I looked at him. Our patients were always well dressed. This man wasn't. He was dirty, unshaven, and wore torn old clothes. In fact, he looked like a druggie... or perhaps a vagabond.

He put both hands against his dirty face and spoke with anger between gritted teeth.'Help me, please... please...' He fell to the floor on his knees. This man was broken. Tears streamed down his face when his eyes found mine. They were desperately searching for some hope. I had to give it to him. What does one have if one has no hope?

I walked closer to him and his stench assaulted my nostrils. When was the last time he had showered? I refrained from screwing up my face in repulsion to his odour, and proffered my hand. Human touch. I bet he was craving the touch of another human.

His sad blue eyes looked at my hand and his face became impassioned, tears streaming down his cheeks. It was like I had touched his heart. I cried inside for this man. What had happened to him to torture his mind and soul?

'Follow me,' I said in a gentle voice. I didn't want to speak with aggression, as sometimes we did with people begging for drugs. It would break his spirit more—if it could break any further. He stood with his eyes glued to mine. I was like a cylinder of life-giving oxygen he desperately needed to survive. 'I'll take you to the shower, arrange some clothes and food for you, and then we can talk. My name is Georgia. Let me take some of your burden from you,' I said, my voice filled with compassion for this man.

He dropped his head into his hands and sobbed

deeply from the centre of his being. 'Ethan... thank you,' he spoke between sobs.

My heart bled for him. How I wished I could make it all better.

I told him to take a long shower to help relieve his stress, then set about finding some clothes for him, and some food: sandwiches from the nurses lounge, and a new bottle of spring water. I fussed about in the room, anxiously waiting for him to resurface.

The creak of the opening shower door drew my attention to the bathroom, and then the refreshing smell of honey and almond body wash preceded him.

He emerged from the shower a totally different person. I couldn't help but stare at this gorgeous man before me. His brown hair was now orderly, his blue eyes sparkling and his skin clean. He covered his manhood with a towel wrapped around his superb torso, his pectoral muscles well defined, his stomach muscles sculptured. His shoulders were broad and powerful. Who was he to look like this?

'Thank you,' he said. His smile reached his eyes and melted my heart. Then he looked down and sadness returned to his face.

'You're welcome, Ethan. I must try that magical shower to see how I exit from it!' I commented, smiling at the beautiful, sad man before me. 'Here's some clothes I rustled up for you. I'll be back in a minute or two, then we can talk.'

I watched his eyes wander over to the clean clothes. He looked at me and nodded, smiling shyly. I smiled back at him then left him to clothe his sculptured body.' "

'Georgia—' I interrupted.

She scowled at me, annoyed by my interference of her reading. 'Cohen?' she said curtly. She definitely was not impressed with my interruption.

'Mmmm... nothing. Go on... I am enjoying the book,' I lied. It was like some stupid romance novel or something. What was the point of this whole exercise? Unfortunately, I had agreed to listen to her story—I was signed in and couldn't sign out till the end. I had agreed.

She held my gaze for a moment before she continued with her reading.

" 'When I returned to the hospital room he stood with his hands in his pockets. The shirt was way too tight, stretched taunt over his broad shoulders and chest. And the pants were oversized, hanging loosely off his hips. No matter, he looked good this way, and definitely smelled heavenly after his long shower.

'There is food and drink for you. Help yourself,' I encouraged as I sat on the chair next to the hospital bed. I had cleared all my research appointments for the day. Ethan's state of mind was high priority. If I could help him, I must. I was now accountable for him.

'Thank-you,' he said with a gentle voice, then reached over to the food.

'You must nourish your body. It's good for the mind and soothing for the soul,' I commented.

His eyes darted to mine, as if I had thrown a poisoned arrow at him.

I held his eye contact and radiated peace from my eyes. He needed to know that I was concerned for him. 'Can I get you a cup of coffee or tea?' I asked. Timing was of the essence. I needed to give him some space after his dislike of my previous comment.

'Coffee would be un-soothing for my mind, Georgia, so I will have tea... please,' he said in a ruffled voice.

His manners were impeccable, but he was using my words to throw back at me. He was in defence mode. What was eating him? I left in silence, holding my posture in confidence. He needed me to be strong for him. He didn't realise it, but I knew it.

When I returned with his tea he was sitting on the bed, leaning against the pillows, one leg bent up, one outstretched. His eyes were closed and his face relaxed. My heart softened for him. 'Ethan, let's talk,' I said, trying to reassure him of my trustworthiness.

He opened his eyes and looked straight ahead, like I had extracted him from a happy place and back to reality—a reality that he did not want to be in.

'Yes... we must talk,' he said. His voice was deflated, and he focused on the food.

'There's something troubling you. I can help you. But you need to let me know what is going on. Is it an external, or internal war? External meaning that something is happening or has happened to you from someone else, or a situation that you have become involved in ... or internal, meaning a war with your mind, body or soul?' I questioned, trying to explain carefully to him. He remained passive as I spoke to him. That is, until I mentioned the word soul. Again, his eyes darted to me, and in them, I saw a fire that raged.

Now I knew what his problem was—his soul. Or was it his spirit? It was not unusual for someone who was on death's door to worry about their spirit. But, for a man this age, this physically maintained, and this alive, it was not the norm. What had he done? Why was he ripping himself apart?

He breathed deeply before he spoke in the quietest of voices with his eyes closed, tensed. 'I believe... that I don't have a soul.'

His face was ashen, gutted, and my own heart twisted for him.

After a moment of silence I spoke to him, keeping my voice tranquil. 'Why do you believe that, Ethan?' "

'Georgia—' I interrupted, again. It took some courage on my part. I didn't want to get that "if looks could kill" stare again.

'Cohen?' her voice was curt again, her blue eyes piercing mine like a dagger.

'It's getting late. The sun's starting to set. When do you want to continue the story?' I asked her, searching her eyes for a connection to the real world.

And then she snapped out of it—out of the book. She was kind and beautiful Georgia again. The Georgia I knew, if only briefly.

She took off her glasses and breathed out like she had been holding her breath throughout the entire reading, and looked around. Then she pressed her lips together and frowned. 'Oh ... yes of course. Right you are, Cohen. I will email you again, Tim. What is it with the late-night emailing, anyway?' she asked in a curious voice.

'It's a long story. But I'll tell you sometime. I've got to go. Watch the trackers follow me. They have odd behaviour! Ah... thanks for reading to me. Your story is... intriguing. I am keen for the next instalment.' I looked into her eyes gauging her reaction to my statement. She smiled slightly and nodded her head.

I smiled crookedly at her and then began my journey home with my trackers in tow.

The smell of a roast chicken dinner seduced me the moment I entered my apartment. My stomached growled. I was hungry. As per the usual routine, I ate dinner, watched sport on television, had a steamy hot shower, and then went to bed. I looked forward to the text from Georgia.

The vibrating Blackberry against my leg was like a cattle prod waking me. In a haze, I reached under the blanket to read the email.

FROM: Georgia Harrison
SUBJECT: The next instalment
DATE: May 15 23:15
TO: Tim Jennings

Dear Tim,

The trackers are indeed very odd.
Do they have undercover spy lessons to
practise their moves?
Thank you for listening to me read my book today.
I am still offering you a get out clause at this point.
I will understand if you ditch me.

Georgia
#thegingerbreadmenarehappytobebackintheoven

FROM: Tim Jennings
SUBJECT: The next instalment
DATE: May 15 23:20
TO: Georgia Harrison

Dear Georgia,

I know my trackers' faces very well.
I like to change my direction to annoy them.
They don't cope with a change of plan very well.
I feel privileged to be given the chance to listen to you
reading your book to me.
I want to know what Ethan says next. You have me hooked!

Tim
#gingerbreadmenarenicerinmystomachwithacupoftea

Send...

FROM: Georgia Harrison
SUBJECT: Gingerbread Men
DATE: May 15 23:30
TO: Tim Jennings

Dear Tim,

Since you are indicating that you are not going to ditch
my readings of the book, I would like to deliver the
next instalment tomorrow.
I never read it by myself. Likewise, I never read it silently.
Where would you suggest we meet?

Georgia
#Iamgoingtomakeyouagingerbreadmantoeat

FROM: Tim Jennings
SUBJECT: Gingerbread Men
DATE: May 15 23:36
TO: Georgia Harrison

Dear Gingerbread Maker,

I am stuck in critical meetings tomorrow. So, I think

we should meet in the evening. How about back
at our very first meeting place. 7.03pm?

And please notice that I spoke of gingerbread MEN in
my stomach—plural.

Tim
#leaveoffthesultanasbutidoenjoytheicing

Send...

FROM: Georgia Harrison
SUBJECT: Sultanas are healthy
DATE: May 15 23:45
TO: Tim Jennings

Dear Tim,

Tea for two would be brilliant with the gingerbread
MAN—singular.

I shall meet you at 7.03pm, where you first surprised me.

Georgia
#Ilikesurpriseswhentheyarepackagedlikeyou

FROM: Tim Jennings
SUBJECT: I don't like to share!
DATE: May 15 23:49
TO: Georgia Harrison

Dear Georgia,

Cookie Monster is my aka, and gingerbread is
like a cookie.
I will see you first at 7.03pm.

Tim
#runrunasfastasyoucan

Send...

FROM: Georgia Harrison
SUBJECT: Challenges
DATE: May 15 23:52
TO: Tim Jennings

Dear, Dear Mr. Tim,

I enjoy a challenge!

Georgia
#wearingmyrunningtrackspikeshoesforbettergrip

Hmmmm, I like a girl who can banter. She definitely has it down pat.

I closed my eyes to enter the sleep zone, wishing for a peaceful sleep—but it was not meant to be.

My dream... Was in black and white. Mostly black. My left eye was the host of the mind-reading implant. When it was first implanted, I had control over it. But it had developed a mind of its own and its electrical impulses overrode my own natural electrical neurons firing in my brain. It owned me. It entered my mind, growing its savage roots there, fighting with my own mind until I was weak and surrendered to the will of the mind-reading implant. Now I had a mission. And it was not my own. I was simply the arms and legs and living body for the mind-reading implant to do as it pleased. And it was black. There shined no light. No colour. Just the blackness of badness. And the only way to overcome it was by death. My death...

Horror surged through my body, and I was alerted to fight. I woke in a profuse sweat, breathing heavily, my heart beating rapidly. I placed my hands over my wet face, then dragged my stiff fingers through my damp hair.

What have I done in the creation a mind-reading implant? It holds no hope for the human race, only destruction. It must not work—it cannot work. It must be stopped. It must be destroyed before it destroys us.

The remaining dark hours of the night ticked by slowly as my mind flitted from the project to my childhood, to my future—if I had one. I couldn't see it—it had been taken away from me.

I placed my hands over my face and cried, protected by the cover of darkness, the buffering of the thick blanket muffling my convulsive crying until I hit the wall of emotional exhaustion— leaving nothing but emptiness inside. I wanted to see a flicker of hope for my life, but the darkness was too strong. Perhaps it was time to wear a metaphorical mask, hiding my face of fear.

Ever aware of my daily surveillance, I escaped from my bed of despair at 6am and headed off to gym, showering after my extensive workout before grabbing breakfast on the way to the CAI building.

I entered my secure office by 9am, exhausted before the day had begun. Today would be pivotal in the meeting with the doctors. I had to play my cards right. I had to play my cards carefully.

I stood by the large glass window and looked out over the city. I refused to look at my graffiti wall of design at this moment.

I couldn't.

I wasn't ready for the vision to enter my head after the nightmare last night.

The streets were busy below, and dark thunderclouds formed in the west already—how apt. I retreated to my computer, logged in and was greeted by the ping of emails.

The only important one being from Miss Rubin. I opened it up.

FROM: Jordan RUBIN
DATE: May 16 09:00
SUBJECT: Conference
TO: Cohen DARCY

Dear Mr. Darcy,

The conference is organised for 11am in your office.

Have your secretary ensure that we have refreshments.

Be organised, or I'll be questioning your viability with the Organisation.

You do not want to disappoint my father.

J.

I leaned back in my chair after reading her correspondence, seething with contempt. She was a power player, using her father's power. What a coward. I opened the employee files and searched for her profile and qualifications. Let's see what she has for herself, and, is it earned or given?

Jordan Elise Rubin
Department: Communications Research Assessment
Qualifications: Classified information: access denied
Contact email: jerubin@cai.com

Given—she had been given the job by her father. It had been handed to her on a silver platter. She had all rights and no responsibility. But well taught in lessons on arrogance and rudeness. The apple doesn't fall far from the tree...

FROM: Cohen DARCY
DATE: May 16 09:10
SUBJECT: Conference 11am
TO: Miss RUBIN

Dear Miss Rubin,

Thank you for your email detailing the time of the conference. Every requirement is met, except for the refreshments. I do not have a secretary. I would be appreciative if your secretary, Miss Reuben, could cater for our needs, with your approval of course.

Kind Regards,
Cohen Darcy

Send...

Within two minutes I received a reply in my favour. Miss Reuben would cater for our meeting as I had requested. This could work to my advantage.

10.45am—Mia knocked on my office door. I welcomed her into my office, and she busied herself with arranging refreshments.

10.55am—Miss J. Rubin entered my office, dressed in a hot pink fitting dress that finished above her knees. She wore ridiculously high stiletto shoes that looked impossible to walk in. I nodded to her to acknowledge her presence.

'Morning, Miss Rubin.'

'Mr. Darcy,' she replied, her voice cold, unwelcoming.

At 11.00am as scheduled, Drs Peterson and Williams entered my office, together.

I shook their hands, introduced myself and Miss Rubin, followed by Miss Reuben. I took command of the meeting at once.

I started from the beginning—the purpose of our meeting, the conception of my idea, and finally the design details, followed by consultation with the professors.

They studied my diagrams in detail and the technology that was to be inserted. The professors took copious notes and conversed with each other in medical speak.

We engaged in long conversations about the engineering, possible positive outcomes and listed all the negative outcomes.

Repeatedly, the professors expressed their doubt about the technology and emphasized they could not be held personally responsible for outcomes that may impede the quality of life of the host of the mind-reading implant.

Once the details were discussed and we were all on the same page, we called for Mr. Rubin to join us in our concluding discussions, to make the final decision about developing and trialling the technology.

I stood back and watched as the professors talked to Mr. Rubin with their intricate knowledge of the eye and brain systems. Once their conversation had finished, Mr. Rubin made his decision instantly; the procedure would go ahead to be trialled. He had already decided what to do, no matter what the professors advised.

After an exhausting six hours the meeting had finished. My head was thumping with pain and I was well and truly done for the day.

I left the office at 5:15pm with a guilty conscience. It was heavy and unrelenting. I was about to waste millions of dollars of the CAI in developing a mind-reading implant, that was guaranteed not to work. And for the sake of humanity, it must not work. I was the only one aware of the flaw that would cause its failure, and it would stay that way. I would take my secret to take to the grave.

The rain was beating down when I ventured through the revolving doors, but as always, my personal taxi driver was waiting for me.

He drove off into the driving rain as I made my way up to my apartment to the smell of dinner. I was getting tired of the game of maximum security, and I did not feel like playing tonight. I wanted to curl up in a corner in the fetal position to console myself. The burden of the mind-reading implant was getting to me, and I needed to step away from it—but, I feared, it was an impossibility.

So, I did the next best thing. I had a long hot shower and let the heat of the water burn the tension away. The flow of the water relaxed my mind so I didn't feel like digging it out with a spoon anymore.

Numerous times I ran my hands through my wet hair in frustration, and then in resignation of the situation. I had to bide my time. I had to stay strong in playing the game better than them. I could not let any cracks appear in my role as the Creative Designer.

Steam from the shower entered my bedroom before I did, then flowed around like a confident inhabitant of the air space. It led my eyes to the time on the digital clock—6:38pm.

Damn! I had to meet Georgia at 7:03pm at Flowers for Fleur! I had forgotten all about it in my moment of doom and gloom.

I quickly pulled on some old, faded denim jeans, a white T-shirt, and a white long-sleeved button-up shirt. I left through the front door of the apartment shoving my sports shoes on my feet.

The rain was still drizzling as I bolted along the streets to the café. The doorbell announced my arrival as I entered, and stopped abruptly once I was inside. I examined the tables carefully, looking for Georgia. I didn't want her to defeat me in the race to the café.

She was nowhere to be seen, thankfully. It was exactly 6.59pm, according to my world time synchronised digital watch. At least I couldn't be accused of being late!

I found a table and sat at it, watching the door for her entry. But 7.03pm came and went, and there was no Georgia. I guess that she couldn't find her spiked running shoes for better grip.

Maybe though, I had been stood up. It wouldn't be the first time in my history of relationships with women. It always ended this way.

Great! Hope sank to the pit of my stomach.

I put my head into my hands at the table and covered my eyes with my fingers. Maybe I could walk the streets by myself for a little bit before I return to my empty apartment? My life just wasn't panning out the way I wanted it to. In fact, it was the complete opposite to my ideal life of the future.

I ran my hands down my face and opened my eyes. And there she was. Sitting opposite me, smiling. How could I not hear her approach the table, or pull out the chair? There was no clanging of the doorbell, and I didn't smell her sweet perfume.

'Hi,' she said in a quiet voice.

'Hi,' I said, smiling crookedly at her, suddenly feeling shy. 'You're late, Miss Harrison!' I commented.

'This is why, Mr. Darcy,' she added, sliding a freshly baked gigantic gingerbread man in front of me. It smelled divine. It looked perfect, and was smothered in coloured icing.

'Georgia!' I exclaimed, impressed by her culinary skills. 'This is amazing! Thank you.'

'I aim to please, Mr. Darcy. And... it's the least I could do for someone willing to listen to me reading my book to them. Repay kindness for kindness.' Her voice was soothing to my soul. She was exactly what I needed tonight.

My Georgia...

I closed my eyes and smiled to myself. What return for

kindness will I receive from the world for interfering with success of the mind-reading implant... for stopping its capabilities from causing destruction among humans? They will never know. Georgia will never know. My smile widened. I was a hero in my own lunch box.

'Something amusing, Mr. Darcy?' Georgia said, her voice low, her blue eyes looking up at me from under her long eyelashes as she poured tea for two.

'Hmmm... I was just thinking that you probably hid the sultanas underneath the icing on the gingerbread man. It's the perfect hideout for them,' I quipped, lying.

'Eat Mr. Darcy. I want to see you squirm in gastronomic delight as you devour this exquisite gingerbread. It's guaranteed to make your digestive juices hum.' She was bossy, but not, at the same time.

'Miss Harrison, I hope that your memory recalls my predisposition to not sharing gingerbread,' I said, and bit into my treat.

Georgia smiled at me over her teacup, her eyes danced with enjoyment.

I closed my eyes as the heavenly taste of the gingerbread caressed my taste buds. I was in gingerbread heaven. It was divine.

'It's... passable... Miss Harrison,' I commented, playing down the deliciousness of the treat.

'Does that mean that you'll pass it to me, Mr. Darcy?' Georgia asked, placing her hand out for me to give it to her, her eyes seductive, trying to convince me to part with my beloved gingerbread.

I looked into her big cornflower blue eyes and shook my head, slowly, then broke off a very small portion of the gingerbread man's leg and placed it into her hand. Our fingers touched lightly, and it sent a warmth through my body. I inhaled sharply at the very nice sensation that lingered in my blood.

My Georgia...

I watched her as she placed it into her mouth, brushing the crumbs off her luscious lips.

'How did your eye appointment go today, Cohen?' Georgia asked.

'It was a pre-appointment. The next appointment is in the Office of Optometrics. We will see how it goes then,' I said, skipping around her question.

She nodded her head at me and then smiled, pulling out the book, resting it on the table in front of her. 'Ready?' she asked, narrowing her eyes at me, checking my commitment to her readings.

'Quell my curiosity, Miss Georgia. Continue the story from where we left off. I want to hear his answer,' I said, looking deeply into her eyes. My voice was low, almost a whisper.

She smiled slightly, put on her glasses, looked down at the book and opened the bookmarked page. She looked up at me again before she began to read, as if looking for reassurance from me. I bobbed my head, closing and opening my eyes in affirmation.

" 'I was manufactured, not created,' he said. His face was forlorn. His fingers dug into his legs.

I sat, watching his body language. He was embarrassingly ashamed of himself. 'What is your definition of manufactured, Ethan?' I asked, feeling compassion for him. Being a product of IVF was nothing to be ashamed of. In fact, his parents very much wanted him if they went through the IVF process. He was the baby they had dreamed of, the baby they vowed to love forever.

'I was a stem cell, ignited into human form by an electrical impulse. I spent my embryonic life contained in nutrient rich liquid suspended in an artificial environment until my coming out—my so-called birth. I do not have a mother, or a father. I just am. I am not born of love. How can I have a soul if I am not the creation of a living egg from a female and the living sperm of a father?'

'Ethan, you are a living being. You are a soul!' I emphasized.

'A cat or dog is living. Do they have a soul? A plant is living. Does a plant have a soul?' he said with acidity in his voice as his eyes pierced mine, searching deeply for answers to his unanswered questions.

'Yes... animals and plants are souls—soul means life—'

'—And created in the realm of the natural paradigm. But I am not natural. I am a scientific product of an experiment in human intelligence. They didn't care for me. They didn't care for me in here.' He put his hand over his heart. 'They basked in their own glory of their dominance in the world of science, their world of science where they are the god. And here I sit. A human soul with no spirit... If I have no spirit, I have no hope—' his voice trailed off in pain.

'Hope for?' I asked, wanting to know the exact root of his problem.

'Hope for something... more,' he answered. His eyes were empty.

'What do you mean by something more?' I asked as my heart was breaking for him.

'I want to experience life after death. I want to be a spiritual being after death. But without a soul—' He choked on his words as emotional hurt was exposed on his face.

He wasn't talking about his soul. Everything that has life has a soul. He was talking about his spirit. My skin prickled. His spirit was strong and shone brightly. I could feel it. I smiled to myself, knowing the great happiness and peace he would feel once his eyes and ears were opened to receive the blessing. In time it will come, and he will fall to his knees in thanks.

I reached over and lightly placed my hand over his. His hand stiffened at my touch, as if he was repelled by it. But then he relaxed and breathed out deeply.

'Ethan, I believe you are talking about your spirit. That is the part of humans which survives after death. In my experience, if you worry about not having a spirit, then you must have one. If you didn't have one, the concept of a spirit would not even cross your mind. Your spirit is strong. I can feel it,' I said, letting the soothing words flow from my mouth like a baby's lullaby, singing to the core of his being.

He looked deeply into my eyes and connected at a spiritual level I knew of, but he was not consciously aware of. Not yet anyway. He pulled his blue eyes away from mine, breaking the magnetic connection. He looked at my hand on his and contorted his face as if in pain. 'I must go now. I'm taking up your precious time — thank you for...' He furrowed his eyebrows and pressed his lips together. 'For your kindness,' he finished, and then started to move off the bed.

'Where do you live?' I asked. He looked as if he lived on the street when he fell into the reception area of the medical research centre. In fact, he looked like a druggie.

He grimaced and shook his head. 'Nowhere mentionable,' he answered, continuing to shake his head. He averted his eyes away from mine.

Was he lying, or ashamed of where he lived?

'Please come back to see me if you feel that you need to. I am here to help — always.'

He looked into my eyes and nodded, closing his eyes as he did so. In the same breath, he left out the double doors and into the concrete jungle. Where to I will never know. I wanted to follow him. I wanted to know that he would be okay. He was a lost being searching for his place in the universe. I hoped that he did not find the wrong place that would ultimately destroy his soul, or his spirit.' "

'Excuse me, sir, were you wanting to order anything else before you vacate the table for waiting customers?' the waitress babbled, extracting me from the characters of the book. I looked up at her clueless, and then to Georgia and frowned.

'No, thank you. I think that we are done here, are we, Cohen?' asked Georgia, articulating her words perfectly. I ran my hand through my hair, trying to break free from the brain fog that clouded my thoughts and coherence.

I raised my eyebrows. 'Yes, I guess so.'

Where had I been?

As Georgia read to me, I lived the words of the book. It was like being spellbound, enraptured. And I had been disconnected abruptly. I wasn't ready to leave the story yet. Where did he live?

Georgia placed her hand over mine. 'It's time to go, Cohen,' she said quietly, and then placed the leather-bound book into her bag and stood. I watched her as if there were two of me. One in body, and one in spirit. Yet, we were not connected.

Without the need to think, I stood and followed her out the door. The bell clanged, announcing our departure, and echoed in my mind as if it were a distant church bell rebounding off the mountains. I shook my head, trying to clear it, and return to reality.

Georgia turned to me at once when we were outside. Her gaze was intense. 'Are you alright?' she asked in a voice filled with concern.

'I think so,' I replied unconvincingly.

She placed her hand on my forehead, and then the side of my face and looked closely into my eyes.

'What?' I asked, my heart beating faster.

'You look awfully tired. Do you feel okay?' she asked, looking into my eyes as she waited for me to answer.

I raised my eyebrows and took a deep breath. 'Yes, I think. And yes, I am exhausted. I didn't sleep well last night. When can we meet for the next reading? I need to eat some more of your gingerbread,' I suggested. I wanted to see my Georgia again.

She looked up at me then blinked and smiled slightly with her head tilted to the side. She touched my forearm with her soft, warm hand, melting my heart and sending tingles throughout my body.

'How about the library—tomorrow night at 7pm?' Her voice was quiet.

I nodded. 'I look forward to it.'

We walked the next three blocks together with her hand linked in through my arm. Her closeness made me feel high. And when we stopped at the corner to part ways, I turned and faced her. A tear ran down her cheek slowly. I looked into her eyes to try to read her mood and figure out the reason for her tears. I couldn't, but I gently wiped the tear from her face with my thumb. 'Tomorrow, 7pm at the library,' I whispered into her ear before I went my own way. I wanted to kiss her. I wanted to wrap my arms around her and hold her against me. But I didn't—I just didn't.

Chapter 13

While I supervised the 3D rendered drawing of my mind-reading implant by a biomedical engineer, I received a phone call from both doctors confirming their interest in the project, detailing the surgery team involved.

The mind-reading implant was on the move towards reality. The only thing holding it back was the manufacture of the implant, which would take about four weeks to complete.

My phone buzzed. It was Mia. Mr. Rubin needed to see me, immediately.

Mia smiled and nodded at me as I walked past her, and the double doors to his office clicked as I touched the handle.

As per the usual greeting, he faced away from me.

'Mr. Darcy—sit,' he ordered in his bossy tone.

I sat in the red leather chair opposite his marble topped desk in silence and waited for him to turn to face me.

He clapped his hands, slowly, sarcastically, and then his chair swivelled to face me. 'Congratulations, Mr. Darcy. I honestly didn't believe you could achieve the mind-reading technology. We are now well ahead of the rest of the field. Our Communications

Company will become the wealthiest, the most powerful, and the most respected company in the field. But, as you know, it's pivotal on one thing, Mr. Darcy—the success of the implant, and the viability with how we can use it.' He leaned forward. 'It is time to trial it. This places me in a difficult position, Mr. Darcy. We have managed to keep the project top secret. Only six people are aware of its existence. We need two of those people to trial the technology. I have chosen you, and laboured over the other choice, but it falls upon my head, as I trust no other person. In four weeks' time, we will meet at the hospital. I will see you there, Mr. Darcy. Do not be late. Good day.' He started to turn in his chair towards the large glass ceiling to floor window.

I cleared my throat to draw his attention. 'Mr. Rubin, I request that you turn to face me. It is about the implant.' I waited for him to turn back to me. I refused to leave his office unless I had said what I needed to say to him.

After half a minute, he turned his chair aggressively towards me.

'Mr. Rubin, I will be the only one to trial the device. I created it and I will run the risk of blindness or death on my own. I do not want you to trial the device until the technology and surgical process has been refined. You are risking both your sight and health, Mr. Rubin. It is still highly science fiction in its conception, and highly unpredictable with the outcome,' I implored, knowing the device would not work, unbeknown to him.

He raised his eyebrows at me. 'Mr. Darcy... so little do you know—I can't trust you. You could easily have the implant fitted, and then report to me that it does not work, when in reality it does. This way, if I am also fitted with the device, only the truth will be known. Do you understand, Mr. Darcy? Do you under - stand?' he repeated slowly, sarcastically.

'Clearly, Mr. Rubin. But let it be known—I have warned

you. And if it all goes wrong, you were in control of your fate, not me. Good day, Mr. Rubin.' I left his office, under my terms.

As I passed Mia's reception desk, she handed me a folder. 'Mr. Darcy, this folder contains all the information you need to know about the hospital procedure. Read it carefully today. Do you understand?' she asked, widening her eyes at me and nodding her head at the same time.

I took a deep breath then let it out. 'Yes… I understand, Miss Reuben,' I replied, and then left to return to my own office.

I opened the orange folder and found the hospital admission forms, times, dates, fasting information etc. I also found a small white note. No names, just a time—8pm. I understood.

The large glass doors of the university library opened when I approached them at 5pm, two hours before my book reading with Georgia. I had my own research to conduct. I wanted to know about the possibility of an eye contact lens that could organically grow into the eye to connect to the brain for mind intrusion, or the possibility of an interocular (external) contact lens that could wirelessly connect to the electrical impulses of the retina and move through the neurons to mind read. Was it a freaky possibility, or was technology not ready for this type of connection to the human brain yet?

The world of the eye, brain and contact lens technologies was intriguing and had taken me prisoner at the study table in the library. It had rendered me totally oblivious to all that surrounded me and captured me in the world of science-fiction.

I made my decision. My Mind-reading implant would be different to Mr. Rubin's, which was destined to fail by my will. My mind-reading implant would be an eye lens that is organic, and grows into the blood vessels of the eye, making electrical connections to the brain to allow mind-reading through the other person's retina. It only required eye surgery. There was no brain surgery involved, so it was a much safer option, but still with obvious risks. Professor Thomas was the world leading doctor in this area. I needed to contact him after I had engineered the technology.

Visually, my brain started building the mind-reading technology and storing it away for use. Having a photographic memory and strong visualisation abilities always allowed me to travel far with my creations. I was completely assimilated in my world of "science fiction meets reality" when the scent of a floral perfume broke through my disconnection with my surroundings.

Georgia was here.

I stared at my notes and drawings and listened to where she was. I had no idea until she touched my shoulder, ever so lightly. She walked around the desk and sat opposite me.

She smiled with a look of merriment on her face. I smiled back at her gently, wondering what was so amusing. 'Am I entertaining you, Georgia?' I asked, becoming self-conscious.

She leaned in closer. 'Your hair is all ruffled. It's kinda delicious,' she whispered.

I ran my hand through my hair, trying to control it somewhat. I must have had my hand resting in my hair as I was researching. I hope I haven't scared her off with my wild look. 'Are you going to attempt to eat it, Miss Harrison?' I asked quizzically.

'Maybe later it you're lucky, Mr. Darcy—come, I know the perfect place where we will be alone,' she said.

I raised my eyebrows and followed her through the library maze until she stopped at a dead end in the library. The books were old, and their information was out of date. They were like the dinosaurs of the library: extinct.

We sat down on the floor at the very end and Georgia's face lit up like we were seven-year-olds, hiding in a secret tree house, or behind the garden shed.

Her beauty blinded me sometimes, and this was a time that it did. I smiled back at her and tucked a stray curl behind her ear, touching her lightly. She took a short sharp breath. Maybe she did like me more than I thought. She was very hard to read.

Georgia pulled the book out from her bag, plus a brown paper bag. She kept the book in her hands and handed the brown paper bag to me. I knew what was in it before I opened it. I could smell the ginger spices escaping from the bag like it had been held prisoner. I broke off a piece and put it into my mouth, then broke off another piece and offered it to Georgia.

She opened her mouth for me to place it in, surprising me. I gently wiped a crumb from her soft bottom lip with my finger, and tried to ignore my emotional response to the intimacy of the act.

I should have kissed her. It was the perfect opportunity. But I didn't. I needed to know how she felt about me before I made an idiot of myself kissing her. What if I had read her signals wrongly?

I was here just to listen to her read from the stupid book. That is what I had agreed to. We were not out on a date, or even dating for that matter. Our paths had only crossed because of the book.

I looked back at the gingerbread man to break off another piece to eat.

'I thought that you didn't share your gingerbread, Cohen. That's twice now that you have shared it with me,' she remarked.

I smiled crookedly, my eyes on the legless gingerbread man. 'It's the way I test it—for poisoning—you know. Gingerbread men can be very sneaky,' I said as I looked up at her.

She was smiling at me, melting my heart.

'Read to me, Georgia. Where does Ethan live?' I asked, encouraging her to start reading from the book.

She gazed into my eyes for a long moment before she looked down, put on her glasses and opened the book. She didn't notice me take a sharp intake of breath as my feelings for her escalated. She was like a drug, and I was beginning to get addicted to her.

My Georgia...

"'And that was the last that I saw of him. Like ships that pass in the night. A fleeting second in a lifetime of thirty-two million seconds. He left me downhearted. I wanted to go to a dark corner and release my tears for him. I wanted to tell him he did have a place in the universe, and that he would be alright in his journey of life. We are never alone—never. I wanted him to feel the amazing grace and presence of our Giver of Life. One can never come to being without His approval. I wanted him to know. But I never told him. He may remain lost in his closed dark world of self-doubt, self-loathing. I prayed he would come back. If he didn't, I had failed in my belief and my compassion for humanity.

I paused while I gathered my composure, and then returned to my day's work. How will I forget him? How will I forgive myself? Life goes on I reminded myself...' "

A tear fell from Georgia's eye. She looked up at me through her long eyelashes with her face full of grief. I took a deep breath, moved by her sadness. Then I pulled her close and wrapped my arms around her and held her against my chest, feeling her quiet sobs as her tears wet my skin.

I kissed the top of her head, and we sat in complete silence as I comforted her.

I stroked the ends of her hair with slow movements of my hand, closed my eyes and connected to her presence touching me, her body warm against mine.

I sent healing thoughts through my mind, hoping to enter the realm of spiritual comfort.

After a moment she pulled away from me, looked into my eyes and whispered, 'Thank-you.'

A deep longing for her came from the core of my being. I held my breath and tilted my head to the side then nodded gently to her. I didn't know what to do next. Should I talk to her? Should I say something? Or should I wait until she spoke first?

If only I knew—if only I could read her mind—frustrating.

She leaned over and placed her hand on my heart, lightly.

'Go with your heart, Cohen. Don't over think,' she said quietly.

Was she answering my unspoken question? How did she know?

I closed my eyes and breathed out. Then I felt her hand on the side of my face. It was so warm, so full of energy. I opened my eyes slowly and looked at her as she trailed her finger along my jaw line before pulling her hand away. Our eyes were locked in each other, knowing.

What was this control she had over me? I felt like she had touched my heart, my mind, and I wanted to melt her into me to have her forever.

She looked back to the book while I continued to drink her in. Then I leaned my head against the wall behind me and closed my eyes.

I don't do relationships. Do I?

Her seraphic voice entered my head when she continued to read.

"'Hours turned into days, and days into months,
but there was no sign of Ethan. He was forever
in my mind, day and night. I searched his name

and history everywhere I could possibly think of, and there was no record of him, anywhere. There was no reference to his name, and no registered birth. He did not exist—apparently. I had to forget about him. There was nothing I could do for him anymore. I had my chance and blew it. I prayed I had planted a seed of hope in his mind in our one and only conversation. All things are possible with the Giver of Life. It was in His hands now. All things are possible...

And then one day as I worked, he was there. He appeared, standing in front of me—emotionless. His eyes were desolate and full of self-loathing.' "

Georgia stopped reading the book at the sound of my irritating watch alarm.

'Sorry,' I mouthed to her and winced. 'I have to go to meet someone,' I tried to explain without sounding harsh.

Her eyes widened in what—fear? She tilted her head down and frowned. Disappointment had covered her face like a cloak. My heart twisted. Had I hurt her by potentially leaving? Or was it something else?

If only I could read her mind—what was she thinking?

I ran my hand through my hair, torn between staying with Georgia and with meeting with Mia. But Mia had been adamant, and our point of meeting was branded as urgent.

I couldn't stay with Georgia, even though that was what my head and heart were screaming out at me to do.

I stood then, breaking my magnetic connection to her. It hurt, physically.

I proffered my hands to help her off the floor. She continued to look down at the book, her chin trembling. She sucked in a breath, took off her glasses and tucked the book into her bag, flung it over her shoulder and then placed both of her hands in mine. They radiated a tingling sensation throughout my body and made me feel a heightened sense of being.

My heart was singing, bathed in pure happiness.

Her eyes were wet when she looked up at me. 'Tomorrow?' she asked, full of hope. How could this woman who gave so much hope and energy to others be looking to me for hope?

My heart grew arms to hug her. 'Absolutely,' I answered in a gentle voice. I looked down and found her hand to hold in mine, and walked back through the library maze with her, intoxicated by our closeness that seemed to have developed.

We stopped to part ways outside the university library. She faced me and placed her hand over my heart again. She smiled at me and turned on her heel and left.

I watched her, wanting to run after her. But I didn't. Reluctantly, I turned and made my way to the bar to meet Mia— Mia the red head.

As I sipped my scotch, Mia's low voice greeted me. She led me to a dark corner of the pub, looking around suspiciously before she talked to me.

'Cohen, we have stepped up security for you. Word is, on the street, that he plans on taking you out of the picture once he has total control of the technology, and has you sign over the copyright of the mind-reading implant. He has eradicated any evidence of your presence on the earth on digital storage. Trust no-one. Watch your back. We are tracking your whereabouts and watching people tracking you. You will be protected. You are crucial to Mr. Rubin's impending imprisonment. We will have him locked up and the key thrown away. Prepare for a rough ride.'

Mia left in haste. Quietly and stealthily.

I finished my scotch before I headed off along the street, strolling along to my apartment. I felt like yelling, "Human Target Here!" But I knew I was safe until after the surgery, and until after I had signed the documents over to him. *If I was dead though... I* thought, *he couldn't claim the designs and patent as his own—could he? I needed to amend my will.*

I hit the hot shower as soon as I entered my apartment. My head was turning over the information and designs for my own organic mind-reading implant.

I went to bed, but could not sleep.

The Tim Jennings Blackberry vibrated against my leg.

FROM: Georgia Harrison
SUBJECT: Meeting
DATE: May 17 22:07
TO: Tim Jennings

Dear Tim,

You are just like a gingerbread man.
You keep running away from me.
Meet me at the park tomorrow.

Georgia
#thankyouformeetingmeeachtime

FROM: Tim Jennings
SUBJECT: Point Of View
DATE: May 17 22:10
TO: Georgia Harrison

Dear Georgia,

One day I will meet the fox.
Do you know what she looks like?
I look forward to meeting you at the park tomorrow.
Tim
#iwonderwhatthestorywouldbelikefromethanspointofview?

Send...

FROM: Georgia Harrison
SUBJECT: purple flowers
DATE: May 17 22:15
TO: Tim Jennings

Dear Tim,

I told you not to over think things.
Sometimes it's best to follow your heart.
Can you meet early tomorrow morning?

Georgia
#wheredidyougetthenametimjenningsfrom?

FROM: Tim Jennings
SUBJECT: Childhood Memories
DATE: May 17 22:18
TO: Georgia Harrison

Dear Georgia,

Have you ever been told that you ask too many questions?
What time tomorrow morning?
Or do I even need to ask that question?

Tim
#iwonderhowethanwouldtellhisstory?

Send...

FROM: Georgia Harrison
SUBJECT: purple flowers
DATE: May 17 22:15
TO: Tim Jennings

Dear Tim,

I told you not to over think things.
Sometimes it's best to follow your heart.
Can you meet early tomorrow morning?

Georgia
#wheredidyougetthenametimjenningsfrom?

FROM: Tim Jennings
SUBJECT: Childhood Memories
DATE: May 17 22:18
TO: Georgia Harrison

Dear Georgia,

Have you ever been told that you ask too many questions?
What time tomorrow morning?
Or do I even need to ask that question?

Tim
#itisthenameofmychildhoodimaginaryfriendifyoureallymustknow!

Send…

FROM: Georgia Harrison
SUBJECT: Purple
DATE: May 17 22:22
TO: Tim Jennings

Dear Tim,

Meet you under the wisteria vine. You know what time.

Georgia
#youreallyareverycuteMrDarcy!

I smiled to myself and turned off the Tim Jennings Blackberry. Georgia was a very nice distraction to my complicated world. And that thought stayed with me as I drifted off to sleep...

Chapter 14

Isat under the wisteria vine with the magnificent purple blooms suspended above me like a cascading waterfall, and waited for my Georgia to arrive. My heart literally jumped for joy merely at the thought of seeing her again. It shouldn't be this way. I don't do the girlfriend thing.

But then, my elated feeling was overshadowed by the reality of the mind-reading implant, and where I was possibly headed with it all.

I knew what I had to do. I had made a deal with Georgia to listen to the book in its entirety, to the very end. And I wouldn't break my word. Then, I would distance myself from her, slowly, so I wouldn't break my heart, or hers—that is, if she had grown to like me. Maybe I was just someone for her to read the book to, and then she would just say thanks very much, it was nice knowing you.

If so, be it. The less heartbreak the better.

But I knew my heart would break. I should have listened to myself—I don't do girls.

I picked up a purple flower from the ground and ran my

fingers over the petals.

She was here. I could smell her perfume.

'Penny for your thoughts, Mr. Darcy.' Her voice was soft. I looked up at her. She had a faint smile on her beautiful face while her blue eyes caressed mine.

'You're late,' I said, my head tilted to one side in a questioning manner.

'You were early,' she replied as she rested her hand on my shoulder and sat beside me.

'And you know this how?' I asked, curious to hear her answer. I didn't see her anywhere near the great purple wisteria vine when I arrived with my trackers.

She looked down and smiled gently. 'I was early, too,' she answered, looking up at me through her long lashes.

My eyes wandered to her lips. I wanted to kiss her.

'It's a beautiful morning,' she said, changing the subject, thankfully.

'More beautiful now that you're here,' I added, looking into her eyes. I hoped she didn't mind my complimentary comment.

What was she thinking, or feeling? I wish I knew.

She smiled at me and pulled out two containers of tea, and one croissant filled with ham and melted cheese. 'Tea for two, Mr. Darcy? And I brought a croissant for you,' she said, smiling.

'You don't need to feed me every time I come to a book reading, Miss Harrison,' I said. 'I come willingly to hear the continuing story you are off loading on me,' I added in jest.

She stopped and looked sharply at me, and started to shake her head from side to side.

I had hurt her.

'You honour me with your presence, Cohen. I must give you some sort of incentive to keep listening to the stupid book,' she said. There was not an ounce of humour in her voice.

I opened my eyes wide in surprise at her comment. The

stupid book—she had taken my very words!

I looked up and laughed. 'The stupid book,' I repeated after her in an English accent, smirking. 'Why do you call it that?' I asked, watching her face carefully as she answered. I thought she had written the stupid book.

'Because it… owns me. I can't be rid of it until its contents are out, and then I can move on from it. Perhaps then it can become fuel for your fire,' she said, no qualms about it.

I contemplated her reply. The stupid book becomes more intriguing by the minute.

'I was under the impression the book is your diary or journal,' I put out there.

'No. It—,' she couldn't answer my statement.

'Found you,' I finished her answer. I looked at her, saddened by her burden with the stupid book. I decided to change the topic of conversation.

'Georgia, I drew this for you,' I said, and handed my piece of artwork over to her, with a purple wisteria flower.

'Oh,' she gasped. 'It is so beautiful—thank you. There's much more to you than meets the eye, Mr. Darcy. Now I am enraptured and honoured to be in your presence,' she said, embarrassing me.

If she knew what I was about to do with the mind-reading implant, she would not think that at all. I looked down at my tea and croissant and with a small smile. 'Read to me, Georgia,' I said gently, changing the subject again, looking into her warm blue eyes.

She nodded, put on her glasses and took a sip of tea before she took the book out of her bag.

" 'Georgia, I… I… please let me talk to you again,' he said, his eyes desperately searching my face for my consent.

'Let me finish with this research paper. Sit over there and I'll be as quick as I can. No—on second thoughts, come with me while I finish up with the research for today,' I said, my voice and mind racing as adrenalin surged through me. He was here. This was my second chance.

'Here, eat while I work,' I encouraged him as I took my paperwork and sat at a desk in another room.

'I do not come for food for the physical body. It is my mind that is hungry. Things you know of, and I don't,' he said emphatically.

His words stopped me in my tracks and froze my pen on the spot. I turned to face him.

His hands were behind his head and his face was impassive. Or was he angry? It was hard to tell.

'Talk, Ethan,' I stated, words no more, no less.

He looked at me and considered me before he added to the dialogue. 'How do I get a… spirit?'

I looked at him, bewildered.

'One does not "get" a spirit like buying it from a shop, Ethan. It's given to you, as a free gift from the Giver of Life. You are living, Ethan. You are a soul. It's the essence of humanity's being. It is who we are. It's what makes us feel emotions. You have a heart, a mind, a body. You cannot have these things without a spirit, which is the part of humanity that connects with God. It seems to me that you are purely thinking about the process through which you were created. The process doesn't matter. If the Giver of Life did not want you here on this earth, then we would not be here having this conversation. It's that simple. You. Have. A. Spirit. A connection to God. Cherish it,' I articulated explicitly to him.

He rubbed his hands over his face and through his hair.

'But I can't feel it here!' he said in anger, almost yelling at me and putting his hand over his heart. 'I feel empty... in here. I feel nothing.' His voice was rough and pained.

I reached over and placed my hand over his heart as a tear fell from my eye.

He looked at me, confused.

I wiped my own tear away and looked into his eyes. My heart was hurting for him. 'Tell me about your life, Ethan. I need to know,' I said, desperate to find the reason for his self-loathing and his belief of being a human without a spirit.

He put his head against the wall and squeezed his eyes shut. 'I can't tell you,' he forced out between gritted teeth.

'Can't, or won't?' I asked, knowing he may not be ready to deal with his past yet.

'Won't,' he replied after a while. He looked down and pulled his eyebrows together.

'You need to release your past. Set it free. If you keep it inside it will chain you down forever, keeping you in the darkness. You don't have to tell me. Write it down and burn the paper, tell a friend, a stranger who will listen, a pet, bash it into a pillow, take it to the top of a mountain and get rid of your past hurts, shout it out until you have no anger left inside... and... and cry until you are emotionally exhausted. You don't have any room inside your heart to receive goodness and kindness with your past overflowing like a toxic waste,' I said in gentleness.

He looked at me, taking in every word I spoke. Then he looked down at his hands. 'Can I ask you one more thing, Georgia?' He had tears in his voice.

'Absolutely — go ahead,' I replied, hoping this

was not the last time I was going to see him. He had a lot of baggage that needed disposing of, and I could help him do that.

'Will you hold me?' His eyes were anguished.

Astonished, I nodded to him. He moved towards me, and I wrapped my arms around him and pulled him closely against me. He smelled of body odour, unwashed clothes, and his hair was full of old perspiration, but his breath was clean and sweet.

He let out a choked cry and began to sob against me, deeply.

I cried with him, for him, and let my tears drops fall upon his face, mixing with his. I could feel him squeezing his eyes shut against me as he let out the deep grief from the centre of his being.

He was a broken man.

I held him in my arms with my eyes closed, giving up silent prayers for this beautiful man. Once he had shed his last tear and the last of his heaving sobs ceased, he moved away from me, averting his eyes away from mine as if ashamed of himself.

'Ethan... I help people. It's what I do,' I said softly, trying to lift him higher.

'You do it well then,' he said after a moment of silence, in a voice that was barely audible.

'Go and take a long warm shower. Let out more tears. You haven't finished yet. That's why you're feeling this way,' I encouraged.

He looked at me and nodded, turned and entered the shower.

He exited an hour later.

If we had made any gain before he entered the shower, I didn't see it now. He presented as a gorgeous physical human being. But his face, in all off its sculptured beauty, was still full of sorrow.

My beautiful, lost Ethan. How long will it take for your healing?

He gazed at me when he saw me then smiled, crookedly.

My heart skipped a beat.

'Thank you... again... Georgia,' he said with shyness as he looked at his broken watch. 'Gotta go... things to do... places to go. You know how it is,' he offered.

I smiled and nodded at him, wondering if he would come back to visit me again.

I doubted it. Men don't like crying in front of others—they think it's a sign of weakness. But it's far from that.

'I'm here for you, Ethan—whenever you want,' I offered back to him, and gave him a warm hug.

He hesitated before he enfolded his arms around me, gently, and kissed the side of my head.

I stepped back from him and watched as he walked out the door. 'Good-bye, Ethan,' I whispered for me, for closure. I knew the pattern for those who seek refuge. Once you start to get to know them, they pull away and disappear from your life. We were done, according to him anyway—' "

'Georgia, did you seek me out? Did you plant the book in my apartment?' I interrupted, my eyebrows furrowed.

'Cohen,' she retorted sharply. 'How can you say that? How can you accuse me of doing such a thing?'

She was hurt. She slammed the book closed, gave me a shove, removed her glasses then stood, and stormed off.

I should have gone after her. But I didn't.

Instead, I watched her as she left the parklands, followed by a tracker—not mine.

When I realized she was in danger, I took off after her.

The wisteria flowers became a purple blur as I ran after her. For one, I wanted an answer. She had left me feeling exasperated and frustrated as she hadn't told me how the book came to be in my apartment! And two, I had to tell her that she had a tracker.

I slowed as I approached her and put my hand on her shoulder once I was close enough to her. She was still in a huff. I could feel it. Her mood surrounded her like a storm cloud, brewing. We stopped walking.

'I'm sorry. I apologize. It's… just things are kind of weird—you know…' I stepped forward and hugged her closely, not in affection, but to whisper into her ear like she had done to me once at my apartment door. 'You have a tracker—he is over to your left. Memorize his face—it is not optional,' I added.

I heard her gasp. 'Great! Another complication!' she said with acid in her voice.

'Meaning?' I asked, annoyed with her.

'Everything—' she lifted her hands, '—about you is complicated. Every time I want to meet you to read to you, it must be in public, and… and you have trackers, and the trackers have trackers. The only time I can text you is late at night. And then there's that thing where I have to read from the book to you because you can't seem to see the words! What's going on with you?'

'I can't tell you, yet. But I will when I'm in the clear—' I whispered into her ear.

'—YOU are frustrating!' she hissed in my ear, 'but the book can't stay away from you,' she added softly.

She took a step away from me and looked into my eyes. So many questions were reflected there, and fear, and love…

I saw love.

It connected to my soul, filling me with a warmth that I had never known. I wanted to pull her into my arms again and kiss her tenderly.

But I didn't.

Not here, not now.

'Georgia, you are the one who is frustrating. The book can't stay away from me? That doesn't even make sense. I see no rhyme or reason why you have to read it to me. Why can't you read it to your boyfriend, or a girlfriend?' I asked. My voice was tense.

She looked away from me and then down to the ground.

What have I said now? I grabbed her hand and started to walk with her.

'Where were you heading to?' I asked in a low voice.

'Anywhere... as long as it was away from you!' she answered.

'I'm sorry. I didn't mean to offend you. It's just that the circumstances are so... so...' I stumbled.

'Intriguing,' she finished and let out a sigh.

I nodded and took a deep breath, then brought her hand to my lips, and kissed it with the lightness of a feather.

'Read to me again,' I requested to keep her near to me. I didn't want to say goodbye. Yet.

A vacated park bench was beside the azure blue lake where ducks floated in gracefulness and pelicans sat judging the shenanigans nearby.

Georgia sat first and I sat beside her, our legs touching. I leaned forward, resting my elbows on my knees as she put on her glasses and read.

" 'I ran back to my research room and grabbed my coat, then took off out the automatic double doors. I had decided to follow him. I didn't know where this little adventure would lead me to, but my inner conscience was telling me to go. I stayed back fifteen metres behind him, trailing him like a spy. He walked like a man who knew his destiny.

He walked like a man full of self-confidence who was satisfied with his lot in life. He was so unlike the man I had conversations with, in the research hospital. Did he mask his emotions to hide his misery, his doubt about life? Or maybe he had a multiple personality disorder. What if he was just playing me, and I had fallen for it—hook, line and sinker?

I hate being so gullible. I always believe people at face value, thinking the best of them, believing that they had a good heart.

He continued to walk through the city streets and to the park near the bridge that led to the other side of the city.

It was dark there at this time of the afternoon because of the tall buildings blocking out the sun, and not a soul was to be seen. He took the pathway that led to the pedestrian walkway over the bridge, but then detoured down a side path. I followed him over the unstable dirt track, stumbling a few times over loose rocks.

He headed towards the bridge pylons. I hid behind one of them and watched Ethan enter through a blanketed doorway, concealing what lay beyond.

It was deathly silent and cold. An hour went by as I observed from behind the pylons, obscured from the eyes of those who entered and left the blanketed doorway of mystery.

It was not a place of prestige, high society, or even the hideout of a violent gang, but one of a place of squalor, of people poor in wealth, health and spirit. Their faces reflected the pain and torture etched on their hearts and minds.

I swallowed hard. This was almost too much to bear. I wanted to go in there and announce that there was room for them at the inn, luxury, food for the body, mind and heart. And that there was a healing peace and a happy future for them all, no matter what has happened to them or what they have done. We are all people. We have all made mistakes, or have been dealt a major blow, sometimes through no fault of our own.

I wiped a tear away and inhaled deeply as I tried to control my emotions from boiling over with heartbreak.

But then, an alarming scream from a girl startled me. She screamed over and over again, chilling me to the bone. I couldn't stand here and listen to it any longer. I had to enter the blanketed doorway and help the girl from the pain she was so obviously suffering.

In slow premeditated steps I approached the doorway, then peeled it back, revealing a dark cavernous community dwelling. The lighted candle led me directly to the girl. She was covered in perspiration and her eyes screwed shut, in pain.

Hovering over her were three men.

Rage fuelled my body now as I moved at speed towards her to rip the men away from her.

She screamed out again.

'Push,' a gravelly voice said. What? They are encouraging each other.

'No, she is bleeding,' another said.

What have they done to her? Please, please, stop!

'Doc, what shall we do?' the first one asked with concern in his voice.

I moved into a better position to see the faces of the men to be able to testify against them for the hideous crime that they perpetrated, but I froze. Ethan was there with the two others.

No, no, noooo! Please stop! I heaved with revulsion and nausea.

I looked down at the girl. She was heavily pregnant, and in the throes of childbirth.

'Doc, tell us what to do?' a man asked again.

He was a doctor? Ethan was a doctor?

I knelt next to the teenager and ran my hand over her forehead.

'Breathe... it's okay...' I said to her in hushed tones.

I looked up and my eyes met Ethan's. He looked at me with disdain. His eyes were cold and callous, making me shudder and my skin prickle. Immediately I removed my eyes from his and concentrated on the girl labouring in front of me.

'I'm going to look at how your baby is going, is that okay?' I said in a calm voice.

She nodded at me, her eyes pleading for help, desperate for relief from the pain of childbirth.

Moving next to Ethan, I could see the cause of concern. There was blood, maybe too much. I placed my hand on her belly, gently rubbing my hand over the baby and speaking quiet words of assurance. I could see a tuft of the baby's black hair at the birth canal. The baby would be here soon, very soon.

Immediately my nursing instincts kicked in. 'When you feel the next contraction, push as hard as you can. Your beautiful baby is minutes from birth. You are doing exceptionally well. Breathe... breathe... breathe...' I encouraged, while looking into the eyes of Ethan.

The girl screamed out.

'Now push, as hard as you can—1,2,3,4,5,6,7,8,9,10— nearly there. The baby's head is out,' I said as I encouraged her and wiped her forehead.

And with the next contraction, the baby was born. A beautiful princess.

The baby's cry echoed through the cavern and the homeless peoples erupted in a happy cheer. I wrapped the baby up in some old material, while Ethan attended to the girl.

I could see him rapidly working to stem the bleeding. But he had no medical equipment to stop the flow of blood.

At once, he stood and picked up the girl in his arms, then hastily left the dark cavern these people called home.

Under the cloak of darkness, I trailed Ethan. I carried the sweet baby in my arms while he carried the girl. He hailed a taxi and Ethan directed it to the secret entrance of a hospital, the hub of the Doctors of Compassion.

There was a hive of activity that seemed to stop, and then flowed in slow motion as soon as the Compassionate Sisters saw a bleeding young girl and a newborn baby enter, followed by a hyper speed of doctors ferrying her off for examination.

I followed her in. I held her hand as she was examined, whispering words of assurance and brushing her long hair for comfort.

She gripped my hand in fear. Ethan placed his hand upon her head and closed his eyes as if in prayer — but I knew it was not. He was breathing deeply and evenly.

The doctors stopped her bleeding, and her life was no longer threatened.

She fell into a peaceful sleep. I kissed her forehead, blessing her and her newborn baby, a gift to her.

'Leave the room, Georgia,' Ethan ordered,

concealed in his aggressive voice. He followed me out with his hand on the small of my back, pushing me urgently until we were outside the door. 'What are you doing?' he yelled at me, mad as hell.

I was angry with him. How dare he treat me this way? 'No! What are YOU doing?' I counter questioned him with my hands on my hips, fuming anger from my eyes.

He turned around and ran his hand through his hair.

'YOU had NO right to follow me!' he yelled.

'THAT girl would have DIED if I didn't happen to be there, Ethan!' I yelled back.

He looked at me full of fury, and was about to say something, but stopped himself.

'I want some answers, Ethan. You have deceived me,' I spat at him.

He pulled a cell phone out of his pocket, shocking me. He was leading a double life. Maybe he did have a split personality. He ordered a taxi.

'When the cab arrives, get in it and disappear. You saw nothing tonight—no bridge, no people, no girl, no baby, no secret hospital—understood?' he said in a low threatening voice, then ran off into the dark shadows.

I stood alone in a poorly lit, deserted street with noises that were unfamiliar to me, unnerving me. A cool breeze brushed against my skin telling me that I was unwelcome. I wrapped my arms around myself for comfort, wanting to cry out at the hurt of deceit from a man I had opened my heart up to. But he had reared his ugly head and devoured me—I was now a woman scorned. I never wanted to see him again.' "

Georgia's voice wavered. I looked over at her as she lifted her head and removed her glasses. A tear ran down her face.

I closed my eyes. 'I'm sorry the book is painful for you to read. I wish that I could see the words so I could read it myself, and save you from the sadness you feel.'

I sat up and put my arm around her, and pulled her to my chest as she sobbed some more. I felt protective of her, like she was mine forever. But I knew she was not. I could never fall in love and live happily ever after with a wife to adore and cherish till death do us part.

CAI would see to that. They would see to it that I lived a long and lonely existence, wishing for my life to end to extinguish the pain.

'I'm sorry, Georgia, but I need to go,' I said quietly against her head.

'Are you meeting the redhead again?' she asked.

I inhaled sharply. How could she know that I saw Mia last night? 'And you know about the redhead because...' I asked.

'I followed you last night,' she added matter of factly.

'Oh, you're in the habit of following men then, are you?' I stated. 'She's a work colleague, and I probably shouldn't have given you that information. Now you know too much.' I kicked myself for what I had revealed to her. *Stupid! Stupid!*

'I'll email you, Tim,' she commented.

'I'll look forward to it,' I said, and smiled coyly at her. I stood, and walked away.

Chapter 15

The shower is the perfect place to conceal tears. And mine cascaded down to my feet, washing away my deep sorrow. I had fallen in love with her. There was absolutely no doubt whatsoever. I had been trying to deny my feelings. But— she was the light in my life. She made me feel alive as I have never felt before.

But we could never be together.

So, being with her was like a form of self-torture, punishing myself.

I placed my hands over my face and screamed in frustration, in anger, and then breathed out deeply and released my self-pity.

I went to bed in the darkness, metaphorically speaking. The darkness of my heart, my mind and my future. I had to fight it. I couldn't let it suffocate me, because then, Mr. Rubin wins, and I was damned if I was going to let him win!

I felt a surge of optimism. A cause worthy to fight for, and the darkness left me.

All things are possible.

At 11.15pm, the anticipated vibration of the Tim Jennings

Blackberry buzzed my leg. I pulled the bed covers over my head and opened my email.

FROM: GEORGIA HARRISON
SUBJECT: hearts, flowers, tears
DATE: May 18 23:15
TO: Tim Jennings

Dear Tim,

I don't have a boyfriend.
Beautiful men are far and few between.
Maybe I'm too picky. However, I do have some amazing girlfriends that I could match you up with if you were looking for a date, or even a partner for life.
Thank you for letting me stain your shirt with my tears.
You have the patience of a saint.
Are you able to meet me again tomorrow?

X Georgia
#weirdmenmagnet

FROM: Saint Tim
SUBJECT: Weird men magnet
DATE: May 18 23:19
TO: Georgia Harrison

Dear Georgia,

Because it is Sunday tomorrow, I can meet you and your tracker at any time. If you name the place, I will avail myself as I am a Saint.
Am I also a weird man?
X Tim
#thetearcatcher

Send...

FROM: Georgia Harrison
SUBJECT: Trust
DATE: May 18 23:25
TO: Saint Tim

Dear Tim,

I'll meet you under the wisteria vine again—early, at
the breaking of dawn.
What is the description of a weird man?
You are more of a mysterious man to me.
I know nothing about you, yet, I trust you implicitly.
We have nearly finished the book.
See you tomorrow.

X Georgia
#mysteriousmenareattractive

FROM: Tim Jennings
SUBJECT: Purple
DATE: May 18 23:30
TO: Miss Harrison

Dear Georgia,

When you have solved the mystery of a man,
is he still attractive?
Purple is the colour of good judgement. It is the colour
of people seeking spiritual fulfillment. If you surround
yourself with purple you will have peace of mind.
Purple also symbolizes magic and mystery.
I will see you as the first rays of the sun peep over the
horizon in the east, under the cascading spiritual flowers
of the wisteria vine.
I do not want to finish the book. I want it to go on forever.

X Tim
#ihatesayingafinalgoodbyetopeople

Send...

My energy drained when I realized that perhaps tomorrow may be the last day I would see Georgia. She would finish the stupid book and then our verbal contract, our connection would be done.

I sighed with a heavy heart. It was probably better this way. My life was about to get messier with the mind-reading implant.

It would be better if we were done...

I shut off the Tim Jennings Blackberry and fell into a disturbed sleep, waking well before the sun shined its first rays, giving me time to gather my thoughts before I headed back to the park to meet my Georgia. For the final time.

She wore a deep purple, long-sleeved shirt with black pants. She sat with her eyes closed under the radiant purple wisteria flowers, the green leaves vibrant in this twilight hour before the dawning of a new day. Her face was peaceful, and so beautiful.

How I wanted to kiss her…

Without a sound, I moved in closer to her and placed the bouquet of pink roses under her nose.

Her face lit up as she smiled.

'Cohen, you're here,' she said quietly with her eyes still closed, her smile growing wider.

'Yes,' I whispered, 'I'm your weird, mysterious man you attracted.'

She giggled. It was the sweetest sound. Then she opened her eyes and looked into mine. I drank her in. If this was our last rendezvous, I wanted to memorise everything about her.

She took the bouquet of roses from my hand and her fingers brushed against my skin, setting a tingling trail where she had touched me.

'I was hoping we could have breakfast together, later,' I said nervously, berating myself for my unease around her today.

'That would be nice,' she answered, and placed her hand on the side of my face and kissed my cheek.

Her lips were soft and warm, and made me feel weak.

'Thank-you for the beautiful roses. I love them.'

I lowered my head and smiled. She would be somebody's girlfriend one day. But not mine.

The fascinating purple and pink colours of the twilight morning sky changed and disappeared, leaving a crisp blue skyline as Georgia opened the book and put on her glasses. Perhaps for the last time.

I watched her face as she read. I wanted her beauty burnt into my memory to keep with me forever.

> " 'Georgia...' It was his voice. I kept my eyes on the paperwork in front of me. If I made eye contact with him, I was likely to use unkind words that I would regret later. Instead, I took a calming, deep breath.
>
> 'Dr. Ethan—' I replied coolly, refusing to look up at him.
>
> '—I have come back for my chicken soup for the spirit, as you advised,' he said in a smooth voice.
>
> 'There are very good counsellors around, psychiatrists, psychologists, dogs—' I offered. My voice was monotone. I was still bruised from his animosity at me a while ago.
>
> 'It is you who I seek to talk to. It is you who can fill my need as no one else can. I have tried to stay away from you since the last time our paths crossed. But I am finding it impossible. I will not leave until I talk to you,' he said with an assertive voice.

I looked up at him and narrowed my eyes. How could I not help him? It is what I did. It is who I was—a guide for those who seek.

'Where would you like to talk to me?' I asked in a softer voice.

'At the park, near the bridge, there is a seat under a dead tree. 4pm. Don't disappoint me, Georgia,' he directed, and bowed his head slightly before he turned and left.

Huh! Arrogance as well—not a pleasant trait to possess.

He was waiting for me under the dead tree as we had agreed. He was leaning forward with his elbows on his knees, and his hands were threaded through his messy brown hair. His face and hence his mood were unreadable.

'Ethan,' I said and sat beside him.

He removed his hands from his hair and turned his bearded face towards me and nodded in acknowledgement.

'Thank you for coming. I am gratified by your presence,' he responded as the afternoon sun rays accentuated his blue eyes. 'I wished for my occupation to remain anonymous to you, but as it turns out, my wish has not been granted,' he started.

'You did speak of your high intelligence at our previous meetings. But I would not have guessed your occupation according to your attire or your state of mind. You looked more like a drug dependent,' I added.

'I choose to dress like this to fit in with the people I help. I need to be seen as one of their own.

And it works well. I'm not sorry if it offends you. I'm working with people who desperately need help, and have no money, no energy, and see no way out of their living hell. This physical life on earth—repulses me!' he explained. He looked out over the water that flowed beneath the bridge.

'You help them? You help them to forgive others and themselves? Yet you do not use the same playing field for yourself—how is that?'

'I have no spirit, Georgia. I have no control over my eternal destiny. But they do, and I want them to know it.'

'Only because you choose to see it that way. I look around and see the beauty, the goodness, the love that conquers all the things that repulse you. It's your frame of mind—the way that you choose to think. But you should know that, you're a doctor!'

He remained silent—like wisdom without words. 'I've called you here because I need to tell you about my childhood, as you suggested, to free me of the chains that link me to my past. I want to see the beauty, the goodness and the love you see. I want to feel it in here.' He put his hand over his heart and pain shot across his face.

My lost Ethan.

I so wanted to pull him out of the maze of darkness and into the light that will fill his life and make him feel peace. 'I'm here, and I'm listening— no judgement. Nothing can shock me, or scare me,' I encouraged.

He looked out over the water for some time before he started.

And I waited. Good things come to those who wait.

'I was manufactured, as I have told you. My

earliest memory is of many men surrounding me, talking, questioning, talking, attaching electrodes to my head to measure brain activity, taking blood test after blood test, and listening to educational audios as I went to sleep each night — subliminal learning. I had no motherly influence. No mothering, no touching. I was tended to by male scientists, focused on my intellectual ability and my physical health. My emotional health was deprived. I didn't know it at the time. How could I? It was the only world that I knew.

'By day, my learning was accelerated with one-on-one teachers, scientists, instructors and computers. By night, my mind was filled with knowledge through audio books and the audio of sleep-learning.

Then one day... a female teacher came to my learning room. I was fascinated by her. She had long hair — it was far different to the short hair and balding heads of the scientists. Her face was attractive and full of... compassion. Her voice was tender. And she touched me, on my shoulders and hands to help with learning. It was the first time that I remembered being touched without a probe or some other scientific or medical tool.

'My world had been so sterile, so cold, emotionally. I felt confused by the new emotions I was feeling. I wanted her to touch me again and again. I craved her hands on me, like some depraved animal. She made me smile, and I liked it.

'Smiling was unfamiliar to me, as was the emotion of happiness. I wanted to be like her — kind, and helpful. I am what I am today because of her. Those qualities of compassion soaked into me like I was a thirsty sponge.

'Then — they took her away. They took the light of my life away. And my world collapsed in on me. The darkness invaded and covered me like a suffocating blanket. I now knew there was more to life than what the scientists had me believe. They had sheltered me from the reality of life, from the real world. I was empty. And the void was taking over.

'I completed my medical degree by the age of eighteen — they had chosen my life for me. And then, when I got the chance, I escaped from them.

'I hated them, Georgia, and what they had done to me. I was purely a cloning experiment that, in their eyes, was a success. I was super-intelligent and showed no signs of the compromised immune function and higher rates of infection, tumour growth, and other disorders that had been previously seen in cloning of animals, or the early attempts at human cloning.

'Physically, intellectually I was a success. But emotionally I'm a complete and utter mess. I don't belong here. I don't belong anywhere. I am lost in the darkness. Lost without hope of anything. I need you to help me... please...' his voice cracked in emotion and tears welled in his eyes.

I placed my hand onto his shoulder. My heart was breaking for him. He placed his hand over mine, and lowered his head, silent.

To be honest, I didn't know what I could do for him. He had led a deprived and sad life, guided by men of science who should have known better. They were accountable. If they had neglected his emotional well-being, he was not a success in my eyes. Emotional health is the most important of the human attributes, above physical health, above intelligence. One is nothing without emotional health, a sense of knowing who you are and your worth to society—giving care to others and receiving it—compassion.

'Ethan, you have spent your entire life with scientific, medical methods. You know no other way. And now you choose to spend your time with others in a poor state of mind, health and wealth. I cannot see how you can see the world in a different light when you are so immersed in depressing situations of others around you,' I said, trying to put what I saw in perspective.

'But, Georgia, I help people. That is what I do, like you,' he responded. 'I don't want to walk around in a world where there is happiness. It reminds me of what I do not have, and what I never will have. I feel nothing in here.' Once again, he put his hand over his heart and twisted his face in pain.

'Balance, Ethan. You need to balance your working world with a world of opposites to this world where you are helping people, continuously. You are helping people yet denying yourself. You are allowed to be happy. When did you last go to the beach?' I asked him.

There was silence as he looked out over the flowing water.

'Never,' he replied, swallowing.

'Never, ever?' I said, going for clarification of never.

He shook his head. 'I've seen the beach in books, on television, in the virtual world I was raised on. I don't need to go to the beach,' he explained as an excuse for his lack of experiences.

'Oh, my goodness, Ethan! Do you truly believe that a virtual beach is like experiencing a real beach? Your unintelligent intelligence beguiles me,' I said in shock.

'It's what I have felt—all my life,' he answered, ashamed of his admission, hanging his head.

'You feel an emptiness. It does not have to stay that way. You keep shutting people out. Let them into your life. Let them give to you, instead of always giving to them. You must learn to like yourself, to love yourself. You need to let yourself do that. You are worthy. Just by being alive you are worthy. Life is a gift. Open it up and feel the freedom, your wholeness. Give yourself permission to do that. You are the one who is in your way. You feel alone, don't you?'

He nodded, concentrating on his knotted hands.

'You know, many people, conceived naturally feel that way. That feeling is not isolated to your "manufactured beginnings".'

He turned his head and looked at me, his expression unreadable. 'I know the statistics, Georgia. You are not telling me anything new here. I want a spirit. I want to feel peace. I want to feel complete, satisfied. I want… eternal life,' he spoke in hushed tones.

'You are talking about your spirituality. Seek and you will find,' I answered him in a whisper, looking deeply into his eyes.

He stared at me, searching. Searching my eyes, searching my face. If he could reach in and search my heart and mind, I'm sure he would have done that, too.

I leaned forward and kissed his forehead. 'Knock, and the door will be opened to you,' I added softly before I stood and placed my hand lightly on his shoulder.

And then I left him as the darkness of the

evening crept in. I turned back to see his silhouette on the park bench under the dead tree, but he had vanished. The breeze blew my hair as a warmth hugged my body. I had finished what I had to do with him. I closed my eyes then and turned to walk home.

Would I see Ethan again? I felt the answer was no. My heart was telling me so. He had taken from me what he was looking for, and I prayed that the piece of information I gave him completed his jigsaw puzzle perfectly, with perfect love." '

Georgia closed the book, took off her glasses and turned her head away from me. The time had come for us to part. The story had ended.

'Did you ever see him again?' My voice was low.

She turned her head to me, slowly, and shook her head with minimal movement. 'No,' she answered, and brushed a tear away.

'What now?' I asked, the empty feeling in the pit of my stomach becoming larger. My time with Georgia was finite.

She looked down at the closed book and ran her fingers over the stamped leather word.

'I really don't know. But I do know that I have to give this book to you now? There's something in it that is connected to you.' Georgia looked up at me with serious eyes. She leaned forward and put her head on my shoulder.

I didn't know what to say to her. I only knew that my heart was tight. I didn't want to say goodbye. 'Breakfast time,' I said, trying to sound positive. I stood and proffered my hand to help her off the seat.

She placed her hand in mine and stood close to me. 'The book belongs to you now. You are the Keeper of the Book.' Her voice was a whisper and her eyes penetrated mine as she moved her face closer, slowly, looking at my lips.

Our lips touched. Lightly. And a warmth entered my body, and an addictive high of emotion. Our kiss was slow and gentle. My chest fluttered as her soft lips caressed mine.

I pulled away and placed my hand at the side of her face then moved my lips to hers, kissing her again, deeply, letting my heart connect to hers.

She ended the kiss and looked into my eyes. 'Say it!' she said. 'Say it, Cohen.' The intensity of her eyes were burning into mine.

I didn't know what she wanted me to say. I didn't know whether she wanted a declaration of love. I only knew I couldn't tell her of my love because of my fear of rejection. And, most of all, I couldn't tell her because of the mind-reading implant.

So, I said the only thing that I could. 'I am the Keeper of the Book.' I said it.

Did it mean the end of Georgia and I? Us?

Was it the kiss to seal the deal?

What had I done?

I stepped back from her and ran my hand through my hair, confused. I was neither here nor there. Stuck in a place I did not know. Was I in some sort of a relationship, or not? She was calling all the shots, and I wished desperately that I could read her mind!

'Tea for two, Georgia,' I suggested to her after a moment, and we walked in silence.

I looked up. The once perfectly clear sky had clouded over and threatened to rain on our journey to our very first meeting place. And perhaps, our last meeting place.

My heart started to ache.

Stupid book!

Chapter 16

The clang of the doorbell heralded our arrival at Flowers for Fleur Café. Immediately I inhaled the welcoming aroma of coffee, tea, and the delicious products from the bakery.

Georgia sat at the table for two by the quaint window facing a small courtyard while I ordered tea for two, a gingerbread man, and an enormous cupcake decorated with pink flowers.

The bouquet of roses I had given her earlier lay across our table, and Georgia stroked the soft pink petals, absent-mindedly.

'Penny for your thoughts, Miss Harrison,' I said quietly to her as I sat in the opposite chair.

She smiled shyly and closed her eyes. When she opened them again her smile was gone. 'I feel so lost, Cohen ... so empty now the book has been read,' she said in a quiet voice.

'Separation anxiety?' I suggested to her.

She looked out the window with sadness in her eyes. 'Perhaps ... but is it from the book, or you?' she asked.

'It doesn't have to be both—does it?' I questioned. I had no idea of the protocol that apparently came with the stupid book.

'The rules are clear. He who hears the book then becomes the Book Keeper, who you shall see no more,' Georgia whispered as if tempting misfortune.

I put my hand over hers and looked into her beautiful blue eyes. 'Rules are meant to be broken,' I suggested, as panic started to spread through my blood.

Our tea for two arrived with the edibles. Georgia looked at the cupcake and smiled.

'More flowers for you, Miss Harrison,' I said, smiling softly at her as I poured the cups of tea.

'Thank you,' she mouthed to me with her head slightly to the side, melting my heart that was in the process of breaking.

I snapped off the gingerbread man's arm and offered it to her. 'You are the official Gingerbread Taster,' I said and looked into her eyes.

She took the gingerbread and placed it into her mouth. She chewed slowly, rolled her eyes in delight and smiled, lighting up the room.

My heart skipped a beat and silence descended upon us. I looked down at the table. This... all of this... would come to an end. I looked up at Georgia. She pulled her eyebrows together and a tear trickled down her face.

Georgia pulled her reading glasses and a pen out of her bag. 'I nearly forgot. The Book Keeper is also the reading glasses keeper, and the pen keeper.'

I frowned as I took the glasses and the pen, and put them with the book. I took a deep breath then. It was time for me to go. I hesitated. 'Dinner… and a movie… tonight... to celebrate,' I said then stood, and left her at the table, the clanging of the doorbell announcing my departure.

I shoved the book under my arm and the glasses and pen into my pocket as I trekked back to my apartment. The dark clouds hung in the sky with an ominous warning.

Upon entering my apartment, I placed the book, glasses and pen on the bookshelf in the study room. It belonged there, with its own family of books.

I took out Tim Jennings Blackberry to email Georgia.

FROM: The Keeper of the Book
SUBJECT: Evening twilight
DATE: May 19 11:11
TO: Georgia Harrison

Dear Georgia,

I will come and pick you up when it is
neither daytime nor night-time.
Dinner followed by a movie.
Flick me your address please.

Cohen
#ireallyhatesayinggoodbyetothegingerbreadmanmaker

Send...

FROM: The Ex-Book Keeper
SUBJECT: The Gingerbread Man's Address
DATE: May 19 11:13
TO: Tim Jennings

Dear Tim,

Twilight is such an amazing time of day.
A connection to peacefulness.
From Flowers for Fleur Café—follow the Gingerbread
Men with hearts.
I will await eagerly for your knock on the door in the
rhythm of the Gingerbread Man chant.

Georgia
#ithinkthatiwanttobreaktherules

I closed my eyes and sighed. I knew I wanted to break the rules. But, I also knew we could never be together. The desires of my heart would never be fulfilled—emotionally, or physically. The mind-reading implant would see to that.

Five hours stood in the way of seeing Georgia again today. The sport on television held little interest for me to pass the time away, and my mind was agitated, hungry even, needing to be filled with knowledge.

But of what?

A cool breeze flowed through from the study room. I entered the room to close the window, sure that it would start to rain soon. I pushed the window down and stilled. The book had entered my mind.

The ridiculous book!

I turned around and looked at it, shaking my head. I didn't want to engage with the book again. Ever. I had given the book to the bookshelf. The bookshelf was now the Book Keeper!

I ran my hand through my hair as frustration dripped from my face.

Bloody Book!

I walked over to it and reefed it off the shelf, grabbed the glasses and pen and then walked out of the study room with heavy feet like an immature child expressing my huge dislike.

An echo bounced off the wall as I slammed the book onto the kitchen table with a thud. Inflicting a little pain onto the book made me feel a little better. Maybe I should punch into it to feel a whole lot better?

Tempting...

But instead, I took a calming breath. The fact was, I was now the Keeper of the Book. I was the Keeper...

I ran my hand over the brown leather. The raised surface of the insignia felt warm, hot even, while the rest of the leather cover was cool.

Odd.

Underneath the three interconnecting circles were some words—Latin, I think. It said 'Mutato nomine de te fibula narrator'. I had no idea what it meant. And I didn't want to know. Ignorance is bliss for me in this instant.

I opened the book up and put on the glasses. Inside the leather cover was white, inkless paper, so perfect in its hue that it hurt my eyes if I looked at it for too long. I squinted to keep up the eye contact and turned the pages. They were all exactly the same; until I came to the page with Geogia's information on it. Where it was once inkless, just indentations, I could now see the writing. A hue of blue. I took off the glasses, and the writing wasn't there.

I lifted the glasses and inspected them closely. Forensic glasses with ultraviolet light.

I focussed on the pen—invisible ink pen.

I guffawed then looked up at the ceiling in disbelief. I really thought there was something mysterious about the book. All along it was just smoke and mirrors. But what of the story?

I lifted the book to my nose. An old musty odour spoke of its age, mixed with Georgia's sweet rose perfume. I shuffled through the pages again with the glasses on.

There were words and sentences and paragraphs on each of the pages.

I raised my eyebrows and wondered what to do with the book now... and how was the book and me connected?

Do I need to start to write in it?

Do I leave it on the shelf for a century or three?

It had been nothing but trouble from the moment it invaded my life without an invitation. I pushed my hand through my hair and left the book alone on the table. Watching sports on television seemed like an awesome idea after all. At least it was a mindless pursuit that didn't challenge my intelligence. And it wasn't something mysterious, until of course, my evening with Georgia.

As the time approached for my last evening with Georgia, I changed into black pants and a long-sleeved white cotton shirt, rolled up to just below my elbows. Georgia hadn't seen me dressed this way—a little bit fancy; a little bit up market. It was the perfect way to dress to celebrate our short time together.

The dark clouds hung heavily in the sky as I walked to the Flowers for Fleur Café to find the first gingerbread man. And there he was, attached to a street light post, gingery in colour with a red heart with a C in the middle of the heart.

I smiled. Georgia knew how to make me feel happy. I loved her. But I could never tell her. There was no future for us.

I followed the seven gingerbread men to her residence. She lived in a modern establishment with high security. The last gingerbread man had a number on his heart '789'. So, I pushed the corresponding button on the intercom.

'Cohen, you're here!' Georgia's voice flowed through the intercom like a melody. 'Come through, seventh floor, number eighty-nine. See you soon,' she said.

My heart started to dance. I put my hand over my chest and patted it. Be still my beating heart.

The elevator rose to the seventh floor smoothly. I exited and strolled down the corridor until I came to door number eighty-nine. The golden numbers were highly polished. I took a deep breath and knocked on the door with our secret code from the gingerbread man story... run, run, as fast as you can...

The blood drained from my face when my eyes met with Georgia's the moment she opened the door. She was beautiful. Her wayward brown wavy tendrils were controlled in an updo, and long pieces of hair framed her face. She wore a spaghetti strap black fitted dress that ended just above her shapely knees and the black high heeled shoes matched perfectly, showing her lovely ankles. She also draped a soft blue shawl over her shoulders and around her upper arms.

Her eyes captured me, soaking me in as I was her. 'Cohen,' she whispered to me, smiling shyly.

I returned her smile with a gentle smile of my own. Perhaps I should not have come.

I wanted to kiss her.

To hold her.

To keep her.

'You look beautiful, Miss Harrison,' I said, trying not to sound nervous. Which I was—very. How does a beautiful woman do that to you?

'Thank you,' she said and looked down. Surely, she must know how desirable she is.

'Shall we go. I have a dinner reservation I must attend with someone important in my life,' I added to break the uncomfortable silence between us.

'I hope that she, or he—is nice?' she responded, playing along with my words.

'She—is nicer than I could ever have imagined,' I said and looked deeply into her eyes. If I just had the courage to move closer and lightly place my lips onto hers...

'Let's go then, Mr. Darcy. I am dying to meet her,' she said as she pulled the door closed behind her. She put her arm through mine, walking closely to me along the corridor.

Her sweet rose perfume intoxicated me tonight. I must remind myself not to inhale it too deeply, lest it weakens my self-control with her.

The doors of the elevator glided open, and we stepped inside the elevator with others.

She stood next to me and leaned on me. She removed her arm from mine and then ran her hand up to the back of my neck where she lightly ran her fingers over my skin. Warmth spread through my body and my brain scrambled for a moment.

I closed my eyes but opened them when the elevator doors opened at ground level. I took half a step away from Georgia, looked down for her hand and took it in mine as we left the elevator and the foyer of the building.

I hailed a taxi, opened the door and slid in the back beside her, giving the destination to the driver.

Georgia sidled up next to me and rested her leg against mine, and put her hand on my thigh.

I didn't want her to do that. But I did want it. I wanted her in my life for good. Saying goodbye to her tonight was going to be emotional torture.

'You look amazing tonight,' she said to me in a low voice.

'Thank you. I thought I should dress to my new title as "The Book Keeper",' I added in jest to take me away from her dangerous effect on me. I looked into her smiling eyes. She was happy. Was it because of me, or because she had finished reading the book to me and thus parted with the book. Maybe the book had been a burden on her as well?

Her hand felt so warm and delicate in mine as we entered the restaurant. I knew I could easily hold her hand forever. I ignored the thought as the waiter led us to our reserved table. It was beautifully decorated with fresh light pink flowers and two glowing candles. It was perfect for Georgia.

I watched her beautiful face as she read the menu. No glasses. How could I be so lucky that our paths would meet?

'Let's share one dessert and eat it first before the rest of the meal,' I suggested.

She looked up at me with a look of shock on her face. But then she giggled quietly and nodded.

'How about the Warm Chocolate Puddle Cakes?' she suggested.

I was surprised that she didn't choose the Decadent Ginger Cake with Crème Anglaise. But if her heart desired the chocolate dessert, then that is what we would have.

'Excellent choice,' I agreed in a low voice before I smiled crookedly at her.

The waiter appeared to take our order. After he had noted our order, mentally, he bowed his head to me, then bowed it to Georgia as he left us.

Suddenly I felt tongue tied.

I got up from the table and walked around to her, offering my hand to her.

'Will you dance with me?' I asked. My voice was shaky as I looked into her blue eyes and waited for her to take my hand. I breathed deeply as her warm hand touched mine with the lightness of a feather. I enclosed my fingers around hers and drank in her beauty in as she stood before me. My heart raced at the thought of holding her close to me.

The butterflies jittered around haphazardly in my stomach as we approached the dance floor. I slowly turned to face her and pulled her close to me as we assumed the waltz pose. There was gentle, slow music playing in the background, but I couldn't hear it. All I could hear was my thumping heart, and feel Georgia's body moulding into mine as her sweet rose perfume intoxicated me like a magic spell.

She rested her head against the side of my neck. I delighted in her nearness and lowered my head and kissed her bare shoulder, twice.

She moved her hand up behind my neck, sending warmth through every cell in my body. I was blissfully trapped by her presence, and I didn't want to escape, ever.

And then the music stopped, and our closeness was torn

apart, ripping my heart strings the tiniest fraction.

I looked into Georgia's warm eyes and then over to our table. The Warm Chocolate Puddle Cakes had just been delivered and were awaiting us.

Georgia's fingers lightly trailed down my forearm and then into my hand. She entwined her fingers through mine.

Please don't.

Once we were seated, I picked up my wine glass, swished the red wine around to release the flavours and held it to my nose to inhale the scent, and raised it. 'To the Book Keepers,' I announced.

Georgia smiled and clinked her glass against mine, and we savoured the fruity flavour. I handed Georgia the dessert spoon so she could have first dibs on the Warm Chocolate Puddle Cake.

She removed a piece of the cake, but then offered it to me, placing the spoon into my mouth. It was a very intimate gesture, based on trust, and dare I say … love.

'Mmmmm—heavenly,' I said as Georgia smiled at me and then placed a portion of the dessert into her own mouth, closing her eyes as she devoured her spoonful.

We continued the routine in silence, looking into each other's eyes until the last crumb of the Warm Chocolate Puddle Cake was gone.

'Thank you,' I whispered.

'For what?' she asked.

'For coming out with me tonight,' I said in a low voice.

'It was the least I could do after you listened to the book through to the end,' she said.

Ouch! A kick in the guts. She was only going out with me to return a good deed for a good deed.

I nodded my head at her and tried to conceal the hurt on my face. I needed to change the subject...

'Tell me what to do with the book now that I am the Keeper,'

I requested.

Our main meals appeared on the table. But I had lost my appetite, with my hope. I shouldn't have hoped to be with her anyway—I don't do girlfriends, or books! Being here with her tonight was futile. I was punishing myself.

She took a sip of her wine. I could see she was choosing her words carefully.

What is it with the book?

She put her cutlery down on her plate and her face became serious.

'Cohen—it's the rule that you must write your full name and birth date into the front of the book. After the ending of my story. It uses the ancient concept of Naming as a prophetic word spoken over an individual's life, shaping both identity and character. Once you do this, it will all become clear—that is all that I am allowed to tell you.' She stared into my eyes, and I saw fear inching its way inside her large black pupils.

I dared not ask her another question about the book. I heeded the warning and took a deep breath. 'So, what now for you after closure on the book?'

'Relief. The book is kinda freaky to tell you the truth. You will know what I mean soon enough. But strangely, I feel sort of lost without it... like it was part of me.' She shook her head as if ridding her mind of an unwelcome thought and frowned. 'I guess I will just continue on with my life as per usual, hoping that my prince will come and I will live happily ever after,' she added in an impassive voice.

I was shocked by her words. Any man would be honoured to have her in his life.

'It will happen. I know it will. Your prince charming will come and sweep you off your feet and carry you off into the sunset. You deserve the best,' I encouraged her with all my heart.

She looked at me with sad eyes. 'Thank-you, Cohen. And

what about you—now that our story time has finished?' She picked her voice up, sounding more cheery.

'Same old stuff,' I said. 'My life was much more interesting when you walked into it.'

She smiled at me then reached over and touched my hand.

I wanted to dance with her again, but I had lost my confidence. She had come to return a good deed, not because she wanted to.

'Movie time—let's go,' I announced. I stood, grabbed her hand and led her outside into the static atmosphere. The clouds still hung low, building up and threatening to unleash their moisture, perhaps even a disgruntled rumble or two.

And it would be very soon.

Chapter 17

She entwined her fingers through mine as we sat in the safe darkness of the movie theatre. Her hair tickled my cheek as she rested her head upon my shoulder, the green-apple scent reminding me of summer.

I closed my eyes for a moment, relishing the closeness we had, but for a moment in time. It would not last. It couldn't.

I wished the movie would never end. But it did. And it was time to disconnect from each other, unwillingly on my part, but a necessity, on my part. I stood and took her hand in mine. It would be nice if she would hold my hand as we said our goodbyes to each other. The final touch.

The final goodbye...

Just our fingertips connected as we made our way through the crowd and out onto the street. Lightning flashed, followed by a loud peal of thunder as the rain smashed down.

Georgia stood closely next to me, protected from the rain by the street roofing. There was no way we could walk home in this deluge.

Her large blue eyes looked into mine. She was anxious.

'Taxi,' I said. It wasn't a question.

She took a deep breath and nodded.

I stepped into the violent downpour of rain and hailed a taxi. When it stopped, I opened the door for Georgia to scuttle in, then I followed suit, as wet as a fish.

As the taxi drove off to Georgia's apartment, I heard her giggle. 'You find me amusing in some ugly way?' I asked her.

She covered her lips with her hand, but her eyes sparkled, then she looked out the window.

I brushed my hand through my wet hair to gain some sort of control over it. As a superhero might have. 'My mission was successful,' I whispered into her ear as I leaned towards her.

'And so was mine,' she said in a quiet voice, turned her head towards me and looked into my eyes. I took a sharp breath when she looked up at me through her eyelashes, twirling a lock of hair around her finger.

No Georgia... no ... you and me can't be a "we".

'Mine was to keep you as dry as possible,' I added.

'Mine wasn't,' she whispered, smiling.

'Touché!' I said, and placed my hand on my soaking wet shirt glued to my chest.

The rain was torrential when we arrived at Georgia's apartment building. I unbuttoned my shirt and climbed out into the storm. As Georgia climbed out after me, I removed my shirt and held it over her as we ran to the building entrance. It was the gentlemanly thing to do.

We stopped under cover, breathing heavily, laughing together. That is, until she touched me.

She put her warm hand onto my bare chest.

I looked down at her hand and then into her eyes.

'Come to my apartment to dry off before you head home,' Georgia said.

I put my hand over hers, holding it to my chest, but I did not answer. I looked out at the storm. It was getting worse. 'Okay,' I replied, wondering if prolonging my time with the beautiful Georgia Harrison would be a mistake.

She released the security door and pulled me in behind her. I left a trail of water droplets throughout the foyer as we made our way to the elevator and waited in silence, and then in uncomfortable silence as we rode the elevator unaccompanied to the seventh floor.

Georgia walked briskly to her apartment. But I lagged behind, questioning my decision to accept her invitation. I should have chosen to be kind to myself and gone home. Then I would have avoided any emotional detachment pain that was certainly coming my way.

I crossed my arms over my chest as coldness started to set in. But as I entered Georgia's apartment, the warmth welcomed me. I could hear flames dancing in a fireplace.

She turned and faced me, walking backwards, her eyes making a piercing connection to mine. She held out her hand for me to take. And I took it, like a bee attracted to a flower. I could not resist her pull.

Our fingers touched. My fingers tingled where she touched, and a fire seemed to start deep inside me. I took in a sharp short breath, trying to resist my strong attraction to her.

She led me to her living room where the fireplace was glowing and inviting, calling me near. I put my wet shirt over a wooden chair. It would dry with the heat of the fireplace.

Georgia took my hand and guided me to the floor in front of the warm fire, pulling me down in front of her. She held my eyes in hers and moved her face towards me. When our lips touched, she closed her eyes, softly.

I pulled away from her. She was dangerous, and I could feel her giving herself to me.

Her hand moved around to the back of my head and into my

hair, and she kissed me again. This time firmly, building up to a hunger in her fervent kiss.

Warmth throughout my being. I pulled her closer and deepened the kiss. Her moan of pleasure ignited my desire.

Her hands caressed my shoulders, my back, my chest, my stomach, and travelled down to my belt. She started to unbuckle it and unfastened my trousers.

I so wanted this.

But I pulled away from her.

She looked at me in a state of confusion.

'Georgia… I… I can't do this with you,' I said to her. My husky voice told her differently.

She put both of her hands on my chest. They were wonderfully warm, electrifying every cell that lay beneath her touch.

'Can't… or won't?' she asked. Her eyes watered.

I closed my eyes and took a deep breath. She was so frustratingly hard to resist.

'Won't. You are not my wife,' I answered and looked into her eyes.

She removed her hands from my chest like I was made of fire. 'You're married?' she asked, her eyes wide.

'No.' I shook my head. 'I only want to be intimate with my wife. I feel very strongly about it,' I tried to explain without hurting her feelings. I twisted my commitment ring on my finger.

'Cohen—' she whispered. She placed her hands back onto my chest.

I pulled her against me and held her in my arms. 'I'm sorry. I feel like I have disappointed you,' I whispered against her head with my eyes closed. I concentrated on controlling my desires of the flesh… I could take her here. A moment of weakness—for that brief pure ecstasy. It was so tempting…

'Don't apologize, Cohen. You are so much more than I could ever have expected. I am the one who is sorry,' she said.

I kissed her head. 'Don't be hard on yourself. You probably have men eating out of your hands,' I said.

She sighed. 'No one has attracted me like you. And then it turns out I can't have you.' Her voice was laced with sadness.

'Your purity will be the greatest gift you can give your husband. Knowing you are untouched... he will love you all the more, and your past loves and intimate memories will not come back to haunt you… or your husband,' I said with a gentle voice.

A deafening clap of thunder rattled the windows of the building, and the power went out. Georgia tensed in my arms. I kissed her forehead and released a slow breath against her skin.

'Stay with me,' she whispered.

I bent my head down further until my lips found hers. I kissed her gently and pulled away, squeezing my eyes shut in sheer frustration. Georgia…

She wrapped her arms around my neck and pressed her body into mine. 'Stay…' she whispered again.

I paused before I spoke. 'I can't,' I whispered into her ear.

But then her lips were on mine again. She kissed me with passion and urgency, a hunger that could not be sated.

I moved my hands into her hair as our lips locked. I returned her kiss with depth, then pulled away for a moment in time. 'I have to go…' my voice cracked. I stood.

Georgia took a deep breath and rose. She slid the straps of her dress off her shoulders and her evening dress fell to the floor. She stood before me in her naked beauty. Her pale unblemished skin singing to me. She was a stunning.

I turned away from her. 'Georgia…' I said. My voice was pained as I spoke. I knelt on the floor with my hands over my face, hiding my agony from her.

My heart was tormented. My heart wanted the pure passion now. I wanted to be temporarily lost in a world of ecstasy.

But my mind was restraining me, putting up a fierce fight

to resist the moment of pure passion that would be so easy to participate in.

I ran my hands through my hair and scratched a nails into my scalp with purpose. Physical pain would haul me from my despair. I stood and walked to the fireplace and grabbed my shirt, then walked towards the front door.

I stopped to button up my shirt.

Her hand rested on my shoulder. I glanced a look to her. She had put her dress on. 'I'm sorry,' Georgia whispered.

I stopped midway through the last button of my shirt and stared at the closed door for a second, before I put my hand on the doorknob and turned it, opening the door to my escape and back into my comfort zone.

I'm sorry Georgia, but you are not my wife—

Dark storm clouds continued to unleash their fury in the nightshade hours as I walked home in the pouring rain. Nobody could see the tears that rolled down my face hidden by the heavy rain.

My heart hurt, my head hurt, and my body ached for her. *Live my life with no regrets…*

And I knew I would regret my moment of my weakness, my moment of indiscretion with her when I met the love of my life. The woman whom I would love for eternity, cherish and adore with my whole heart. The woman whom I would want to wrap my wings of love around and protect her with my life.

I will know her when she walks into my life. *I will know*—I had to believe that.

I started to run in the pouring rain to numb the emotional pain.

When I unlocked the door to my apartment, drops of blood on my shirt caught my eye. It was from my scalp that I had scratched on purpose. It was akin to my breaking heart.

But our parting was for the best. My life was about to change tomorrow—for the worst. It was the date for the mind-reading implant surgery.

I made my way to the shower, stripped off my clothes and stepped under the stream of hot water.

I felt nothing where my heart should have been.

No happiness.

No fear.

No hate.

No love.

Nothing.

I was like an empty vessel. It was like my body was undergoing metamorphosis in preparation for the mind-reading implant tomorrow.

I closed my eyes and slid down the tiled wall and sat on the shower floor. The warm water cascaded over me like a waterfall, washing away my human-ness from me.

My heart was now void, and my mind was now empty.

I was ready.

Chapter 18

Complete darkness surrounded me when I awoke from a nothing sleep with my nothing heart and a nothing head. I closed my eyes for a moment. There was no going back. I had committed myself to being the guinea pig. I could lose one hundred percent of sight in my right eye if the design components and organic combinations were incorrect. But if the engineering of this design was flawed, it had to be me who should pay the price of blindness, not someone else.

The weight of my backpack surprised me when I loaded it onto my shoulders and left the bedroom and headed toward the front door to go to the hospital. My personal taxi would be arriving at any moment.

I ran my hand along the wooden dining table as I walked to the front door, and my fingers accidently grazed Georgia's book.

"You must write your full name and birth date in the book—it will all become clear."

Georgia's words bounced around in my nothing head, echoing in the vacant space. I stopped momentarily and considered the deed I must do according to Georgia, the previous Book Keeper.

Was I bound to it as the new Keeper of the Book?

Rules were meant to be broken right?

Bloody book!

I held my breath and moved forward on my journey to the front door, but stopped.

A prominent bang sounded as my backpack hit the wooden floor. Infuriated, I turned and marched back to the dining table. With the pen Georgia had given me, I wrote my full name and birth date after the ending of her story, on the pure white page of the book. I put on Georgia's glasses and checked what I wrote.

Cohen Seth Darcy
1.9.91

I closed the leather cover, lay the pen and glasses across the book and returned to the front door, hoisted the heavy backpack over my shoulder and left to the waiting taxi in the street.

Next stop—the hospital.

Time seemed to be moving forward like I was being sucked into a vortex. There was no escape, and certainly no waking up from the nightmare.

The rain continued as we travelled along the busy roadway. And it beat down upon my back like a thousand whips as I walked to the entrance of the hospital.

The admission into hospital, pre-op and the journey into the operating theatre remain a blur. Perhaps I had subconsciously shut off my mind to cope with what I was about to do.

But betrayal of my employer was a necessity, a must do.

And betrayal of humanity was unforgiveable, an enormous burden that would weigh upon my shoulders and heart forever.

Would I survive the ramifications of what I was about to do—this emotional burden that could possibly lead to self-destruction?

My life was now a ticking time bomb, and the timer had been started.

Perhaps it was my destiny, and the timer had been ticking since the moment of my conception…

The the darkness of anaesthesia overcame me.

Under the eye patch, pain seared through my right eye like acid burning my skin. A headache reared its ugly head above my eye, causing nausea. I didn't open my good eye yet. I didn't want to. It would mean that I would have to face reality, and the cold hard truth that I was now humanity's number one enemy. I wanted to remain in the dream state where anything that happened was not real, and hence, I was protected in my cocooned surrounding.

As I lay in my hospital bed, the steady beat of the heart monitor began to annoy me. I wanted to rip the noisy machine off its mountings and smash it onto the floor.

Peace—I wanted peace!

But which peace?

Peace from silence of sound, or peace in my spirit?

Frustration and anger grew inside of me. I felt trapped by life circumstances, and the beeping of the heart monitor started to pick up pace. Within seconds, I heard the sound of running footsteps approaching, and voices murmured over me.

Then the sound of a female voice trying to persuade me to open my eyes.

Crap! I liked being in a state of suspended animation.

No expectations.

No accountability.

No pressure.

'Mr. Darcy… Mr. Darcy,' the angelic and calm voice called while I felt the touch of a warm hand on my shoulder.

With great effort I opened my left eye. My right eye had heavy bandaging forcing it to remain closed. 'Ah…' I groaned as the pain scorched through me.

'How is your pain, Mr. Darcy, on a scale of 1-10?' the angelic nurse inquired.

'50!' I spat at her through gritted teeth.

'Good to know, Mr. Darcy. We can help you with that,' she said in a calm and reassuring voice. She placed a cylindrical device in my hand and guided my thumb to the top of it where there was a button.

'When your pain is too much, push this button. You will feel much more comfortable,' she explained. I felt her push my thumb down on the button, and almost immediately my body relaxed as the pain was numbed with a controlled dose of morphine. The world was instantly a better place.

'Thank you,' I whispered.

She nodded and smiled at me with her clear sparkling green eyes, her patient care radiating from her.

The patient-controlled analgesia was my best friend for two days. After that, I had to take oral pain relief.

Day four saw the removal of my eye bandaging. It was neither pleasant, nor inspiring.

Dr. Thomas instructed me to keep my eye closed as the bandage was removed, and to wait for the good doctor to tell me when and how to open my eye to see the world again.

I did not expect the instant, violent spinning sensation and nausea at the release of the pressure of the bandage on my eye. Vertigo. Debilitating. Like torture.

I struggled to keep the contents of my stomach down and breathed steadily through my tight lips to subdue the urge to vomit, and after a short while the spinning ceased. Now I was acutely aware of the gritty feeling covering my eye, and then the cool sensation of the skin being cleaned around my eye.

'Turn the lights off, please,' instructed the doctor.

'Cohen—breathe out, and then slowly open your eyes. Blink slowly when you feel the urge.'

I nodded my head slightly, acknowledging his instruction.

It was success or fail time.

Eyesight or blindness?

Temporary or permanent?

I exhaled through my pursed lips until very little air remained in my lungs. And then I focused on the muscles around my eyes and opened them with absolute control.

My compromised eye lagged behind the healthy eye as I opened them. But open it was, accompanied by the air attacking it like acid, tears welling and running down my face.

I blinked slowly, in pain, then tried to categorize exactly what I could see.

It wasn't clear what I saw, if I could see at all.

Darkness surrounded me, even with my good eye. But that was the plan, to introduce light to the implanted vision slowly, and to let my eye adjust to working with the new implant over the iris.

The doctor had not spoken. His silence was both irritating and frustrating. I needed to know what he was thinking. It was a pity the mind-reading lens was not operational at this moment. It would have been the perfect test for it.

As each hour passed by, the light luminosity increased, until it was glowing at full wattage.

I sat, bewildered. My vision was perfect in my surgery eye, with not a single defect in the field of view.

The good doctor performed the VEP test determining whether the optic nerve was working properly, the ERG test for the retina response to lights of different brightness and colour, and the EOG test for eye movement as well as my visual acuity.

All good.

'Cohen, the outcome of the procedure appears to have been a success at this very early stage. But I still refrain from declaring it successful officially until after six months. During this time, your vision may fluctuate. You may have glare, or see halos during the stabilization period. I want to see you every four weeks for observation and fine tuning if needed. Do you have any questions?' Dr. Thomas asked while his eyes scanned my implanted eye the entire time, his finger and thumb on either side of his square chin.

'No… no questions. Thank-you, Dr. Thomas,' I answered, wondering how much the good doctor knew about the purpose of my implant, and would he be killed if he knew too much information?

I held out my hand to shake his. He took it and I nodded to him in thanks.

The soft pillow cocooned my head as I looked out the window at the bright blue sky.

How long would it be? How long would it be until I discovered my new mind-reading ability?

Would it be activated by an electrical impulse, a chemical drop to my eye, or will it fuse with my own blood vessels and nerves using the body's own combination of electrical and chemical processes in the nervous system?

Only time would tell.

And only I would know if it happened.

I ran my hand through my hair at the realization that I was free to leave the hospital. It felt surreal. I had walked in completely human in every way. And now I leave with a piece of technology fusing itself into the intricate electrical system of my body to work as one with my own neurons.

What would I be classified as now? A cyborg, a neuro-techno freak, a tech-med-borg?

What would it take away from me, and what would it give me?

At least I would be the only one who would know if it worked. And then at least, I could work with it, or shut it down in denial.

Play the game. Play it better.

I grabbed my backpack and hurled it over my shoulder, then promptly left the hospital room.

I stepped out into the daylight, the rays of the sun attacking me like a spotlight in a search and rescue operation. Except I wasn't missing or lost. Shielding my eyes with my sunglasses, I lowered my head and stepped up the pace to my personal waiting taxi, and promptly arrived at my apartment in no less than thirty minutes.

The aromatic smell of a roast dinner cooking in the oven greeted me, reminding me of the infuriating fact that I was under surveillance.

My heart took a nosedive at the disappointment of reality.

This was my life.

I ate dinner alone, accompanied by the book on the table. Another reminder of the reality that I had walked out on a perfectly beautiful woman.

I rested my head in my hands as I contemplated the mess my life had become. I pinched the top of my nose between my eyes with my thumb and index finger as I squeezed my eyes shut. Then groaned loudly as pain seared through my right eye.

Reality check, again.

The good doctor said I would feel like this—downtrodden and beaten. Bed and sleep was the best place for me right now. A place where I would be oblivious to everything I hated about my life right now. A place where I felt no pain, no joy, just the peacefulness of sleep and a state of being unconscious to reality and the emotions presently suffocating me.

Within two minutes of climbing into bed, sleep descended upon me like a thick fog, until I was conscious no more.

Bliss.

Chapter 19

Sleep was meant to be bliss.
A total consciousness of life, voided.
Nothing to worry about.
Nothing but restorative healing for the body.

But my dream was alternating. Between black and white images and colour. People's expressions, natural disasters, the sun peeping through the dark, ominous storm clouds, unleashing violent bolts of lightning, and the precious birth of babies surrounded by angelic wings of love. Then there was vision of me dispersed throughout the dream sequence. I was standing alone, the wind blowing my unkempt dark brown hair as I stood atop a mountain looking down at the world, confused and frustrated by the mess, and distressed by the screams for help by humanity.

But I couldn't help them. I looked down at my chest and found a gaping hole where my heart should be.

My heart was… gone.

I was alive, yet not. I closed my eyes, praying for heavenly intervention for the earth and its inhabitants. Then I fell to my knees and sobbed, covering my face with my hands. At once, a bolt of lightning descended from the cloudless sky and struck me. The impact was sudden, and there was a violent and loud noise inside my brain like a gun being discharged.

I opened my eyes in horror, only to become aware of a sharp pain in my chest that had seized me. So much for a blissful sleep, logging out of reality. It turned out to be more savage during the state of subconsciousness. I ran my hand over my face and wiped off the perspiration that layered my skin like a mask.

I sat up and immediately placed my hand over my chest, making sure it was complete. I lowered my head, closed my eyes and felt the steady beating of my heart.

I smiled to myself, amused by my sheer stupidity.

I am still me, and the mind-reading implant can't change that—I won't let it. I squeezed my eyes shut, but a sharp pained shot through my right eyeball again before it receded.

Breathing deeply, I headed for the shower to wash away the nightmare, and the fear that struck at my very soul.

The day brushed over me in a blur as I struggled to focus my vision and the headaches coming and going. It went on like this for twenty-eight days before I went to see the assigned doctor for my eye service.

The sterile consultancy room was dimmed as I entered. He appeared before me as if by magic, startling me. He held out his hand, greeting me. I took it in mine and nodded briefly to him.

'Mr. Darcy. How is our magnum opus?' he questioned, studying my eye in close detail as if it was the only important part of my being.

'As Dr. Thomas described it would be, but I believe the fluctuations between perfect vision are becoming less prominent,' I answered with honesty, eyeing the good doctor trying to read his body language, wondering whether I could trust this doctor, or not.

'Good, Mr. Darcy. Sit in this chair while I exam the progress of healing, and its cohesion to your own molecular structure,' Dr. Paddington instructed, manically focused on my right eye, as if it were a being of its own.

His obsessive focus fascinated me. His attention to detail and fussing over of notes and illustrations annotated with medical abbreviations was impressive to say the least. He did not speak as he examined me but moved with quick precise movements proceeding through test after test. His facial expression was unreadable, almost robotic like.

Then he sat back on his chair and folded his arms across his chest and stared at me.

'It is unbelievable, Mr. Darcy—it is ready. The implant has become one with you in remarkably short time. It could never have been predicted to fuse so quickly.'

Nervousness washed over me instantly while he spoke. I needed more time to assimilate the fact I had a mind-reading implant working as one with my mind.

I wasn't ready.

The good doctor stood and walked away from his chair, unlocked a drawer and removed a pair of glasses. He returned to me with excitement like a child on Christmas morning.

'These—' he started to say, and then ran his fingers over the black frame of the slim design spectacles, '—glasses, will engage your mind-reading technology. Without the glasses you are a person without ability.' He handed them to me and indicated for me to put them on. 'But you must wait for an electrical reaction in your brain signalling your oneness with the device. It will come to you as a brilliant flash of light, and the sound much like a gun blast, I believe. There is no knowing when this will occur, or even if it will occur,' he added.

'Will this reaction occur during consciousness or subconsciousness?' I asked.

'It is not known, Mr. Darcy. This whole implant technology

is a first. It is only predicted that this may happen based on knowledge in biomedical-nanotechnology, and the electrical circuitry of the human body. Have you already experienced something such as this?' he asked, looking at me sideways.

'No,' I lied. 'But I will be in contact with you once it occurs,' I added.

'Ensure that you inform me of the occurrence as soon as it happens. It is a vital piece of information in the study, Mr. Darcy,' he added in an assertive voice.

Play the game. Play it better.

'Any questions before you leave, Mr. Darcy?' he asked. His voice was cooler now. He did not wait for me to respond to his question. 'I will see you in four weeks, unless you experience the fusion, and then I will see you immediately, no matter what time or day. Is that understood… Mr. Darcy?' He looked into my eyes with a threat.

I narrowed my eyes at him, understanding him perfectly, and nodded.

I was not a person to him. I was an experiment.

The coldness of the door handle reflected the coldness of the heart of the good doctor. He was no longer good. He had changed his demeanour. Was this his true self, or had something occurred to cause this change in his personality?

Whatever had caused the change, I did not intend to find out.

Chapter 20

The stupid spectacles sat beside the stupid spectacles of the book on the table. They all had two things in common. I avoided them, and I hated them.

I don't do books. I don't do girlfriends, and now, I don't do forensic book-reading glasses, nor mind-reading glasses.

I lied my way through the next five eye doctor appointments, convincingly telling him that the fusion had not occurred.

His impatience and frustration grew with each appointment, as did his copious note taking. The appointments grew shorter with each unsatisfactory outcome, until at the last appointment he simply sat and stared at me with his arms folded over his chest, disappointment covering his face like an ugly mask.

He took a deep breath, then stood and led me to the door, his shoulders slumped, his eyes focussed on the floor.

The once good Dr. Paddington had cleared out of his mind, and a desperate doctor had entered, intent on finding a positive outcome no matter what it took.

I almost felt sorry for him. He had been a pawn in this game as much as I was. And although this was where we were innocently connected, I could not involve him in my plan of deception aimed at CAI.

In my own way, I was protecting him with my deceit.

The ridiculous revolving doors mocked me as I entered the CAI building for the first time since the transformation.

The reception area on the twenty-eighth floor where my office was located had not changed, except my office had. I could no longer enter it. It was locked.

I about turned, re-entered the elevator and travelled one level below to the sterile, white reception area.

White Girl, Mia greeted me. 'Good afternoon, Mr. Darcy. Mr. Rubin is waiting for you. Enter his room at once,' Mia squeaked in her bubbly, fake voice.

I looked at her and bowed my head in affirmation of her direction, then with quiet confidence, entered the room of the man whom I despised the most in the entire world.

His red high-backed leather chair was turned toward the window, facing away from me as was his typical, arrogant, repulsive manner.

'Mr. Darcy… long time no see,' he boomed as he turned in his chair towards me. 'Sit!' he commanded, charm oozing out of every pore—not.

Play the game. Play it better.

I sat on the said chair. He came and sat on a chair opposite me, ominously close, looking into my eyes, searching for signs of the implant for sure.

'What am I thinking… tell me,' he threatened in a low voice, barely audible to human hearing.

I blinked, slowly, and appeared to focus on reading his mind, furrowing my eyebrows and narrowing my eyes after a short while.

'Nothing, Mr. Rubin. The good doctor said that it would take time. As yet, I have not had success with the implant. I'm still having trouble with my eyesight, and may have to wear glasses for focus. And you? Have you been able to read minds with your mind-reading implant?' I questioned him, my voice calm, non-threatening.

He stared at me as though I had just stabbed him in the chest with twenty knives, twisting each one of them individually.

'Because of you, Mr. Darcy, I almost died, and am now blind in my right eye... because of you!' He was seething. His face grew red with fury, and he spat as he talked.

I swallowed, hard. 'You were thoroughly informed of the risks of the technology, Mr. Rubin, before you took it upon yourself to trial the mind-reading implant. You also signed the disclaimer on the contract. I'm sorry this has occurred to you. It's also possible that I will also lose my sight,' I said.

He breathed out deeply, his hands raised in the air. 'Get out of my office, Mr. Darcy. You disgust me. The only time I ever want to see your face again will be when your mind-reading implant is working, or when you are dead!' The venom in his voice was clear, his eyes piercing me like a dagger. His malice was making him as ugly as sin.

I stood and bowed to him slightly before I turned on my heel and left his sanitized, freezing, psychotic office. His eye burned into my back like the fire of hell.

As I briskly walked past Mia, I smirked at her.

'Good day, Mr. Darcy,' she chirped in her squeaky voice, and then cleared her throat, signalling to meet her at the club tonight 9pm. Then she sipped on a glass of water covering her coded message to me.

The icy wind chilled my bones as I exited through the revolving doors. And there was my taxi waiting for me. Obviously as hated as I was, I was still the corporation's most valuable employee.

The warm smile of Max settled upon me. I knew I could trust this man. His loyalty to me had grown during our time spent together in the taxi. I may need him one day—perhaps even in a matter of life or death.

He delivered me faithfully to my residence. The familiar view of the wooden dining table beckoned me as I entered my apartment under the eyes of the limited view surveillance cameras. There, the mind-reading glasses sat beside Georgia's glasses and pens and book.

I ran my fingers over the smooth timber towards the mind-reading glasses, tapped my index finger twice and then picked them up.

With apprehension, I placed the glasses onto my face, unsure of what to expect once they were in place. I was disappointed, and relieved, to find they changed nothing in my field of vision, or my mind. I walked around the apartment talking myself into feeling normal whilst wearing them. Like any other person who wears glasses.

On a whim, I removed the glasses, placed them in my pocket and left the apartment in haste. I headed to the café.

The bell jingled announcing my entrance, and I sat at the counter for a light drink before being shown to a table.

The café was crowded. Of that I was glad.

I pulled the glasses from my pocket and put them on.

Nothing—I heard nothing.

But what had I expected? A jumble of voices invading the peace and quiet of my mind, straining above each other to be heard?

I looked down at the counter, disappointed.

'Sir, what would you like to drink,' a young female voice

asked.

I looked up at her, directly into her eyes.

And it started.

'Mmmm… very nice, attractive… I wonder if he's taken?'

I narrowed my eyes at her. 'Juice… orange juice, please,' I answered, amused by what I had heard.

She raised her eyebrows at me. *'Odd… he is ordering juice? I was sure that he would go for a beer…'*

The communication broke off when she turned to grab the drink. I chuckled to myself.

Oh, good doctor… it works. Clearly. Remarkably. As planned.

As the time passed in the café and I played with my new toy, I discovered the mind-reading implant only worked with eye-to-eye contact. And I had to focus my concentration acutely to engage in the mind-reading at first, and then it seemed to continue like second nature.

The mind-reading ability kept me captive, surprised and even shocked by the thoughts created in the minds of people. Some thoughts were chaotic, some carefully planned, some thoughts were carried through, many were not, some even sang in their minds as they went about their conversations.

After two and a half hours I removed the glasses and squeezed my eyes shut, exhausted from my brain being overloaded with excessive noise from others.

I left Flowers for Fleur Café and wandered along the street, enjoying the cool wind against my skin, until I entered the club to meet Mia. I was unsure about wearing the glasses in her presence.

I decided against it.

Again, she sat in a darkened booth at the back of the bar. Two burly men were with her. Her red hair was hard to miss. She gave me the nod to join her, and then greeted me with a kiss on either side of the face like we were old friends.

'Cohen, you are looking well,' she said, her low voice in stark contrast to her squeaky, bubbly persona of the sterile white office.

I smiled at her. 'I am well, thank you, Mia,' I replied. Maybe I should put the glasses on, as a test of her integrity. I squeezed my eyes shut and rubbed the skin between my eyebrows, as if I was straining my eyesight. Then I reached into my pocket and put my glasses on. 'My eyes are still causing havoc with me since the operation. Oh… I can see you better now. You are no longer a blur,' I lied, smiling at her.

She smiled back, her eyes wandering over the ugly frames. How much would she know about the surgery, and was she updated with my progress from the good doctor?

'Why do you look at the glasses like that?' I asked as if in a very normal conversation.

'Are they the glasses your eye specialist gave you?' Mia inquired, narrowing her eyes at me.

I had direct eye to eye contact with her, but her mind was silent. 'Yes, he is aware of my trouble focusing and so gave me these to help,' I answered.

She raised her eyebrows at me. 'Really? And he did not tell you what these glasses had the potential to do?'

So, she did know about the glasses, about the plan. She was keeping her mind void of thoughts for my sake. She was very good at it. Had she done it before? Are there others like me?

'No,' I lied. 'The... implant—is not functional, yet. He is baffled by the outcome, but is still hopeful it will kick in, so to speak,' I added.

Mia inhaled deeply and looked into my eyes fully. *Never tell a living soul if it does work. I hope you hear me. Save yourself, because no one else can, or will.'*

She had pushed her thoughts to me with purpose. I wanted to nod to her in confirmation of receiving her thought. But she was a living soul, and hence a danger to me and herself. She was protecting me—but from what, or whom?

'Cohen, this is our final meeting. There is nothing more that I can do for you. You are released from our program of intelligence and protection. However, we will continue our surveillance of Mr. Rubin. Out of respect for you, if there is a problem heading your way I will contact you. Thank you for meeting me here, tonight,' her words were said under duress. Had she been given an order?

She proffered her hand.

I shook her hand, looking into her green eyes, searching for her thoughts. *'Their choice, not mine. I am following orders. Peace be yours.'*

I kept my face without reaction.

I looked down at the table. 'Thank you for meeting me to update me on the program. I must thank you and yours for watching over me when you did. I am indebted to the program for that,' I replied, then dropped her hand and left the club.

As my feet hit the hard pavement outside of the club, her words pierced me like a sword—*no longer in their program of intelligence or protection.* So, I still had trackers, but they were not on my side.

I now walked alone. One of a kind. Being watched. A target. The hunted.

They were waiting for their move, or my move, whichever came first. I was caught in a perpetual game of chess. Except this was real.

I returned to my apartment with a feeling of foreboding. Paranoia would have to become a weapon of choice if I were to survive. I was bound by the chains of CAI, imprisoned until they decided how to deal with me. There was only one way to win.

Play the game. Play it better.

I took my Tim Jennings Blackberry to bed with me. I wanted to email Georgia to see if she was okay after I had walked out on her. It seemed like a lifetime ago. But it was still foremost in my mind.

FROM: Tim Jennings
SUBJECT: Stormy Night
DATE: December 7 23:00
TO: Georgia Harrison

Dear Georgia,

I need to know that you are okay.
You stir my soul like no other.

Tim
#doyouknowhowharditwastowalkawayfromyou?

Send…

FROM: Georgia Harrison
SUBJECT: Soul Food
DATE: December 7 23:05
TO: Tim Jennings

Dear Tim,

It was my fault that you walked out on me.
I thought you would never speak to me again
and I had lost you forever.
I hope you are well.

Georgia
#luckywomanwhohasthekeytoyourheartxx

FROM: Tim Jennings
SUBJECT: Connections
DATE: December 7 23:15
TO: Georgia Harrison

To My Georgia,

How could I never speak to you again?
We are connected through the book, remember.
I hope you are well.

Tim
#iaminneedofyourtheraputicgingerbreadmen...please.

Send...

FROM: Georgia Harrison
SUBJECT: The Gingerbread Men
DATE: December 7 23:22
TO: Tim Jennings

Dear Tim,

The Gingerbread Men left me. They said I had
treated you cruelly. They share your apartment
with you.
Perhaps you could return them to me.
I miss them badly.

Georgia
#emptynestsyndrome

FROM: Tim Jennings
SUBJECT: The Boys
DATE: December 7 23:26
TO: Georgia Harrison

Dear Georgia,

The Gingerbread Men much prefer
looking at you than me.

Can we meet at the place where fate brought us together?

Tim
#dinglybellsteafortwoandgingerbreadmenimissyou

Send…

FROM: Georgia Harrison
SUBJECT: Flowers for Fleur
DATE: December 7 23:30
TO: Tim Jennings

Dear Tim,

Tomorrow.
I can't wait any longer to see my Gingerbread Men.
Georgia
#don'ttellthemthatiambringingthefoxwithme

FROM: Tim Jennings
SUBJECT: The Sky is Falling
DATE: December 7 23:32
TO: Georgia Harrison

Dear Georgia,

Evening. 7:03pm.

Tim
#don'tbringthefoxitwillscarethegingerbreadmenaway

Send…

FROM: Georgia Harrison
SUBJECT: Fox Taming
DATE: December 7 23:36

TO: Tim Jennings

Dear Tim,

The fox will be disappointed.
See you at 7:03pm.
My time.

Georgia
#gotmyrunningshoeswithspikesready

Bittersweet. My hunger for the sweetness of Georgia would end in bitterness. But I had no choice.

I fell asleep to the depressing reality that I would never have a partner to share my life with—the mind-reading implant had seen to that.

Chapter 21

The door bell jingled. Georgia.

I stood inside the café near the back wall and watched her as she made her way to the bar. She wore a dark three-quarter length coat. Her wavy hair flowed around her shoulders and framed her beautiful face. I watched her as she read the sticky note I had attached to the bench.

"The gingerbread men are waiting. You're early, Miss Harrison."

She pulled the note from the top of the bar and turned around, her eyes scanning the café until she found me. Then she broke into a smile that lit up her face. My heart cartwheeled and increased in speed, and I inhaled deeply to cope with the visual feast I had laid my eyes upon.

I walked towards her, watching her the entire way. If she was going to run, I would catch her and hold her against me, breathing in her beauty and sweetness that attracted me like a bird to nectar, intoxicating me.

She walked toward me and hugged me. Tightly.

Maybe it is me who will have to run away...

'Cohen,' she whispered into my ear, making my heart sing.

I stepped back a little from her and handed the freshly baked gingerbread men to her. She looked down at them and smiled before looking up at me, mouthing a thank you, her lips drawing me close.

I needed to taste her. But I dared not.

I grabbed her hand and led her to our table. The original table of our first meeting.

'Tea for two, Miss Harrison?' I asked.

'Yes, please,' she said, smiling and shaking her head from side to side.

I wondered what she was thinking. I also wondered if it was appropriate to read the mind of someone who you were connected to—there must be parameters or rules that go with the mind-reading implant.

I already knew the answer to my question. It was a resounding no—you definitely do not read the minds of loved ones, family or friends. But logically, Georgia and I could never be an "us", and I would say my last goodbye to her tonight. So hypothetically speaking, I could use the mind-reading implant with her.

I lightly brushed my fingers over her hand as I went to order our tea for two. When I returned, I sat down opposite her and put on the glasses.

'You got your eyes checked then, Mr. Jennings,' she said. Her eyes followed the black frames around my eyes. 'It makes your eyes look blue-er, especially the right eye.'

"I never noticed that before. Glasses make you look highly intelligent. Perhaps a bit like Clark Kent—Superman…" she thought.

'Yes, I finally had my eyes checked, and tadaaaa—I only need to use these sometimes,' I explained.

"Cohen—" she whispered emotionally in her mind. 'They suit you in an odd way, Mr. Darcy,' Georgia said, furrowing her

brows.

'Thank you, Georgia,' I replied, and smiled coyly at her.

"Don't look at me that way. I want to kiss you," she thought.

I looked down, breaking the mind-reading connection. Perhaps it was not a good idea to wear the glasses. 'So, what have you been doing lately? It has been a while since I last saw you.'

Her chest expanded as she breathed in and then she looked into my eyes. *"Missing you... badly,"* she thought. 'Working mainly, back to the same old ho-hum of my life before it became exciting, reading the book to you,' she said. There was a sadness in her voice.

I wanted to hold her and make everything alright. 'Well, I have brought the gingerbread men back to you. They will keep you busy, running away as they do,' I said, trying to add some cheer to the conversation.

Her lips curled up when she looked at the gift-wrapped gingerbread men, I had given her. But her face was miserable. It was almost too much for me to take in.

I was relieved I could not read her mind at that very moment; our eye connection was broken. It would probably tear my heart apart if I knew.

I sat back and ran my hands through my hair, looked up at the ceiling, and then closed my eyes and removed the glasses. I couldn't enter her private thoughts anymore. It was just... wrong. It revealed her true feelings as opposed to the mask she wore to see me.

The rules to the mind-reading implant were becoming clear. If I did not stick to the rules, it would be detrimental to me and my relationships with those who I hold dear.

As if on cue, our tea for two arrived.

At once, we both reached over to pour the pot of tea and our hands touched. I froze, looking at Georgia's hand, trying to deny the chemical and physical attraction I felt for her.

I looked up into her eyes. They were filling with tears. I wanted to jump over the table and take her in my arms and kiss her with the passion that was simmering inside me.

Instead, I breathed out and leaned over towards her and kissed her lightly on the lips, diffusing some of my intense feelings for her.

When I pulled away, I wiped a tear from her face with my thumb, and looked into her blue eyes. I sat back in my chair and watched her as she poured our tea. She unwrapped the gingerbread men and broke off an arm and fed it to me. I reached over and broke off the other arm off and fed it to her.

I was in love with this woman. She moved me in every way. She was my soul mate. I knew it. And I would do anything for her. Including pushing her away from me to protect her life.

Bittersweet.

'How is the book going, Keeper of the Book?' Georgia asked.

'The book is a book. It sits around doing what books do— nothing!' I replied.

'Did you write your name and birth date in it?'

'Yes.'

'Then it is far from doing nothing. It's been activated, Mr. Darcy,' Georgia whispered with intensity in her eyes.

'And?' I asked, raising my eyebrows, returning her intense gaze.

'And… and that's all that I can tell you, Cohen. It will become clear at its appointed time. Then all will be revealed to you,' she added in a low tone.

I inhaled sharply and looked away from her.

I didn't want the leather-bound book.

It was just another complication in my life.

The cool air kissed my cheek as I stepped out of the café.

I turned to Georgia. 'Walk with me,' I said, my voice serious.

She looked into my eyes and nodded, and walked beside me.

I looked down for her hand and took it in mine. I closed my eyes as the feeling of warmth, softness and an electrical connection flowed through my body.

I wanted to hold her hand forever.

We walked on in silence, a comfortable silence, like two people whose hearts beat as one. There was no need for words, just her closeness was all I needed.

The spectacular white fairy lights adorning the trees of the park led us to the pond. I stopped and put my arm around Georgia's shoulders, and looked over at the reflection of the full moon on the water.

'Georgia…' I whispered, 'it would be safer for you to stay away from me.' I closed my eyes and inhaled the refreshing strawberry smell of her hair.

'But you are wrong, Cohen. When I am with you, I feel safe and protected, like nothing bad can ever happen,' she replied, turning and looking into my eyes.

'Then you are deceived. You put your life at risk by being with me. Right now, there could be a bounty on my head, and a hit man with his silenced firearm pointed directly at us,' I said in a low voice close to her ear.

'Why would you have a bounty on your head, Mr. Darcy?' she asked.

'Because of my knowledge of a certain device,' I added, not wanting to give too much detail. 'But I would shield you with my body if we were under attack. I won't let you get hurt,' I said, my voice calm.

'You would take a bullet for me?' she asked, her voice incredulous.

'Yes, without a second thought,' I said. My lips were close

to hers and the electricity that flowed between us was like a lightning storm. *I could just…*

'Cohen…' She moved her lips to mine and kissed me lightly, pulled away, then kissed me with intent.

She ran her hand lightly up my chest and around to the back of my neck, entwining her fingers through my hair.

I pulled away from the kiss and ran my thumb lightly over her lips while I looked into her eyes. 'Georgia, we cannot be—' I said, shaking my head. 'I'm sorry.'

She placed her hands on either side of my face and looked into my eyes before she closed hers, releasing a tear.

'I'm sorry,' I whispered. I pulled her against me. I never wanted to let her go. 'I'll walk you home before it begins to rain.'

'Let's,' she whispered, her voice wavering.

We walked hand in hand, like a couple, in silence. And sometimes, she would rest her head on my shoulder. And sometimes, my lips would find the top of her head to kiss.

Bittersweet.

We stood at the entrance to her apartment building as the first drops of rain started to fall. It was how my soul was feeling at this very moment, crying tears of sorrow, of what ifs… if only circumstances had been different.

But, if the circumstances were different, would we have ever met?

Perhaps everything was as it should be, torturing my mind and heart, wanting to reach out to her, and melt into her with my world and hers, as one. It was a taste of what it could have been. A taste of bliss. A taste of happily ever after, except mine would never come.

I stood facing her, at first looking into her cornflower blue eyes until I could stand it no more. My heart was already aching for her.

I closed my eyes, trying to block out the pain, to disconnect my emotional connection to her.

But then I felt her soft lips upon mine, her gentle tongue outlining my bottom lip until I parted my lips letting our tongues dance seductively.

The world disappeared from around me as a tingle travelled down my spine and then settled filling my desire for her. I placed my hands on either side of her face, and slowly pulled away from her, opening my eyes to look into hers as our hearts connected eternally.

'Thank you for everything,' I said. My voice was rough.

'Everything?' she asked with a look of confusion on her face.

'You made me believe in love again, and that is everything,' I added, looking into her eyes.

'But…' she said, knowing what was coming next.

'But… another time, another place, I would be down on one knee asking you to marry me,' I said, trying to remove the emotion from my voice.

'Another time, another place, Cohen… I would say yes,' she added, making it more difficult for me. I rested my forehead against hers and closed my eyes, not wanting to do what I needed to do next. 'I've got to go,' I whispered.

'I know, Mr. Darcy,' Georgia whispered back. 'Get rid of the trackers and the information so you can lead a normal life, with me.'

'You make it sound easy, Miss Harrison,' I said with an Irish accent.

I grabbed her hand and placed it over my chest so she could feel my pounding heart.

'This is what you do to me,' I whispered.

'Back at you, Mr. Darcy,' she remarked in a low voice.

I held her hand in mine and then brought it to my lips and kissed it lightly, and looked into her eyes deeply, for the last time.

She blinked and nodded.

I kissed her forehead and then left in the pouring rain.

It was déjà vu all over again. The rain always poured down when Georgia and I parted ways, mirroring my emotions pouring out over her. Full of regrets and lost dreams.

I dragged myself up the steps to my apartment and headed directly to the shower where I could drown my sorrows until I was emotionally exhausted.

At least I would sleep soundly, if there was anything to gain from my broken heart.

Chapter 22

The loud rumble of thunder woke me from my sleep. I immediately placed my hand on my chest to make sure that there was no hole there like in my nightmare.

It was a routine now. Every morning I woke and felt my chest. My beating heart eased my mind and put me in good stead for the rest of the day. I was still human, and I still had a heart capable of compassion.

I worked hard at gym class. I felt revitalised, ridding excess energy of my emotional separation from Georgia—again. I ate breakfast at Flowers for Fleur Café before heading back to CAI.

I was unsure of where to park my butt considering I had been locked out of my office. Come to think of it, I was unsure whether I actually worked for this company anymore.

I decided to head up to see White Girl on the sanitized twenty-seventh floor, outside the repulsive office of the wicked Mr. Rubin. She knew everything that went on in the building—she had her sources. She would know the directive about my office, surely.

The elevator doors opened, and White Girl stood smiling,

her grotesquely white teeth lighting up the room, almost blinding me.

'Mr. Darcy, welcome. It is nice to see you, again. Please follow me to your seat,' she squeaked with her irritating voice.

Today, I found her presence unnerving. She was obviously aware of my movements, otherwise she would not have known I was going to enter the sanitized foyer of the twenty-seventh floor.

Was I still being tracked by her informers, or was it the CAI informers?

What game was she playing, and whose side was she on?

I nodded to Mia and sat on the oppressive white seat. I picked up a newspaper to read, then put on my glasses as if my vision was blurred, my motives hidden behind the guise of reading the newspaper.

I looked up over the top of the newspaper and directly at Mia, waiting for her direct eye contact. I only needed a brief eye-to-eye to get inside her head. I hoped she would not look away too quickly. I wanted to know what was going on here on the office floor dominated by Mr. Rubin.

Mia continued with her administration work. She glanced at me several times, but not for long enough for me to make mind contact.

But then the opportunity came. She turned her head towards me and directly looked into my eyes. Did she know about the glasses, and their purpose?

"Tell no one of your mind-reading ability—you have been warned. Nod your head if you understand," she thought.

Mia continued to hold my gaze. She was waiting for the nod. I did not give it to her. What if she could not be trusted either? I turned my eyes back to the paper I was supposedly reading.

Then I stood and walked over to her.

'Am I seeing Mr. Rubin, Mia, or is this my new and improved office?' I asked quietly. I continued to look into her eyes. Her mind was blank. She was very good at emptying her mind so it could not be read.

'Mr. Rubin will let me know when he is ready to see you, Mr. Darcy. Please be patient,' she requested in her too bubbly voice, and broke eye contact with me.

'Thank you, Mia,' I said with a politeness my mother would be proud of. I returned to my designated seat and put my eyes back to the newspaper.

Forty-five minutes later the slight creak of the door to the Ice Kingdom alerted me to some movement. Three men in black suits exited Mr. Rubin's office. I caught a glimpse of a gun holster with a gun just under the coat of the second man in my peripheral vision.

'Mr. Darcy. CAI's most wanted. Get your ass in this office!' boomed Mr. Rubin.

Nice. Good to hear he hasn't changed. He was still the epitome of rudeness.

'It's your lucky day, Mr. Darcy,' he blurted out, poking me in the chest with his pointy finger, the smell of alcohol was on his breath.

'And how is that Mr. Rubin, may I ask?' I inquired with my hands in my pocket, narrowing my eyes as I looked into his.

'I have decided to spare your life for a little longer… Mr. Darcy. I have found your little wifey, and have decided she would be very useful to us with our research,' he declared with a deceitful smile. *"A beautiful brunette—delicious—"* he thought, loud and clear.

I started to shake my head vehemently. 'Mr. Rubin, your source of information is wrong. I am neither married, nor engaged.'

'Then perhaps a girlfriend with benefits, huh?' he added, winking at me. *"Long nights in bed satiated by se—"* he thought.

'—Not even that, Mr. Rubin,' I responded before he could

finish his thought. His vulgar mind repulsed me to the point of nausea.

'What is wrong with you, boy… are you a deadbeat?'

'Mr. Rubin, where is my office located?' I asked, distracting him from his train of drunken thoughts.

His mood changed suddenly. He became irritable. He picked up his scotch glass and hurled it at the wall, splintering it into a thousand pieces. 'Get out of my office. Do not show your face here unless I request it. Understood?' he spat at me in a low acid tone.

'Clearly,' I replied, then stood within inches of his face. 'I warned you about the mind-reading implant. I told you I would trial the implant and suffer the consequences should there be any. But you did not trust me and had to have it implanted into your own eye and brain. You are the way you are by your own choosing, Mr. Rubin!'

I turned away from him and walked out of his office. I nodded at White Girl as I walked past her desk, entered the elevator and ascended one level to the twenty-eighth floor. I scanned my hand as I normally would do, and the door unlocked. I was back in my own office.

It remained the same. Nothing about it had changed.

I closed my eyes and breathed deeply. *What am I doing here?*

It visualised the office was like a prison cell, with one tiny window allowing a pinpoint of lightshine into the small square room. I was looking at the rays of light deliriously, wishing I could fit through that tiny pinpoint in the wall. I was clawing at the brick wall to escape. But all that transpired was the ripping of my nails from their nail beds. Pain was supposed to be searing through my body—and my blood, it was being smeared over the walls. But I was numb—numb to the bone—and my sanity was the only thing that escaped—from my mind.

Play the game. Play it better.

I sat at my desk, slumped, and put my head into my hands.

Funnily, none of the superheroes had the ability to read minds.

Did their creators know it would be a burden too heavy to bare?

Did their creators know they would find pure hearts and minds as rare as hen's teeth, and that those perceived as good, in reality, may not be as good as the mask they wore.

If I had to continue with intruding on the minds of others, voluntarily or otherwise, there is no doubt I would lose my sanity, my own mind, in the process. There is no good in the ability to read another's mind, only destruction of the self.

I have effectually cursed myself. Alone, I have put myself into this position. I only have myself to blame, and my stupidity in allowing the greed of others to define my future.

I will take my secret to the grave.

No soul will ever know of my mind-reading ability.

To humankind, I am a mere man. Average Joe.

Nothing special.

Nothing exciting.

A ground dweller. That was what I was. A lowly ground dweller. A safe, lowly ground dweller.

But is that what I truly wanted? To be like a wallflower?

Sadly, I did not know what I truly wanted. All I knew was that the mind-reading implant must be used for truth and justice. And once I started to lose control, or feel as if I was losing my sanity, that was the time to end it all—in some shape or form.

Not with my life, but with the mind-reading implant.

It would be easy to remove my right eye and destroy the technology that had such a harmful potential.

I did deserve a happily ever after, didn't I?

A loud sound alerted me to a presence outside my office. I opened the door to see Mia talking with police.

'This is the one who you need to arrest,' she said with aggression.

The police entered my office.

'Mr. Cohen Darcy?' the police officer asked.

'Yes,' I answered.

'We have a warrant for your arrest. Either you walk out of the building calmly with us, or we will handcuff you, sir. The choice is yours,' he instructed.

I put my hands in the air. There was no way I was going to be handcuffed.

I looked into Mia's eyes as I walked past her. She had betrayed me. *"I am doing this for your own protection, Cohen. You will be safer in jail. Mr. Rubin is losing the plot. I have done this to protect you."* Her thoughts were loud and clear.

I nodded to her in thanks.

She nodded back at me.

The journey to the police station was long. The officers did not make conversation. They walked me into headquarters and placed me into a cell.

Periodically, an employee from the police department would sit and talk with me. Sometimes they were in police uniform, other times not. Sometimes it was a psychologist, sometimes a detective.

Nobody mentioned why I was being held in a cell. And I remained there under close watch for three weeks before they started to take me out of the cell. Occasionally I sat in on questioning sessions with detectives, who were trained in asking the necessary questions to persuade an alleged criminal or victim to giving a statement of truth.

The process was long and drawn out, often physically and mentally tiring for the detectives and the alleged criminal or victim.

At one stage, a detective walked away from the interrogation table and leaned up against the wall.

'May I?' I asked, and gestured to the alleged criminal.

He nodded at me.

I slipped my glasses on and sat opposite the suspect. Immediately our eyes made contact and I could read his thoughts. I started my tactics for questioning, luring him into the truthful confession of carrying out the crime. The case was closed, and arrests were made.

This first break through led to other cases I became involved in to solve. And in no time, I was a fully pledged plain clothed police detective.

I moved out of my CAI surveillanced apartment and into shared accommodation with another policeman, named Jack.

Thanks to Mia, my life had now taken a different pathway. I could use my mind-reading implant for the purposes of truth and justice. Only Mia and I knew the truth to my apparent "gift" as the police department called it.

I also had permanent protection from the Police Force and legally carried my own firearm.

This was as good as my life was going to get. The chains the CAI had been severed.

I was free. And I was eternally thankful.

Chapter 23

A year later...

1 1:07pm. My Tim Jennings Blackberry emitted a once familiar sound that announced the arrival of an email. It had been such a long time since I exchanged emails in the cover of darkness to avoid being exposed.

I reached over to my lamp and turned it on before grabbing the Blackberry. I should have eradicated it from my life a long time ago. But I couldn't bear to part with it yet. It was my only connection to Georgia. Our exchanges of texts were still on the Blackberry. Not that I would contact her again, even though my life was "normal", and safe—I still loved her.

FROM: Georgia Harrison
SUBJECT: ?
DATE: December 30 23:03
TO: Tim Jennings

Dear Tim,

Hi.

X Georgia

I leaned my head back against the backboard of the bed, closed my eyes and smiled. I hadn't used the alias of Tim for such a long time. It brought back good memories of Georgia, as well as the sadness of our parting.

I opened my eyes and focused on the dancing lights on my ceiling. I didn't know whether I should reply to her. Would it be like opening an old wound? I did shut her out of my life for good. But it was a long time ago. She was probably married now. She should be.

FROM: Cohen Darcy
SUBJECT: Greetings
DATE: December 30 23:07
TO: Georgia Harrison

Dear Georgia,

Hi, back at you. Smiling.

X Cohen

Send…

The softness of the pillow cocooned my weary head as I closed my eyes, still with a smile on my face. I placed my hand over my heart as it accelerated at the mere sight of Georgia's name. The remaining strength of my love for her surprised me. She was my love, but I had consciously chosen to suppress my feelings for her.

The Tim Jennings Blackberry vibrated in my hand and I

opened up emails again.

FROM: Georgia Harrison
SUBJECT: You replied :)
DATE: December 30 23:12
TO: Tim Cohen Jennings Darcy

Dear ?

I am glad you are smiling. It is infectious.
I am smiling too. And crying…

Georgia
#thegingerbreadmenarejumpingupanddownwithhappiness

FROM: Cohen Darcy
SUBJECT: Apologies
DATE: December 30 23:15
TO: Georgia Harrison

Georgia, forgive me for making you cry.
Please take my cybertissue and wipe your tears away
before your sadness becomes contagious.
When you are sad, I am sad.
I am no longer Tim Jennings.
I have been freed from the chains of my previous employer.

Cohen
#thegingerbreadmenneedtogotobed.itislate.

Send…

FROM: Georgia Harrison
SUBJECT: Cybertissue
DATE: December 30 23:20
TO: Cohen Darcy

Dear Cohen,

They are not tears of sadness, but of happiness.
I would prefer for you to wipe my tears away in person.
I have missed you terribly.

Georgia
#wheneverIclosemeeyesIreliveyourlipsuponmine<3

FROM: Cohen Darcy
SUBJECT: Lips
DATE: December 30 23:23
TO: Georgia Harrison

Our lives have changed now.
I have followed your busy social life in the media.
I'm sure you have a man who has stolen your
heart and worships the ground you walk on.
I miss you terribly.

Cohen
#ourmomentsofpassionarepermanentlyburned
intomymemorynevertobeforgotten<3

Send…

FROM: Georgia Harrison
SUBJECT: Georgia HARRISON
DATE: December 30 23:27
TO: Cohen Darcy

Cohen—I am single, until I find the one.
Even if I have to wait a lifetime.
I need to have tea for two with you—please.

Georgia

#please:usedasapoliteadditiontorequests

FROM: Cohen Darcy
SUBJECT: I love tea
DATE: December 30 23:30
TO: Georgia Harrison

Must I remind you that the book has rules?

Cohen
#pleaseisassweetasthesugarthatIputinmytea

Send...

FROM: Georgia Harrison
SUBJECT: Rules Schmules
DATE: December 30 23:33
TO: Cohen Darcy

Rules are meant to be broken.

Georgia
#IamverygoodatpouringourteafortwoMrDarcy

FROM: Cohen Darcy
SUBJECT: The Meeting Place
DATE: December 30 23:36
TO: Georgia Harrison

When?
The gingerbread men know their way to Flowers for Fleur Café.
Do you?

Cohen
#Iwillpourourteafortwowhenwemeetagain
Send...

FROM: Georgia Harrison
SUBJECT: You Haven't Changed At All!
DATE: December 30 23:40
TO: Cohen Darcy

Mr. Darcy,

Because I really want to see you again, I will brush
over that insult you just catapulted at me.
Tomorrow 10:03am. Don't be late!

Georgia
#oneofthegingerbreadmenisangrywithyouandtheydobite!

FROM: Cohen Darcy
SUBJECT: Run, run, as fast as you can!
DATE: December 30 23:43
TO: Georgia Harrison

Miss Harrison,

The gingerbread men are not the only ones who bite!
See you tomorrow.
Don't be late!

Cohen
#perhapsthegingerbreadmanwilllikethegingerbreadwoman?x

Send…

I turned off the Tim Jennings Blackberry. I badly need some
shuteye.

The rain poured down when I left the apartment with a liquid breakfast in my hand.

Really? This is how the whole episode of meeting Georgia began such a long time ago.

Jack, my partner in anti-crime was waiting for me in the police car. I turned on my Tim Jennings Blackberry, which, I never did in the morning. But today was different.

FROM: Georgia Harrison
SUBJECT: Adrenaline rush
 DATE: December 31 03:03
TO: Cohen Darcy

Can't sleep Mr. Darcy…

FROM: Cohen Darcy
SUBJECT: In the dead of the night
DATE: December 31 05:30
TO: Georgia Harrison

Good morning, sleepyhead. Don't be late!

Cohen
#itallstartedinthistypeofweatheronceuponatime

Send…

The down pouring of rain equated to a quieter day at headquarters. It was a good day to catch up on the endless trail of paperwork. Before I knew it, I found myself at Flowers for Fleur Café.

The dingly-dangly bell no longer announced the arrival of peoples. I missed it, although previously I had found it downright irritating. The café was as busy as usual. It was a popular space for regular customers.

When the door closed behind me, I saw her.

She was standing by the fireplace with her back to me. She wore a burgundy long sleeved fitted dress with a skirt that finished above the knees. The curvy shape of her legs were hugged in fine black stockings. Her ankle boot shoes elongated her legs and her brown wavy hair fell loosely midway between her shoulder blades.

And I could smell her floral perfume.

I would recognise it a mile away.

My heart skipped a beat, and I took a deep breath.

This was my Georgia.

As if on cue she turned and faced me. Her beautiful smile took my breath away. I returned her smile with my own coy smile, and then looked to the wooden floorboards underfoot. I was falling apart before her. How could she disarm me so easily?

By the time I had managed to look up again, she was standing before me, and then hugging me. I wrapped my arms around her and held her. I was melting like the gingerbread man riding on the back of the fox, and I wanted to dissolve into her.

I love you... I want you to be mine...

I released her and she stepped back from me and smiled.

'Georgia,' I said in a low voice while looking into her eyes as blue as a cornflower field.

'Cohen,' she said, but her smile was gone, and her voice was serious.

I took her hand in mine, relishing in the warmth and the softness.

We sat in the wing chairs by the fireplace with a small table between us. She crossed her legs as she sat down and gathered her wavy hair over one shoulder. My heart skipped fifty beats. I couldn't keep my eyes off her.

'I'll order, Miss Harrison. Tea?' I asked in a quiet voice, raising my eyebrows at her.

'Please, Mr. Darcy,' she replied.

I bowed slightly to her and turned, then walked over to order our tea for two. When I turned to walk back to her, our eyes locked and remained there.

I sat down next to her. Her hand was draped over the armrest, her long fingers begging to be touched. I reached over and connected my fingers to hers.

'You are too far away, Miss Harrison. I like to have you closer,' I disclosed in a hushed tone.

I watched as she took a sharp breath, and her eyes connected to mine. 'Cohen,' she whispered as she shook her head slightly.

I became confused, and panicky.

She was pushing me away.

Why was I here meeting her?

'It is too difficult for me to be right next to you. I only want more if I am this close to you,' she explained, clearing up my confusion.

'But being this close, yet far away is making the situation worse. Let's sit on the two-seater sofa,' I said.

She looked down at her fingers, which by now were tangled together.

'No,' she said quietly, furrowing her brows.

'Okay, torture it is,' I added, and sat back in the wing chair with my eyes upon hers.

Perhaps I should put my glasses on? Then there would be no second guessing on what was going on with her. I felt like she had sent me some bait on a hook, and I had taken it.

She turned in the chair and faced the glowing fire, as if shutting me out of her presence.

A feeling of dread crept over me. Maybe I should just stand and leave? 'Georgia, are you okay?' I asked in low tone.

She blinked rapidly and slowly turned to face me with a pained look on her face. 'I need to ask you something… Cohen…

I - I...' she started, looking down at her fidgety hands.

I waited in anticipation of what she was about to say, concentrating on her body language. She was highly anxious.

'I… want to…'

The arrival of our tea for two broke the intensity of her words. We both looked down at the tray of cups, saucers, teapot, milk and sugar.

At once I reached for the teapot to pour our tea, and handed Georgia hers.

'Thanks,' she whispered.

'My pleasure,' I responded. I gave her a gingerbread woman, gift wrapped in cellophane with a pastel pink bow around it.

Georgia took it from my hands and looked at me before her deluge of tears started.

I pulled a handkerchief from my pocket and gave it to her. 'If I had known the gingerbread woman would make you cry, I would never have given it to you. I think you should give it back to me so I can eat it, and then you will stop crying,' I whispered to her.

Then she leaned into me, closed her eyes and kissed me, taking me by surprise. Her soft lips caressed mine, pulling me under. I disconnected from her before I forgot where we were. This was going from sublime to ridiculous. Her emotions were all over the place. I didn't know where I stood with her.

'Better now?' I asked, raising my left eyebrow.

'No. I need more. But that will do for now, Mr. Darcy,' she said.

She placed the gingerbread woman onto the table and looked at me again, her eyes intent on mine. 'Cohen… I have been invited to a prestigious celebration of advances in the field of medicine, and I need to take a partner. Will you accompany me?' she finally asked as smooth as silk.

I put down my teacup and looked at her.

Why me? There would be hundreds of men willing to take her, surely? 'And you choose me over the other thirty men you have dated since we separated because…' I said, waiting for her to finish the statement.

'Because you are the only one I feel totally comfortable with. The others gush over me and crowd me, so I have no space, and want every part of me outside and in—they don't understand me as you do, Cohen,' she explained.

I nodded. She finds me comfortable to be with—this—I take as an insult. 'So… I am the one who you feel safe with then—' I couldn't say anymore. My heart was breaking once more. My chest had tightened. I had hoped I meant more to her.

I stood up and walked over to the fireplace and focused my eyes upon the dancing flames. Right now, would be the right time to leave the café.

I inhaled deeply and about turned to say goodbye. I looked at the table that sat between us. She had placed a gingerbread man next to the gingerbread woman I had given her. I sat in the wing chair once more, but I didn't make eye contact with her.

I couldn't. She would see the pain I was feeling inside.

I picked up the gingerbread man and ran my fingers around the outline.

Georgia placed her hand on the side of my face. 'The gingerbread woman is in love with the gingerbread man,' she whispered into my ear. 'That is why she can't go to the event with any other man.'

My breath was taken away, and I hesitated for a moment before I looked up into her eyes.

She leaned in to me, and kissed me. She pulled away as I was wanting more.

'Georgia…' I whispered with my eyes still closed, my voice breaking.

'Come to the celebration with me, Cohen. I need you there,'

she whispered.

'Yes,' I whispered back, then opened my eyes, looking directly into hers.

She kissed me lightly, and I felt her smile against my lips before she pulled away.

I caught her hand in mine before she sat back in the wing chair.

'I need to go back to work. I've already overspent my time here with you,' I said to her as I kissed the back of her hand, and stood.

She stood with me and put her hand onto my shoulders. Her arms slid down to my waist, and then up towards my chest under my coat.

She suddenly gasped and stepped away from me. 'You have a gun?' she mouthed at me with an incredulous stare.

I pulled her back close to me. 'Yes—I work for the force now. I will catch you up to speed another time. I really must go,' I whispered.

'You will,' she replied, looking into my eyes with intensity.

I kissed her forehead and left the café.

The outside cool air surrounded me and brought me back to reality from the fairytale within. Work was definitely not a preferred place to be right now.

Chapter 24

The Tim Jennings Blackberry vibrated against my leg as I slid into the car.

'Cohen, good to have you back on board,' jeered my partner, smiling at me. 'What was the attraction in the café—a girl?'

I smiled to myself. 'Yes it was,' I said.

'But… you don't do relationships, right?' he continued.

'Apparently,' I added, looking out the window of the unmarked police car.

The rain was still beating against the pavement. The Tim Jennings Blackberry vibrated against my leg again. I was on duty, and I had to ignore it.

We returned to headquarters, and I immersed myself in work. The time went quickly as I continually thought about my Tim Jennings Blackberry. It was at the forefront of my mind. But I couldn't interact with it.

Finally, at 3pm I stopped for a break. I pulled my Blackberry out of the drawer and opened emails.

FROM: Georgia Harrison
SUBJECT: Tonight
DATE: December 31 11:00
TO: Cohen Darcy

Dear Cohen,

Dinner tonight, 8pm?
It is New Year's Eve and I want to spend it with you.

xGeorgia
#thegingerbreadmanandwomanhaverunofftogether

FROM: Georgia Harrison
SUBJECT: Tonight
DATE: December 31 11:10
TO: Cohen Darcy

Dear Cohen,

Please let me know about dinner tonight.
Missing you already.

xx Georgia
#youlookedreallyhotinyourblacktrousersand
longsleevedwhiteshirtcoastandaguntoday

FROM: Georgia Harrison
SUBJECT: Tonight
DATE: December 31 12:30
TO: Cohen Darcy

Dear Cohen,

I need to feel your lips on mine again.
Contact me.

xxxGeorgia
#ireallywantotbreaktherulesofthebook

FROM:Georgia Harrison
SUBJECT: Tonight
DATE: December 31 13:00
TO: Cohen Darcy

Cohen, I will track you down.
I have my ways.
Dinner tonight – 8pm?

xxxxGeorgia
#thegingerbreadboysarearmedanddangerous

FROM: Georgia Harrison
SUBJECT: Tonight
DATE: December 31 15:00
TO: Cohen Darcy

If you happen by chance to open your emails on your
faithful Tim Jennings Blackberry, would you please
respond to my request for a dinner date?
Or, is it that you are indeed old-fashioned, and object
to me asking you out?
Please let me know whatever way,
so I can plan my evening.

xxxxxGeorgia
#whateverhappenedtotalkiginrealtimeonatelephone?

My Georgia...

FROM: Cohen Darcy
SUBJECT: Real telephones
DATE: December 31 15:10

TO: Georgia Harrison

Dear Georgia,

I am old-fashioned in some ways of the world.
I can't have dinner with you at 8pm because I am
working on a case till late and probably well into the
New Year.
You have no idea how much I would love for you to
track me down.
I hope the gingerbread man and woman make
thousands of babies.
You can talk to me in real time on one of the numbers
listed on the police website, anytime.

xCohen
#Ihavebeenthinkingaboutyouallday<3

Send…

FROM: Georgia Harrison
SUBJECT: Rejected
DATE: December 31 15:13
TO: Cohen Darcy
To My Cohen,

Sigh … </3

xxxxxxGeorgia
#youareforeverinmyheartandmindx

FROM: Cohen Darcy
SUBJECT: Sigh
DATE: December 31 16:30
TO: Georgia Harrison

To My </3 Georgia,

I am sorry to disappoint you.

xxCohen
#stillreminiscingaboutseeingyoutoday

Send…

FROM: Georgia Harrison
SUBJECT: Disappointment
DATE: December 31 16:32
TO: Cohen Darcy

To My Cohen,

Which night are you free to dine with yours truly?

xxxxxxxGeorgia
#willwebeabletohavedesert?

FROM: Cohen Darcy
SUBJECT: You can't have your cake and eat it too
DATE: December 31 16:45
TO: Georgia Harrison

Dear Miss Harrison,

Work commitments come between us right now :(
We are about to make a breakthrough in solving the
case.

xxxCohen
#waitingforthecollisionofourlifedestinies…

Send…

FROM: Georgia Harrison
SUBJECT: One Day
DATE: December 31 16:52
TO: Cohen Darcy

Dear Mr. Darcy,

Biding my time until we meet again.
The Excellence Awards in Medical Innovation is this
Friday, 8pm.
You did say you would go with me.

xGeorgia
#hope:tolookforwardtowithdesire

FROM: Cohen Darcy
SUBJECT: My Word
DATE: December 31 16:57
TO: Georgia Harrison

To My Dear Georgia,

I never go back on my word.
I will be there with you.
Give me more details.
It will be the highlight of my week.

xxxxCohen
#special:distinguishedfromwhatisordinary.

Send…

FROM: Georgia Harrison
SUBJECT: My Prince
DATE: December 31 17:00
TO: Cohen Darcy

To My Dear Cohen,

8pm.
City Hall Restaurant.
Creative Black Tie.
Can't Wait.

xxGeorgia
#ihavememorizedyourfaceyoureyesyourlips

FROM: Cohen Darcy
SUBJECT: My Princess
DATE: December 31 17:03
TO: Georgia Harrison

Miss Harrison,

8pm.
City Hall Restaurant.
Creative black Tie.
Can't Wait Either.
Back to work for me :(

xxxxxCohen
#justthesmellofyourperfumeacceleratesmyheartbeat

Send…

A gentle tap on my shoulder returned me to the here and
now of the police headquarters.
Crimes to solve.
Suspects to interview.
Minds to read.
Dreams to dream… later.
The next four days dragged along painfully, like the pulling

of a tooth at the dentist in slow motion.

Friday arrived, delayed. Well, it felt that way anyway.

I hadn't heard from Georgia since Monday, and it bothered me. I missed her quirky emails. I missed our banter, innuendos and heart x-rays.

I pulled out my Tim Jennings cell phone.

FROM: Cohen Darcy
SUBJECT: 8pm
DATE: January 3 10:03
TO: Georgia Harrison

Miss Harrison,

8pm.
City Hall Restaurant.
Creative Black Tie.
Counting down the minutes.

xxxCohen
#Ihavegotmydressreadywithmatchingshoesandearrings

Send...

No reply.

Chapter 25

Coloured lights decorated the arched windows of the exterior of the City Hall Restaurant, while planter boxes of dark-green foliage plants bordered the historic frontage leading to the main entrance.

The large glass door was closed, lest the coldness from the outside world enter the cosy inside world of the restaurant. I entered, enjoying the décor and memorabilia of yesteryear, and headed towards the ballroom.

The stately maitre d' greeted me with impeccable manners, checked my ID, and welcomed me to the function.

The room was abuzz with atmosphere. Men and women were everywhere, beautiful in their creative black tie.

I smelled her floral perfume before I saw her. She stood by the grand piano and her beauty took my breath away. She wore an elegant black satin evening gown. Her wavy-brown, mid-length hair was tamed in a flattering updo. She looked pure, noble and sophisticated.

My Georgia…

I grabbed two flutes of champagne and strode towards her, taking my time, drinking in her beauty and her presence of being. As I came closer to her, she was engaged in a conversation with a dark-haired man. And he kept touching her.

I narrowed my eyes and changed my tact, and approached her from behind. I stopped directly behind her and leaned in to speak into her left ear. 'I could smell your floral perfume as soon as I entered the ballroom, Miss Harrison. You look stunning,' I whispered.

She turned her head slightly to her left as I spoke to her, then turned around and faced me. Her eyes smiled first, and then her face lit up with happiness. 'Cohen,' she squealed, and hugged me, longer than I thought that she would. She stepped away from me then, and her eyes drank me in, from head to toe. 'Mmmm… classic tails, Mr. Darcy. Suits you—very suave,' she stated, taking the champagne flute from me.

I dropped my head with a small smile. 'Thank you. Dance with me, Georgia,' I said in a low voice, holding out my hand for her to take. My senses heightened as her fingertips touched mine. I controlled my breathing to settle my hyperventilating mind.

We discarded our drinks, and I looked into her eyes as I pulled her towards me slowly, and held her close as we danced. Her breath was warm and gentle against my neck. 'Have I told you how beautiful you are?' I whispered.

I felt her smile against my skin. 'I recall the word, stunning, Mr. Darcy,' she whispered back at me, kissing my neck lightly, instantly sending fire throughout my body.

I moved my lips toward her bare shoulder and kissed her, then rested my head against hers. 'Georgia,' I whispered. *I love you…*

'You smell delicious, Cohen. Are you armed tonight?' she asked.

'No. I didn't want to scare you, Miss Harrison,' I said quietly.

'You could never scare me, Mr. Darcy,' she replied and looking into my eyes.

'Good,' I said, and kissed her lips, lingering in the intoxicating sensation of our lip lock.

The music stopped and we were seated for the ceremony.

The awards were detailed, structured and grouped. I sat amongst gifted doctors, surgeons and medical researchers, both men and women united in a goal to help, to heal, to honour, to give hope.

I was humbled by their presence. Their knowledge and discoveries of the human anatomy, and the dedication to their profession that reached out to others was second to none.

And I was mesmerised—by Georgia.

She made my soul sing, my heart melt, and my brain buzz with the liquid of the love potion. I had to tell her. I couldn't keep my feelings for her inside me anymore. It was time to bare my soul, expose my heart, and make the connection of heart and mind with her.

But after the ceremony, she was taken away from me.

A tall dark-haired doctor stole her away. He took her by the hand and pulled her into a close embrace on the dance floor. He held her like she was his, and my heart hurt.

I leaned back in my chair and ran my hand through my hair. I wanted her back with me.

But perhaps, she did not feel the strength of love for me as I felt for her.

Don't over think, Cohen.

I closed my eyes then. I couldn't watch him look at her that way anymore.

Loud screams bounced off the walls of the ballroom. I opened my eyes and looked for Georgia. She was standing alone on the dance floor like a deer caught in headlights.

Her dancing partner was gone and to her right, stood a

masked bowman.

I ran at speed to Georgia and hurled her from the dance floor and backed her up to one of the walls, covering her body with mine. Fear lived in her eyes and in her heartbeat as she stared at me in a state of shock and disbelief.

'Don't move. If I get hit, stay under my body and play dead. It's your only chance of survival,' I whispered to her in a calm voice. 'I will protect you with my own life—I lo—'

I sucked in a sharp breath.

The entry of the arrow into my body was different to what I thought it would be.

I thought that I would feel a sudden intense, sharp and unbearable pain.

But it was not like that at all.

At first, I felt a soft poke. It was nothing really.

And then the intense, internal painful burning sensation hit me, like a hot searing knife moving about inside of me. I held Georgia in my arms as we fell to the floor. I tried to cushion her impact as much as I could as blackness overcame me, and my strength left me.

Then there was nothing.

No memory.

No thoughts.

No pain.

Just—nothing.

Chapter 26

Brain fog stopped me from gaining access to control my body. There was a muddy, sludgy weight that held my eyes closed. I desperately wanted to open them, but couldn't. They wouldn't move.

But I could hear… I think. Or was I dreaming?

There was a beeping sound and the smell of disinfectant. The background noise suggested I was in hospital.

It had to be hospital.

Heaven would be entirely different to what I hear and smell now. Heaven would be pure happiness, pure peacefulness, pure love, freedom from the bondage and restrictions of the human body.

Yes.

I was in hospital.

I had survived the bowman's arrow.

But then what had I lost?

The voices came then. There was more than one.

I could hear Georgia's voice.

She was here.

And there was somebody else.

It was a man. He sounded vaguely familiar, but I couldn't put a name or face to him, yet.

'How is Cohen progressing?' Georgia asked.

'Well. We are reducing his medication to bring him out of the coma. It shouldn't be long now until we can assess neurological damage. His surgery wound has healed well. He has one last obstacle to overcome… Georgia, I missed you last night,' he said to Georgia.

What? Why are you speaking to Georgia like that?

'Mmmmm… I needed time to myself, to think, you know—' she replied to him.

There was no sound as uninvited sleep stole my consciousness again…

Warm skin touched mine. I hoped it was Georgia's hand. The fingers made circles around my knuckles, soothing me. Then the fingers traced down each of my fingers, the whole length to the tip of my fingernail. Only Georgia had ever touched me in this way, and it felt good.

'Georgia—you haven't answered my question,' the male voice said.

So, it was Georgia touching me. I smiled inside my mind. *I love you.*

'Marry me. I love you,' the voice was broken, pained and pleading.

My body shuddered and I sucked in a deep breath. Machine alarms sounded and I heard the room become busy with medical staff rushing around me.

I opened my eyes to the white ceiling. The light was bright and my eyes pained. I closed them again to lessen the sting. Then I opened them again, with less haste this time.

Faces hovered over me and stethoscopes attached themselves to my chest—hands touched my wrists.

'Mr. Darcy—squeeze my hand, wriggle your toes, blink,' commanded a gentle female voice. 'Welcome back,' she said, her voice smiling.

I looked at her and smiled. It wasn't Georgia. I did not know of this person.

The medical staff stood around, crowding me. Their serious faces full of concern were focused on me, causing me to worry.

'Georgia...' I whispered, 'Georgia...'

Then she appeared in front of the doctors. Her face shined inside of me and her eyes strengthened my life force. She placed her hand onto my shoulder. 'Cohen,' she said. A tear rolled down her cheek.

I lifted my heavy hand and brushed her tear away. Then my hand dropped back to the bed. I had used up all my energy. I started to shake my head at her. 'Don't marry him... please don't marry him,' I said, my voice weak.

She smiled, leaned forward and kissed my lips. 'So that's why you woke up!' she teased.

I tried to smile at her with what little energy I had.

'Only the medical staff on Cohen's care are to stay. Would others please leave the room so that we can complete observations on our patient, thank you,' a deep voiced commanded.

Only three white coats remained in the room with me. They asked a series of questions, requested me to move different parts of my body, and completed neurological checks.

I became exhausted and needed to sleep again. But exhaustion wasn't my friend. I wanted to be awake. I needed to talk to Georgia before it was too late. Before I lost her to another man.

But I couldn't fight the sleep. It was too powerful for me. I could do nothing but surrender to it. At least I had spoken to her.

At the very least... sleep to heal...

The voices woke me again—it was Georgia and the irritating male.

The florals of her perfume forced me to open my eyes and look straight at her. She wasn't far from me.

She tilted her head to the side as she looked at me, but she didn't speak. She looked happy, peaceful even, and it worried me.

'You look worried, Cohen. Are you okay?' she asked, touching my hand.

'Physically, yes. Mentally, yes. Emotionally—you tell me,' I answered with a little more strength.

She looked at me and then at him. I still couldn't see him as she was blocking my view.

'Cohen—I want you to meet… Ethan,' Georgia said. Her voice wavered. Was she going to marry him?

My heart started to accelerate—and then stopped when I saw him.

He was me.

I was him.

He was an exact copy of me, except for the style of his hair.

No wonder his voice sounded familiar to me. It was in fact my voice coming from his body.

'Hello, Cohen,' he said simply.

I frowned at him in shock.

Two of me?

I didn't know what to think. I couldn't speak and I couldn't move. It was hard just to breathe. 'How…' I managed to splutter whilst shaking my head.

'Remember the book, Cohen. Ethan from the book—' Georgia said, trying to jolt my memory.

'No—no,' I said, shaking my head, my voice quaking. *He's my clone?*

I squeezed my eyes shut. I wanted him gone. This was a living nightmare.

'I'm sorry, Cohen. I will leave the room… I'm sorry,' Ethan's voice was barely audible. He looked to the floor with disappointment on his face and left the room in silence.

I put my hands to my head and sobbed.

Georgia put her head onto my chest and wrapped her arms around me.

'You can't marry him… you can't marry him!' I blurted out in between heaving gulps of air and my outpouring of grief.

'I said no, Cohen. I'm not going to marry him.' Her words were quietly spoken.

'Good,' I replied, feeling my body relax and a burden lifted from my shoulders.

'You need to talk to him. Technically he's your brother,' Georgia said.

'He's my clone, Georgia. He's more than my brother. He is me,' I replied with anger.

'No. You are wrong—yes, the same physical body, the same DNA, but a different mind, a different personality, a different *spirit*. He is more like an identical twin brother,' she elaborated with presence of mind, expression of thought and the voice of her heart of compassion.

I looked at her and contemplated her words. Could she be right? As scary as it seemed that there are two of me, he is in fact a different person entirely, we share nothing but identical DNA.

'When I regain my physical strength, I—' I started, but couldn't finish the sentence. I felt blood drain from my face and I felt cold.

'You should talk to him, Cohen. He was the doctor at the ceremony who saved your life. The least you could do is thank him,' she suggested.

I placed my hands on top of my head again and looked up at the ceiling before I closed my eyes. It was a lot to take in. It was like the three rings on the leather cover of Georgia's book—three interconnecting rings. Was that representational of Ethan, Georgia and me?

I looked back at Georgia and took her hand in mine and pulled it over my heart. 'Thank you—for staying by my side through my recovery. Thank you,' I said. My heart was breaking. Our connection felt broken in some way, after everything that had happened. Love didn't do this did it? 'I need to be alone now—if you don't mind,' I said in an uneven voice.

Georgia leaned toward me and kissed my forehead. She looked into my eyes and nodded. Then she turned and left my hospital room in silence, without looking back at me.

My entire life was in a spin.

It was engaged in an out-of-control spiral dive into the darkness.

Chapter 27

Springtime is glorious, the warm sun, the flowers, the new life, and new beginnings.

Even the old oak tree I sat under smelled of freshness, holidays and childhood memories.

I was meeting Georgia today, three months after we parted in the hospital room.

Her dress blew around in the gentle breeze as she walked towards me. Her hair was the same wavy, wild-brown that I loved and remembered. Her smile still melted my heart as it always did. And her floral perfume accelerated my heartbeat.

I still loved her, of that, there was no doubt.

And it still hurt, of that there, was no doubt, also.

I stood as she got closer.

She jumped when she saw me and ran and fell into my arms, hugging me warmly.

'Cohen—' she whispered.

I found her hand. 'You look beautiful, as always,' I commented when we both sat at the base of the wise old oak tree. I hoped it would impart some wisdom to me.

'How have you been?' she asked, tracing her fingers over my hand.

I took a deep breath. 'Pretty good, actually. And you?' I asked.

She looked out over the pond thriving with new life, then back to me. 'I've… kept myself busy while waiting to hear from you,' she responded sullenly.

'Oh?' I remarked, surprised by her comment.

'I never thanked you for saving my life, Cohen… so, thank you,' she said looking into my eyes.

'I told you I would take a bullet to save your life, except it happened to be a different projectile. I would do it again if I had to,' I said.

Georgia rested her head against the trunk of the oak tree and closed her eyes. Tears rolled down her face.

'I didn't mean to make you cry. Please forgive me,' I said in a low voice, then pulled out a gingerbread woman from a brown paper bag for her, found her hand and placed it in her palm.

She opened her sad eyes and looked at the gingerbread, then shook her head and smiled.

We sat in silence.

My heart was still hurting. 'You know that meeting Ethan changes everything, don't you,' I said eventually.

'That it has, and I live with my mistake every moment of every day,' she said looking down at the grass.

'It was not a mistake, Georgia. It was meant to be,' I said.

'Perhaps, but I could have changed the outcome of our relationship if you had not met him,' she said. Her voice was laced with regret.

'Did you know I was connected to Ethan the very first time we met when I returned the book to you?'

She nodded her head slowly, looking off into the distance. 'At first… I couldn't believe my eyes. I looked for differences in your physical appearance but there was none. I wanted to know how you were different. I even pulled a hair from your head that first time I hugged you. I kept it to see if your DNA matched.'

'And is that why you continued to see me, to read to me—to see how we were similar, and different? Was it all for Ethan?' I couldn't believe what I was hearing.

'I was absolutely intrigued when we first met, Cohen. But then your differences were obvious. You were not alike at all. They more time I spent with you, the more time I wanted. I became intensely attached to you,' she said.

'So, with your knowledge of the book, did you know we would meet like this. Did you bring us together? Was it all planned? Was I used?' I asked. My voice wavered.

'I never planned it. I never used you. I would never do that to anyone. After learning that Ethan was a clone, I wrote in that book, with the invisible ink, to protect him. I had seen you walking to work one day, and thought you were Ethan, but the closer we got, I realised you weren't him. I had you followed, and that same person placed the book in your apartment. It was kind of a million to one chance that you would decode my details in the front and contact me. And you know… then there was the complication of Ethan. He wasn't meant to fall in love with me,' Georgia said. Her eyebrows were pulled together. She was filled with regret.

I had to look away from her. I was growing more confused by the minute. 'Two of me. Which one wins, and which one loses? Where does it leave me?' Raw sarcastic emotion flowed in my voice. 'I fell in love with you, Georgia. I had never felt that way about a woman before. Ever. I thought you were my soul mate, my happily ever after.' I hung my head. 'But now… I don't know anything. I don't know where I stand with you. I don't know… I don't know… anything but the pain in my chest—the hurting of my heart—the doubt about the reasons why our paths crossed... why it was allowed to happen?' I stopped talking for a bit and breathed out heavily. 'I need to leave. I need time to digest it all. I need time to think… I need time…' I added, my voice low and pained.

I looked into her tearful eyes. I touched the side of her face and traced my finger along her jaw line and over her lips.

Then I stood and walked away from her. I walked away from the love of my life. I left her sitting alone under the extraordinary old large oak tree, and I didn't look back.

I couldn't.

Chapter 28

I walked in the same direction as the breeze. I let it dictate my route. I didn't care where it took me. I just wanted it to blow my burden away.

Far away.

And as I wandered far away, the sound of thunder awakened me from a trance like walk where I had shut everything out of my life. The sky had darkened with a foreboding that made me feel uneasy. It was lurking, menacing exposed bodies out on the open. And I was one of them.

The air became eerily still as the storm front approached. I about turned to walk in the direction of my apartment, until an almighty clap of thunder in front of me sent me scurrying for shelter. Then the wind started. Followed by the horizontal rain.

I stopped under the awning of a building and folded my arms across my chest. I closed my eyes—and sobbed. I tried to tell myself I would find another woman like Georgia.

I tried to delete her from my memory.

But the harder I tried to remove her, the more my memories of her kept flooding my mind, with flashbacks of our time together, and of the emotional connections we made.

I couldn't just walk away from her. I had to give us a chance, after everything we had been through. The hurt of being parted from her was too painful and my world was in disarray without her.

My Georgia.

I took off in the direction of her apartment. I squinted to keep the driving rain from my eyes as I pushed forward through it. Thunder echoed through the tall buildings rebounding and playing in the alleyways, and I ran as though my life depended on it.

I had to speak to her. I had to sort out where we were headed.

Perhaps she was done with me and then that would be the finality of us.

But I hadn't finished with her yet. I still wanted her. I still wanted my happily ever after. With her.

I arrived at her apartment building rain-drenched from head to foot. Adrenaline surged throughout my body as my heart pounded in my chest.

A resident entered the building as I stood outside the main doors, and I managed to enter the building behind them. Past the security.

I entered the elevator in hope that someone would be going to the seventh floor. After ten minutes I was in luck. I straightened my wet clothes and ran my hand through my dishevelled hair and approached her door—number eighty-nine.

I stopped in front of her apartment and closed my eyes.

What have I got to lose?

It couldn't get any worse than the way it was right now.

I knocked on the door and then lights in the corridor dimmed before a loud peal of thunder vibrated through the building. I waited patiently for the door to open.

But perhaps she was not here? Perhaps she had gone running

into the arms of Ethan?

I knocked again, and slowly, the door opened.

Georgia stood there looking at me, shocked at first, and then with eyes full of concern. It was obvious that she had been crying.

'Forgive me. I need to be with you. My days are dark without you in them.'

She grabbed my wet shirt and pulled me towards her. Her lips were on mine then, kissing me, her hands twisted through my wet hair. She pulled away. 'Cohen,' she whispered, and wrapped her arms around me and held me tightly.

I closed my eyes as I returned her embrace and rested my head on her shoulder. Then I lifted my head and placed my hands on either side of her face and looked into her eyes. 'I love you, more than words can express.'

A tear rolled down her face as I moved my lips to hers. I hesitated before I made a light connection of our lips just touching, then kissed her firmly, feeling the deep love from my heart flowing to hers.

'Cohen,' she whispered, melting my heart.

I took a deep breath and lowered myself to the floor on one knee, in front of Georgia. I took her hand lightly in mine and kissed the back of it. I looked up into her eyes. They were filled with tears. 'Georgia Harrison… I have loved you since the first time I laid eyes on you. Marry me…' I asked. My heart thumped as time stood still while I waited for her to answer me.

She lowered herself to the floor in front of me. She was taking a long time to answer, and I started to panic. She put her hands on either side of my face, looked into my eyes and kissed me, lingering, light and sweet. Our lips parted. 'Yes—yes, Cohen—'

Warmth radiated through my being. I tipped my head back with a smile I was unable to contain, then looked into Georgia's eyes before I kissed her. She was my Georgia. I held her against me and shed tears of happiness and thankfulness.

I kissed her shoulder and stood, proffering my hands. Our eyes locked as she stood, and I pulled her against me. Our happily ever after was just beginning.

My messenger alert sounded. I reached for the transponder and read the message: "Urgent". I sighed. 'I have to go. Talk to you soon.' I kissed Georgia, lingering lightly before I ran my thumb across her bottom lip. I turned and left her apartment and hightailed it to work.

Police headquarters was unusually quiet except for the present high-profile case they were working on. Detectives were at a crucial stage of questioning the suspect, but had come to a point of stalemate. The suspect was passive aggressive, cleverly dodging answers to save his butt, or someone else's.

I entered the interrogation room unaccompanied. I introduced myself, asked a few baseline questions to break the ice, and sat back in the chair. I ran my hand through my hair, as if frustrated and out of questions to ask. I pulled out a piece of paper and put on my glasses, a ploy with the intention of making the suspect believe I needed glasses to read.

I looked directly into the eyes of the suspect, made a connection to his mind and began reading his thoughts. From this information I used direct questioning to corner him into declaring nothing but the facts, gaining intimidation power over him with my apparent knowledge.

Within one hour the case was solved, and arrests were made. I had rid the world of injustice, and made the world a safer place to be in, thanks to my mind-reading implant.

I left the office at 10:30pm and made my way home.

It was still raining as I got into bed. I closed my eyes, thankful for the end of an emotionally charged rollercoaster of a day. And thankful that my future with Georgia was going to be sealed.

The vibration of my Tim Jennings Blackberry brought me back to reality.

FROM: Georgia Harrison
SUBJECT: <3
DATE: April 11 23:07
TO: Cohen Darcy

Dear Mr. Darcy,

I can't get you out of my head.
Missing you badly.

X Georgia
 #wearebreakingtherulesofthebook...

FROM: Cohen Darcy
SUBJECT: <3
DATE: April 11 23:11
TO: Georgia Harrison

Dear Miss Harrison,

I can't sleep, dreaming about you and me.
I feel incomplete without you.

X Cohen
#iquestiontherulesofthebookdidgodcreatetherule?
ifhedidn'tthenit'snotatruerule

Send...

FROM: Georgia Harrison
SUBJECT: flowers
DATE: April 11 23:16
TO: Cohen Darcy

To My Sweet Cohen,

You are so much the romantic—have you noticed the
word 'man' in romantic.
Rowomantic just doesn't sound right.

XX Georgia
#youaremakingmydreamscometrue

FROM: Cohen Darcy
SUBJECT: hearts
DATE: April 11 23:24
TO: Georgia Harrison

To My One and Only,

I intend on showering you with hearts and flowers.
My heart beats for you.

XX Cohen
#iwanttoholdyourhanduntilweareoldandgrey

Send...

FROM: Georgia Harrison
SUBJECT: Counting Down
DATE: April 11 23:29
TO: Cohen Darcy

Dear Tim,

Can you talk to Cohen about moving in
with me before the wedding.
And let him know that our wedding date is four weeks away.
I can't wait any longer than that.

XXX Georgia
#ifyoueattoomuchgingerbreadyouwillbecomea
gingerbreadman

FROM: Cohen Darcy
SUBJECT: Patience is a virtue
DATE: April 11 23:35
TO: Georgia Harrison

To My Georgia,

Tim has the same convictions as me.
I will move in with you after our wedding,
after our honeymoon in four weeks time.

XXX Cohen
#ihavealreadydecidedwhereiamgoingtotakemy
beautifulwifeforourhoneymoon

Send…

FROM: Georgia Harrison
SUBJECT: 20 Questions coming your way
DATE: April 11 23:41
TO: Cohen Darcy

Dear Husband to Be,

Breakfast tomorrow at Flowers for Fleur Café.
Can you make it?

XXXX Georgia
#thegingerbreadmenarepackingtheirsuitcasesalready!

FROM: Cohen Darcy
SUBJECT: Overcrowding

DATE: April 11 23:47
TO: Georgia Harrison

Dear Wife to Be,

Tell the gingerbread men it is called a honeymoon,
not a gingerbreadmoon. They are not invited!
See you tomorrow morning 7:03am, Flowers for Fleur Café.

XXXX Cohen
#iamcountingdownthedaysuntilyouaremywife<3

Send…

Sleep descended upon me like a thief in the night, stealing my consciousness, my planning mind and my hopes and dreams. But it was all good. I would be well-rested and could focus on sharing the same vision as Georgia for our wedding day to come.

Chapter 29

My heart was heavy. I had unfinished business. My clone. Ethan.

He had never left my thoughts since that fateful day at the hospital, although I tried to bury him deep in my mind in a place, I thought was inaccessible. But I dragged him everywhere like a dark cloud over my head. A blemish on my heart.

I needed to deal with my inner conflict and the truth I was hiding from. Head on. So, I arranged to meet him, curious about the other me. How similar was he? The thought of a clone of myself terrified me.

And I saw him before he saw me. *Good.* I wanted to look him over.

Having a clone of oneself was absolutely intriguing. Spooky even. Excellent fodder for the nature versus nurture debate.

He stood under the white marquee at the front entrance of the five-star restaurant. He wore black trousers and a white long sleeve shirt.

He looked exactly like me; the way he held his posture and

the way he positioned his head with his chin slightly down. The only difference was the styling of his hair. His dark brown hair was cut quite short, whilst mine was short back and sides, with a longish fringe and sculptured side burns.

As soon as he saw me he gave an uneasy smile, then looked to the ground in front of him.

Was he as nervous as me about our meeting?

The moment he looked back up at me, I smiled and nodded at him. And as I came closer, I held out my hand in greeting.

The moment our skin touched a cold shiver ran down my spine. It was like shaking my own hand—it was weird and odd at the same time, to say the very least.

I kept telling myself that I am not he, and he is not me. We have separate bodies, heartbeats, minds, feelings, spirits, consciousness of thought...

'Ethan,' I said, masking the nervousness in my voice.

'Cohen,' he replied, 'I am so very thankful we could meet.'

'Curiosity got the better of me, brother,' I remarked.

He smiled genuinely, free of the tension that was on his face before, and then indicated for us to enter the restaurant.

We sat opposite each other at the table. Normally, I would observe the table ware and décor and comment on their beauty, if I was with a woman. But I didn't even notice the table setting in front of me. I was busy scanning Ethan's face, his expressions, his mannerisms.

'I must thank you for saving my life,' I said to break the uncomfortable silence between us. I clasped my hands on the table in front of me. Strangely Ethan did the same thing at the same time, but when he noticed what we had done—he moved his hands apart.

'I was glad to be able to help you. Saving lives is what I do. We very nearly lost you to eternity, but I was not going to let that happen!' he remarked.

'Aah... but then you could have had the girl while I played pushing up the daisies,' I added.

He chuckled at my comment, and I felt more at ease with him.

Why was I sitting here in this fine restaurant with my clone? There were so many reasons, but first and foremost was, I wanted to know if he was a good guy. I had always wondered about having a double somewhere else on the earth. Would one be good and the other the exact opposite? This question also related to my clone.

'How long have you known that you were not born of the womb?' I asked, getting down to the nitty-gritty.

'You mean a clone?' he asked, wanting clarification of my question.

'No. I mean, "of the womb". You could have been transferred to the womb of a surrogate mother, had the scientists chosen that path to follow,' I elaborated.

'That's true, Cohen. You have done some research... from the age of seven, my scientist fathers—plural, were very open with me about my coming into being. But I believed the artificial sterile environment I was raised in was the norm for all people. I became aware of my abnormality at the age of thirteen when I started studying medicine, and hence the creation of life.'

'How did you feel when you learned about natural conception of life?' I asked.

'I was… angry, hostile even. The grieving process, you know. But now I have accepted it. I have mourned the loss of a different "normal" type of childhood—you can't go back and change things, you know—' He stopped talking. The pained expression on his face told me that the memories of growing up were still particularly raw. I felt devastated for him, and guilty. Guilt that my childhood was so happy, loving and nurturing.

'I'm glad that we met, Ethan. I don't feel so alone in the

world now, if you can understand that,' I added.

He put his hands over his face, ran his hands through his hair, and wiped away a tear as he looked up at me.

'Me, too. Meeting you means more to me than I can express,' he said. His voice broke with emotion. He blew out air between his lips.

I reached over and clasped his hand in mine. 'Brothers for eternity,' I whispered to him, to stop myself from becoming emotional.

What a scene it would cause in this fine dining restaurant full of well-to-do people. Two grown men who look identical, crying. We were already receiving many stares our way.

'They walk among us you know,' he whispered to me.

'Others? Other clones?' I asked.

'Yes, medically, physically, they are fine. But emotionally, they are lost. They all seek a connection. A connection to people, wanting to know where they fit into the scheme of the world. They are truly lost—they want to know if they have a spirit, or if there is only one spirit for each set of unique DNA, and whether the DNA host is the body for the spirit,' Ethan said.

I sat back and ran my hands through my hair. Philosophically, theologically, this was a tough question. How could they get a clear-cut answer on that one?

'Ethan, clones do have a spirit, in my opinion anyway.' I tried to add to his discussion. 'Do you believe you have a spirit?' I asked, impatient for his answer.

'At first, I was dogged by the same question. Without a spirit, one would not know between right and wrong. Without really feeling it, I mean. It would be easy to learn right from wrong though, like in a text book. I guess I am talking about a conscience here. I have a very strong sense of right and wrong. I also have the need for a spiritual connection. Therefore, I do believe I have a spirit,' he explained.

'You are a living human being. There is no doubt that you possess your own spirit,' I said, supporting him in his reasoning.

As we consumed dinner, we continued in our conversations.

'Have you thought about having a relationship with anyone, besides Georgia?' I asked.

'My relationships with women have always been plutonic. I never tell them that I'm a clone. They would instantly put me into the monster box, I am sure. It's easier for me if no one knows my creation or upbringing. I generally tell them I'm adopted,' he said.

'You are a wise man. I'm proud to call you my brother,' I said.

Ethan put down his knife and fork, raised his glass of wine and held it up.

'Thank you, Cohen. I am the most blessed man in the world,' he added.

I nodded my head slightly at him as I sipped my red wine. 'Will you be one of my groomsmen at the wedding in two weeks' time?' I asked.

'Are you sure you want me to be there?' He raised his eyebrows at me.

'Absolutely. Our other two brothers will be standing with me. So you must be, too,' I said matter-of-factly.

Ethan put his hands over his face. He took a deep breath.

I clasped my hands in front of my face and rested them against my lips, looking at the table whilst I waited for him to compose himself. Then I reached over, and hand-hugged his arm. 'Welcome to our family. The next step is to meet our parents and brothers. But only when you feel that you can cope with it.'

He pulled his hands away from his face and wiped away a few tears.

'Yes. Thank you. My dream is becoming a reality, only through your willingness to reach out to me. It all could have ended differently had you chosen a different path to deal with the information overload that I'm your clone,' Ethan said.

'Tell me, Ethan, you being the doctor here. What is the difference between a clone and an identical sibling, beside the obvious time spent in the womb together?' I asked, eager for his answer.

'Well, according to scientists, the DNA of identical twins is not an exact match due to copy number variations that occur in the womb—some coding is copied twice or is missing, so, identical twins are not exactly identical. On the other hand, a human clone does have the exact same DNA as its host. But, we did not share the same womb, time of birth, or bonding with a mother or father. It's the nurture coming into play. For instance, if I was your identical twin, nurtured in the same fluid of the amniotic sac, born at the same time, would our intelligences be the same? My perceived, and proven high intelligence was nurtured as I was immersed in educational curriculums to advance my knowledge in all things, as was the plan of my scientific fathers. Cohen—we would make the perfect study specimens for the great science debate, which I refuse to be part of, and so should you,' he said. His eyes wandered to the table and a sadness fell over his face like a curtain. I wondered what scientific studies and experiments he had been subjected to as he aged under the care of his scientist fathers.

I nodded my head. There was a lot to think about. But, what it all came down to in the end was compassion. Love for fellow human beings, and helping, not harming. That is all that mattered in this world.

'So... how many babies do you think you'll have with Georgia?' Ethan asked, totally off the previous subject.

I raised my eyebrows and chuckled. Such a funny question. 'You know, we haven't even discussed that aspect of our lives. For now, I will just be extremely happy being married to her!'

'And you, Ethan? When you find the one, how many babies

would you like?' I asked.

He looked down at his half-eaten food. I had hit an exposed nerve and his face reflected his pain.

'I'm sorry. Please don't answer me if you don't want to,' I added, wishing I could backtrack on my question.

He started to shake his head. 'No, not at all. It is a fair question, Cohen... I—did a genetic study on my DNA quite a while ago. I also did so with my semen. I found a permanent change in my DNA sequence—a "de Novo" mutation. It would be irresponsible of me to father a child, knowing that the de Novo will lead to a genetic disorder in the child. So, I consciously choose to never father a child. To protect myself, a potential mother and a potential child, I purposely will not engage in any sort of physical relationship,' he said.

'But, I recall you asking Georgia to marry you. Why? If that is how you feel about procreation?' I asked, confused by his explanation.

He breathed out deeply. 'I fell in love with her. I felt a connection with her, and I felt a longing to be with her. I thought she would make me feel whole. But we were not meant to be. She is yours, Cohen. She is unable to love anyone other than you. I asked her to marry me because I thought I was going to lose her. Panic persuaded me to ask for her hand in marriage. She now understands this, and I'm at peace with it all.'

I pressed my lips together. He was right. 'When you do meet your soul mate and your wife wants to have a baby, I will happily donate my sperm to you. We are one and the same,' I declared.

Ethan clasped his hands in front of his face as I would do. He nodded his head. 'Thank you. That means the world to me. I will consider it when the time is right and discuss it if I meet the woman of my dreams. All things are possible.'

It was interesting where our conversations led us. I certainly did not expect to enter such deep philosophical meanderings. I expected more day-to-day off-the-cuff conversation, where we talked about our similarities and differences. Or perhaps his childhood compared to mine. But it was better not to venture into the past. I think we had both decided that without consulting each other. It was a silent contract between us, so to speak. It was better to welcome the future into our lives with open arms, hearts and minds.

Love never fails.

Chapter 30

The glowing sun rose above the ocean at dawn, painting the canvas of the sky in colours of yellows and orange, bathing the twilight sky in golden light.

I stood in the open-air church with my brothers Tiernan, Hayden and Ethan, by my side.

A gentle sea breeze played among the bows and ribbons decorating the timber posts as the soft music began. Georgia's sister, Jordan, led the procession down the isle. She wore a lapis-coloured spaghetti strap, long chiffon dress with a wrap, and held a white rose posy. Once Jordan took her position for the wedding ceremony, Georgia made her entrance.

All eyes of our small family gathering turned to watch her walk down the aisle, with her hand on her father's arm.

She was breathtaking in her ivory, strapless, organza wedding gown. She was so effortlessly beautiful and graceful. Her auburn wavy hair was perfected into a curly updo style, her light pink rose bouquet symbolic of the very first flowers I had given her.

As she came closer to me the world slowed down. It was only the two of us. Nothing else mattered.

Finally, the love of my life stood before me.

She let go of her father's arm and faced me, smiling shyly, her eyes wet.

I looked down at her delicate hands and took them in mine as I felt my love for her encompass us. It was powerful. Overwhelming. I imagined it wrapping around her like wings, protecting her for an eternity. I felt its energy throughout every cell in my body. It was like a spiritual connection of our souls.

'You look stunning!' I whispered to her.

She smiled at me and a tear fell from the corner of her eye. I took a deep breath and smiled coyly at her, whilst the pastor welcomed us to our marriage ceremony.

Within fifteen minutes we were declared husband and wife before God and our families, and we left the beach church, floating on love.

I never pictured that the Pacific Ocean was so vast. It appeared that it would never end until the French Polynesian Islands of our destination came into view.

They looked small from the air. The dark green vegetation was outlined by the white beaches and the vivid shades of emerald, turquoise, azure and royal blue waters was captivating. Georgia looked mesmerized as we circled Bora Bora before we descended to land.

'Mrs. Darcy, we have arrived,' I whispered into her ear.

She squeezed my hand.

'Mr. Darcy, you are incredible. This is every wife's dream honeymoon. Definitely a thousand hearts and flowers!' Georgia said in a quiet voice, and then kissed me lightly on the lips.

We transferred from the airport to the shuttle boat and then off to the Hilton Bora Bora Hui Resort Spa.

I held Georgia's hand as we walked along the jetty to our Over Water Villa. The deepest blue water of Tahiti was here, and our villa sat over it.

I walked in silence beside Georgia. A gentle breeze played with her hair as she looked out over the deep blue waters of the lagoon. Her face appeared angelic, and her beauty radiated from within her. My heart skipped a beat or ten as I ogled this amazing woman who was now my wife.

We stopped at the front entrance to our Villa.

I unlocked the door and lifted her up into my arms to carry her over the threshold.

She giggled in delight as I performed this age-old ritual with ease. I pushed the front door closed behind me with my foot, and kissed Georgia lightly before I placed her feet back onto the polished wooden floorboards.

She twirled around as she looked at the interior of the Villa. It was nothing short of spectacular. The ceilings were high and woven, and were composed of a wood and white theme. The walls and furniture featured deep, rich woods.

A king size canopy bed dominated the room. It's dark timber contrasting to the white linen bed dressings, and light airy white curtains hung from the canopy, gathered at the four corner posts. It oozed romance.

I heard water lapping underneath the Villa and was drawn to a glass floor panel that showcased the amazing lagoon and marine life below. We both lay on our stomachs to look through the glass.

I rolled over onto my back and looked to my left.

Glass opening doors opened to a large deck area where we could dine or sit on the padded sun-lounges.

The entire Villa was unforgettable. It was what dreams were made of. It would hold in our memories forever.

I reached over for Georgia's hand and moved it to my lips,

brushing them lightly against her skin before I kissed her hand. 'I love you. Here's to the beginning of the rest of our lives together,' I said, my voice breaking with emotion.

Georgia turned her head to the side and smiled at me, melting my heart. 'And I love you—the man who captured my heart,' she replied, before she moved over closer to me.

As the rain fell heavily, Georgia and I sealed our love. Our emotional and physical bond was fused with unconditional love and could not be broken.

Our marriage vows were sacred, and written across our hearts and minds.

Chapter 31

The return to the land of the living after a beautiful honeymoon on the Tahitian Islands was an unwelcome reality.

Moving my possessions to Georgia's apartment was tedious. Perhaps I should have taken her up on moving my stuff before the wedding.

As I lugged the last box of my belongings out the door of my old apartment Jack came running up to me. He held something in his hand. 'Cohen, you left this behind,' he said, huffing and puffing. He held up a brown leather book.

'Oh, yeah, that book!' I said.

He flicked through the pages. 'Strangest book that I've ever seen. Blank pages don't come bound in brown leather covers like that anymore,' Jack said, then he smiled at me. 'I'll miss you, buddy. And I'll be looking for you at work. Don't be a stranger!' he said and patted me heavily on the back.

'Right back at you, and ah... thanks... ah—thanks for everything,' I managed to launch out of my jumbled mouth. I nodded to him and then loaded my car and headed off to my new life with my wife.

I parked the car on the side of the busy road, grabbed the old torn box, and hoofed it across the road. In doing so, I heard the dull thud of an object that had slipped off the top of the box.

Once I reached the pavement, I turned to see Georgia's and now my leather-covered book sitting in the middle of the road. And within ten seconds, a truck came along and ran over it, followed by a car, and a bus. Each time the book moved towards the opposite side of the road until it was sitting in the gutter.

Relieved, I placed the box onto the pavement and prepared to cross the busy road to retrieve it. But at that moment a grey-haired lady picked it up and tossed it into the waste bin. The garbage truck arrived. It emptied the bowels of the rubbish bin into the belly of the truck. And just like that, the book was gone.

This time for good.

One part of me was saddened: the other freed from the burden of being the new Book Keeper.

But life is like that.

One door closes and another one opens.

I pushed my hand through my hair, picked up the box from the pavement and then headed towards the apartment building.

I strode into the apartment grounds rearranging my clothing, hoping I smelt good and didn't look past my use by date after all the moving I had done.

I pushed the buttons to our apartment.

'Hello,' she said.

'Ah… yeah… a delivery of gingerbread for a… Miss Georgia,' I responded.

'You may enter, sir,' Georgia said.

'Thank you,' I replied, smiling.

When I opened the door to the sight of Georgia, I knew that life couldn't get any better.

'Mr. Darcy, where are the gingerbread men you had to

deliver?' she asked.

'They ran away,' I answered and leaned in to kiss my wife.

'Good, the apartment was getting too crowded with them living here as well,' she said.

We sorted through my belongings.

'Cohen, where is the book?' She looked up at me and frowned.

'Well—I did have it with the last box, but an unbelievable catastrophic chain of events separated the book from me. It was totally destroyed. I saw it. It is irreparable. It's kinda sad you know. It did have sentimental value because it brought us together. It was unique. But it is gone, never to be seen again,' I said.

'You think?' Georgia remarked. 'We'll see, Mr. Darcy. It is a book of circumstance—of revelations. Its inspiration lies in its ability to surprise even the true unbeliever. You'll see,' she commented in a thought-provoking way.

'Mutato Nomine De Te Fabula Narratur,' I recited from the brown leather cover of the stupid book.

'With the name changed, the story applies to you...' Georgia whispered.

ACKNOWLEDGEMENTS

It was 2am that I started to write this novel, as I sat in the hospital waiting room in 2016, wondering whether my dad would survive from a potential heart attack. I was concerned, wondering whether his name was in God's *Book of Life*. And hence, the words from chapter one were born.

Dad survived that night, and lived until 2022. The day before his death, when he was in hospital with atrial fibrillation, Mum and I were heading home after sitting with him all morning, to pick up some clothes for him, I heard in my mind to go back and talk to him, three times. I knew what this meant—I needed to have a chat to Dad about what he believed.

I didn't go back to talk to him that day, but prayed for him that night. The next morning, I went to the hospital early and had that conversation with him, and asked if he believed in God. He said yes. 'And Jesus,' I added. He nodded and said he always had believed. I then told him that angels would be with him when it was his time. Dad said to me, 'Nothing's going to happen to me.' Dad died suddenly and unexpectedly that afternoon with Mum and I by his side. I look forward to seeing him again.

Thank you to my readers, my family and friends, who generously spend time reading my books. I pray that they touch you where you need to be touched—heart or mind.

Thank you to my husband, for your forever patience as I repeatedly enter the world of creativity in writing, and the arts. I love you and adore you x ~JW~ ~AG~

~ Many beautiful things Cannot be seen or touched
They are felt within the heart. What you have done for me
is one of them ~

Thank you to my three beautiful children, now adults who have always listened to my crazy stories with gentle and patient hearts. ~ I remember perfectly the day that you were born, when my heart overflowed with deep, endless, unconditional love for you. I will love you forever and a day x ~JW~ ~AG~

And to my *Heavenly Father*. Thank you for being in my life story. Thank you for being the Author of my life story. I couldn't make it through without You. Thank you for Your rescue packages You give me when I am struggling, in the way of people, animals, and nature. You spoil us, even when we don't deserve it. ♡

Soli Deo gloria.

THE GIRL WITH THE FLAXEN HAIR
print book eBook

JANE PICCADILLY bought a mistake-house. In a hurry.
While her perfectly white shoe sunk into something brown and offensive. There was always a mistake-number-one with something new, wasn't there?

And there was always only one mistake, wasn't there?

Dear Alice's little girl, *plain Jane.* The middle of seven sisters. The one who was the least seen, but saw the most. The one who could slip out of a family gathering, and no one would see.
The middle, invisible child.

The one who saw the bodies.

Jane Piccadilly made the mistake-house an un-mistake, and her six sisters moved in—Poppy the librarian, Violet the hairdresser, Daisy the carpenter, Rose the photographer, Zinnia the botanist, and Flora the farmhand.

Then came the letters left at the front door.
And the strange man with a carpet bag who sat on the bus seat.

It all pointed to one thing. The *unravelling.*
Of the mistake house with its secrets.
Of plain Jane, and the threads that held her past and her present,
her trauma and her guilt and her shame deep inside her,
straining and breaking.

The truth always has a way of exposing itself.
Plain Jane wasn't so plain. Was she?

Amelia Grace

YOU BEFORE ME
(Young Adult Fiction)
print book   eBook

Eighteen year old ARI FLORA COHEN is stuck living in a pre-technology time, until she ventures to the forbidden Beyond where she is captured. Finally released, she staggers home through elaborate underground tunnels, reeling from the lie about the non-existence of the world outside her home. What other lies has her mama told?

ELIAS WOLFE GREEN is Ari's protector. He finds her wild and unconventional and disagreeable. Nevertheless, he has a job to do, no matter how many times she tells him she hates him.

Elias follows the rules. Ari breaks them.

Ari has questions. Elias has answers, including the truth about her father who was taken before her birth, but he cannot speak of his knowledge. So Ari must find the answers herself.

She discovers she is living in a time called *The Unfolding*, where the truth of the world is being unwrapped, layer by layer, after the time of *The Boxing*, when the earth was made singular by the covering of the stars and the universe with light pollution and surveillance satellites, when the truth of everything was hidden. She discovers there are four versions of everyone, and Ari discovers, her mama of love and light, is not who she thinks she is.

Distraught, wanting answers, Ari must dress as a boy and return to *The Beyond*. But disaster strikes.

Now you, dear reader, must choose the ending...
Amelia Grace

THE COLOUR OF BROKEN
(Long-listed to be made into a movie, twice)
print book   eBook   audiobook

A dark secret... Yolande Lawrence-Harrison was hiding a dark secret. She'd returned to her hometown of Tarrin to help her ailing grandmother in Flowers for Fleur, where she had to put her engineering career aside to learn the science of flower art.

A note... As Yolande fussed with the pale pink roses in the basket of her grandmother's 1950s Schwinn Cruiser bicycle, she discovered a note. Yolande fumed at the pitiful manners and pure arrogance of the wording, and after numerous exchanges, she became irritated by the persistent, annoying, pig-headed, obstinate human being who wouldn't take no for an answer.

Beware... But when Alexander Parker walked into Flowers for Fleur, her thoughts scattered. However, she refused to inhale the alluring potion he offered. She could see through his projected façade, where his perfection was a practised deceit. She wondered, if she could see through his pretence, could he see through hers? Could he see that she was damaged, hiding a past that ate away at her core allowing the darkness to engulf what was left of her inner light. Could he see that she was the color of broken?

Run... Yolande wanted to run. Away from the flowers. Away from Alexander Parker. But she couldn't. Her grandmother's life was fading as she battled an incurable illness, and Yolande needed to choose whether to fight her past or not, ultimately exposing her inner demons, in order to save her grandmother and herself from the same fate.

(Profits donated to Meniere's Research)

Amelia Grace

ALL THE COLOURS ABOVE
(sequel to *The Colour of Broken*)
print book   eBook

INDIGO FEATHER DANUBE is a neuroscientist studying memories, how to access them, then remove them, digitally.

One day, her parents implore her to attend a reunion at the park of her youth, where TOBIAH BROOKS dares her to climb the Jacaranda tree of her childhood.

But first, she must remember who he is.

They meet before sundown, with Indigo's intention to succeed at the dare, then leave. But his intention is to win her heart. Tobiah orchestrates a secret rendezvous at the Jacaranda tree on the luminous full moon, when it's light enough to see, but dark enough to cloak their presence.
No-one could possibly know they were there once a month. Together. Alone.

Every story has a beginning. At the beginning of Indigo and Tobiah's story, is a girl who meets a boy. A girl who wasn't in the habit of falling in love, until her heart bloomed like a thousand red roses with the scent of citrus, spice, and sweet fruit, surrounded by a dreamy and exhilarating melody of love.

Until... that day that can't be undone.
On that day of the wish that can't be unwished.
And that moment in time... when she learned the truth.

Mirror. Mirror. Two mirrors. Two of me. Who am I?

(Profits donated to Meniere's Research)

Amelia Grace

A DREAM OF LIGHT
print book   eBook

Courage, temperance, wisdom, justice, patience... KADEN BERKLEY repeated the words sealing them into the depths of his consciousness, finding comfort and solace. For two hundred and sixty years he had been trapped on the earth engaged as an immortal human, after being forced to take the anti-aging elixir. Now he is plagued by emotional torment, chained to the laws of gravity and craving to return to the Light. To freedom. To love.

He takes a deep breath and stares at the blue energy mass before he lifts his hand to it, then watches as the fourth state of matter arcs to his finger tips like bolts of lightning. They tingle under the warmth until the plasma retreats back into the glowing blue energy. He wishes it was the antidote to the immortal elixir.

He thinks of MISS FINNIGAN. She has what he wants. He can feel it, vibrating in perfect harmony with his being. It sings to his soul like agonized poetry, reminding him of what he doesn't have. And he wants it. Now. Mortality. Kaden wants to reach out to her but she is forbidden. Their DNA could never absorb each other, cell to every beautiful cell, harmonizing in a melody only they can hear, unless, he finds the missing piece to his immortality that will free him.

He sighs. He wonders how long he will be subjected to this living nothingness cut off from his spiritual homeland. If he doesn't find the missing piece, he will remain an earth immortal, bound to the physical torture of remaining on the earth, unable to return to his true home.

Yet, he will dream of Light, it was his only hope.

Amelia Grace

www.ingramcontent.com/pod-product-compliance
Lightning Source LLC
Chambersburg PA
CBHW010320100726
47906CB00006B/1069